MOON RISING

MOON RISING

M. J. TROW

www.blkdogpublishing.com

plays like Dido, Queen of Carthage, Tamburlaine, the Jew of Malta and Doctor Faustus. He was the 'Muse's darling', 'all fire and air' and the crowds flocked to his dramas at the Curtain, the Theatre and the Rose.

But even before he left Cambridge, Kit Marlowe was recruited into the dangerous and murky world of espionage, perhaps by Nicholas Faunt, secretary to the queen's spymaster, Francis Walsingham. The religious world was split between Catholic and Protestant and there was a price on the queen's head – the pope himself had ordered the assassination of the English whore, the Jezebel, who had betrayed Catholicism. Walsingham's efforts and those of 'intelligencers' like Marlowe, were all designed to keep the queen and her country safe.

Marlowe was a maverick, a whistle-blower, with outspoken views on religion, the government for which he worked and he was critical of the norms of behaviour. Almost certainly homosexual, at a time when that meant execution, he claimed that Christ had a homosexual relationship with John the Baptist. Or did he? Was all that merely propaganda, invented by the ever-growing list of enemies building up by 1593?

This book offers a different interpretation to the death in Deptford. Marlowe knew too much about the Privy Council, the gang of four who effectively ran England under the queen. He openly defied them in his last plays – the Massacre at Paris and Edward II. And they, in turn, were keen to destroy him – 'His mouth must be stopped' – and stopped it was by a trio of agents operating at the highest level.

The brutal murder of a young playwright at the peak of his powers has intrigued and captivated for over 400 years. This compelling journey through the evidence allows us to know, for the first time, who killed him.

Chapter 1

'Marlowe's dead.'

The gatekeeper had been dozing in the May sunshine, bright and warm, promising a perfect spring day. He had been at work guarding the gate all night and he was just resting his eyes; he didn't sleep on duty, of course he didn't. The soft whisper at his wicket gate had made him jump and he didn't like to ask the messenger to repeat himself. Working as he did for Baron Hunsdon, he did hear some things that perhaps he shouldn't hear but … he had better make sure.

'I'm sorry … sir?' The figure was wearing an unseasonably long and voluminous cape, the hood pulled well down over the face but even so, he assumed it was a man inside all that wool. The shoulders, for one thing. But a whisper could disguise any voice. 'Could you say that again?'

The cloaked figure sighed. Surely, news this momentous couldn't come to a clattering halt at the ear of a man too stupid to understand. 'Marlowe's dead.' Within the limitations of a whisper, each syllable was crisp and clear. 'Tell your master.' And with not even a rustle, the messenger was gone, melting into the crowds of people thronging Whitehall as if he had never been.

The gatekeeper was not a man who moved fast or thought fast or did anything at all without due consideration, but this seemed like momentous news. He wasn't sure who Marlowe was, although he had heard the name as he moved invisibly – as all servants must move – through the corridors of power. So, whoever he was, his death would be news, bad or good, to someone, of that he was sure. He took his time standing up. These days, his knees gave him gyp if he didn't take things steady and he didn't want to hobble if he was going to be hobnobbing with the servants closer to the Baron. He knew he wouldn't be seeing him. He knew his place.

The gatekeeper tapped at the door of the under secretary's under secretary.

'Come!'

The gatekeeper hated that. What if he said that if someone tapped on his wicket? The person outside would think that he was having a turn. But nevertheless and pinning a suitable expression on his rather grubby face, he stepped inside. The under secretary's under secretary was sitting at a high desk in the window, to get the best of the morning light. He held a quill in inky fingers and looked rather annoyed at being disturbed, his normal expression. He was even more annoyed when he saw who it was. He was a man on his way up; it didn't do to be seen talking to mere gatekeepers.

'What?' he snapped, dropping ink on the vellum in front of him, which made him even more annoyed than before. He would be scraping at that for the next half hour now. Had this oaf no idea how busy he was?

'Marlowe's dead.' The gatekeeper had decided that he would deliver the message plain and unadorned.

Another drop of ink joined its fellow, this time unnoticed. The under secretary's under secretary gaped.

'Marlowe's dead? What, *Christopher* Marlowe?'

The gatekeeper shrugged. 'I dunno. He didn't say. S'pose so.' Truth be told, he had no idea what the man's other name was. But if this quill pusher said it was Christopher, then no doubt it was so.

The under secretary scrambled down from his perch and approached the gatekeeper; the two men met in the doorway, one chosen for his brawn, the other his brain and for a moment they made an unseemly tangle of mismatched limbs before the secretary broke free and made for higher offices at the ungainly shamble of a man who spends his time hunched over a desk.

The gatekeeper watched him go and shrugged again. He had had no expectation of how his news would be received, but this was perhaps more than he could have hoped for. When the secretary almost fell arse over head taking the corner at the end of the corridor too quickly, that was a bonus the gatekeeper had not dared to hope for. He gave a little chuckle and went back to his stool. His knees were ready to have the weight taken off and he went off duty in an hour. Time to catch forty winks before he went home to the wife and kids. He settled down with a sigh and leaned back again on his sun-warmed wall. Too much excitement, that was the trouble with this job. Just too much excitement sometimes.

The stars shone down on Lord Burghley that morning. They radiated outwards in their spangle of gilt paint on the azure of the high dome. He pushed the papers away from him, across the table and sipped his Rhenish. The Queen was at Placentia, far enough away not to bother him today. That whippersnapper Essex would be jousting somewhere, knocking seven bells out of a hapless opponent. And Ralegh … well, he could forget about Ralegh. The great Lucifer had well and truly blotted his escutcheon when he got his leg over Bess Throckmorton, but to have married her as well! What was the man thinking? No, Ralegh was no more than a whisper now, an afterthought.

Which left the way clear for his own dear boy, darling Robert. True, the man only reached his father's shoulder and true, the Queen persisted in referring to him as her 'elf', but his back was broad enough (if nearer the ground than most men's) and he'd weather the storm. Then he, Burghley, could lay aside the cares of state and amble around the grounds of Hatfield on his wee donkey, reading Aristotle. It was spring now and he could almost smell the hawthorn, heavy as honey on the air as the birds …

'Did you order this?' A barked demand brought him out of his reverie and he gulped his wine. A tall man stood, quaking with fury, at the door of the Star Chamber. For all he was 67, the intruder's beard was only now remembering to turn grey.

'Good morning, Henry,' Burghley said. He held up the decanter. 'Rhenish?'

'Rhenish, my arse! Did you order it? It had to be you.'

Burghley tried the formal approach, in that the friendly one clearly hadn't worked. 'Baron Hunsdon, perhaps you would be good enough to tell me what you're talking about.'

Hunsdon crossed the room in three strides. 'Marlowe. He's dead.'

Burghley blinked. 'Marlowe?' he replied. 'Dead?'

'There seems to be an echo in here,' Hunsdon snapped.

The Queen's chief adviser wasn't usually a man lost for words, but that was about the size of it that May morning. 'How do you know?' He hadn't got to the top of the greasy pole of politics by not checking his facts.

'A man in a cloak told my gatekeeper, who told it to my under secretary's under secretary …'

'You have an under secretary?'

Hunsdon bridled. 'Of course I have. Haven't you? Doesn't everyone?'

Burghley shrugged and waved a hand. It was too early to begin arguing about who a man had in his household, but still … he may need to look at his servants; he seemed to be falling behind and, in his world, appearances were everything.

Hunsdon counted on his fingers, gathering his thoughts. 'Yes, under secretary. And he told my gentleman of the wardrobe – because I was still in bed, of course – who told …'

'We don't need the whole list,' Burghley interrupted. 'This clearly all starts with Faunt.' In Burghley's world, everything started with Faunt. Whether he had asked for one or not, he poured Hunsdon a large one and topped up his own.

'Many things do, in my experience,' Hunsdon said, slumping down in a chair and taking a swig. 'I thought you'd fired him.'

'You don't fire a man like Faunt,' Burghley shook his head. 'He's like the shit on your pattens – you can wash it off, but the smell will always linger. All right, he was Walsingham's man, not mine …'

'I thought you *were* Walsingham these days,' Hunsdon cut in. 'Queen's spymaster; invisible ink, all that cloak and dagger nonsense.'

Burghley held up his hand. 'We'd be in a sorry state without espionage, Henry,' he said, 'but, as you know, I cannot divulge.'

'On Her Majesty's Secret Service, eh?' Hunsdon sneered. 'Well …'

'What the hell's going on?' There was another man at the door, younger than Hunsdon, but greyer of beard. Bright-feathered flies and bait dangled from his belt.

'Good morning, Charles.' Burghley's quiet reveries were now well and truly shattered.

'I'm confused,' the newcomer said. 'There I was, sitting by the river, minding my own business with a hook and line when I heard …' He looked at the two men in front of him. He could trust neither of them further than he could throw them. 'Marlowe. Is that right? Left for dead in the street?'

'No,' Burghley said. Then, he wasn't so sure. 'Henry, is that right?'

Hunsdon threw up his hands. 'We're going round in circles,' he said.

'I thought we agreed …' the latest arrival chipped in, 'and, as Lord High Admiral, I really think …'

'But you don't, Howard, do you?' Hunsdon interrupted him. 'That's the bloody point. And the Armada, can I remind everyone, was a long time ago,'

Howard of Effingham was alongside the man, his jaw flexing, his eyes bulging. 'You'll take that back, Hunsdon. If you weren't such an old pantaloon, I'd horsewhip you!'

'Old?' Hunsdon was on his feet. 'Pantaloon? I'll have you know …'

'… That you fathered a bastard child recently by a

woman young enough to be your granddaughter. Yes, we all know.'

Hunsdon's hand was on his dagger hilt. 'Emilia is married to Alfonso Lanier …' he roared.

'Oh, yes, that monkey musician you paid to take her down the aisle. Just because you can't keep it in your Venetians …'

'Gentlemen, gentlemen,' Burghley thundered in a tone of voice he hadn't used for years and a small flake of gold detached itself from the ceiling and spiralled gently down through a beam of sunshine. 'None of this explains what happened to Marlowe.'

'Marlowe?' another voice queried as a panel in the wall slid silently sideways and a diminutive man entered. 'Kit Marlowe? What about him?'

The gatekeeper and his wife had been married a long time, mainly because he worked all night and slept all day. Their seven children bore testimony to the fact that they occasionally met in the middle, their wide age range to the fact that it happened infrequently. The two with red hair and the one with the neighbour's squint were simply never mentioned – why rock a boat which weathered life's storms reasonably well with just the odd leak here and there? He threw off his working clothes and settled into the still warm dent that his better half had left in the straw mattress.

'Good night at the palace?' she asked, tying her cap strings.

'Mmph.'

As replies went it didn't tell her much but as she had heard it morning in, morning out for more years than she cared to count, she ignored it. But suddenly, he opened his eyes and looked at her, making her jump. He never did that.

'Bit of news,' he said. 'Marlowe's dead.'

'What?' She went pale.

'Yeah. Dead as a nit, they say. Run over by a cart in Horsemonger Lane.' And without another syllable, he was flat on his back, snoring like a grampus.

'Jenkins!' She shook him to no avail. 'Jenkins! Wake

up! Do you mean Kit Marlowe? Marlowe the playwright?' She pulled him upright, but his head just lolled and she let him fall back. Not even the crack as his head met the board of the bed woke him. 'Damn your eyes,' she muttered, but she knew it had to be him, the sprite of light and air who she often saw out in the streets along the river. There was no other Marlowe whose death would be news. Marlowe's dead – that was no way to start a day.

Dr Gabriel Harvey was at Lincoln's Inn that day, enjoying some particularly fine West Country cheese he'd sent for days earlier. He buttered his manchet bread and was about to take a bite when there was the most almighty hammering on his chamber door.

'Come in.'

A shabby-looking man stood there with a satchel in his hand. 'Dr Harvey,' he half bowed, 'I wouldn't normally bother you with this, but …'

The Cambridge master held up his hand. 'Rudierde, if it's that tosh you've been hawking around the stationers for what seems forever …'

Edmund Rudierde looked affronted. 'Do you mean my *Thunderbolt of God's Wrath Against Hard-Hearted and Stiff-Necked Sinners*?'

'Something like that,' Harvey sighed.

'No, no. But I have, funnily enough, added a postscript. The ink's still wet.'

'Joy,' Harvey smiled, but only with one side of his mouth and without troubling his eyes.

'It's about Marlowe.'

'Who?' Harvey asked.

Edmund Rudierde may have had a one-track mind, that track being far to the left of Martin Luther, John Calvin and John Knox, but he knew Harvey's links with Kit Marlowe and that was why he'd come. 'Your nemesis, Doctor,' he said, waiting to be asked to sit down. 'The bête noire.'

Harvey raised an eyebrow. 'That's French, Rudierde,' he said. 'A little Papist for you, surely?'

The Puritan ignored the slur. 'Dr Harvey, Christopher Marlowe is dead.'

There was a pause, the manchet bread still nowhere near Harvey's lips. For a second, what looked like pure ecstasy crossed the man's face. Then all was calm and matter-of-fact again. 'What was it – the plague?'

'The Lord *does* move in mysterious ways,' Rudierde assured him, knowing the Lord as intimately as he did. 'Not content with sending his thunderbolts to close the theatres … But no, Marlowe's death was altogether more sordid.'

Harvey smiled and patted the stool beside him. 'Do tell,' he said.

Rudierde smiled too. He *knew* Harvey would be interested. He leaned towards his man, a conspirator to the ends of his fingertips. 'You know of course that this Marlowe was a filthy play-maker.'

'Of course.'

'That he called Moses a mere conjuror …'

'I'd heard that.'

'And that even our Sweet Saviour was …' there was a break in his voice, 'a seducer and a deceiver of the people.'

'I'd heard that, too,' Harvey nodded.

'Well, only yesterday, this brain-sick fool, mouthing his blasphemies and profanities in public, met someone of a finer mould in the street.'

'Where was this?'

'Shoreditch.'

'Go on.'

'Marlowe quarrelled with the man, who must have been one of us …'

Harvey wasn't sure he wanted to be equated with the Saints, but if the death of Kit Marlowe was gruesome enough, he was happy to go along with it.

'… because the man saw Marlowe whip out his knife and he grabbed it and turned it into the blasphemer's brain. Even then, he shrieked and cursed before yielding up his stinking breath.'

'Are you quoting yourself, Rudierde?' Harvey tapped the satchel, 'from your still-damp postscript?'

'Um … well, yes. I could probably beef it up a little.'

'Don't bother.' Harvey turned back to his meal. 'But thank you for your news. See yourself out.'

The fish queue wound its way around the bollards on the quay of the Queen's Wharf as the women of Whitehall waited for the men of Tilbury to land their catch. Agnes Jenkins hugged her news to her for as long as she could. She felt somehow that while it was unshared, it was possibly still not true. She had argued with herself all the way down to the quay. Marlowe was too fleet of foot, too wily to be run down by a cart. But the way the carters behaved these days, as though they owned the roads, who was proof against their flying wheels, her inner self snapped back. Crushed, with all his life before him. She could feel the tears welling again and concentrated on watching the fishermen make fast. Jenkins would have been happy with a bloater, but she thought she would treat him to a herring for once – perhaps he would have more detail when he was properly awake. She would stop at the chandler's on the way home and buy some oats to roll the fish in – she knew he liked them that way.

'Agnes! I said, are you listening?'

The gatekeeper's wife blinked and focussed on the dumpy woman standing in front of her. 'Sorry, Dorcas,' she said. 'I was miles away.'

Dorcas Middledew nudged her friend with an elbow which was surprisingly sharp for such a well-cushioned woman. 'I'll say you were. Watching that one with the yellow cap, was yer? He's well set up, I'll give him that. I could teach him a thing or two, on a dark night with a following wind.' She plied the elbow again and Agnes moved away out of range. As Dorcas had been servicing most men in a five-mile radius since she was twelve, this wasn't a surprise. A fresh-faced fisherman from Essex was unlikely to know all the tricks she did.

'What were you saying, Dorcas?' Agnes hoped a bit of polite conversation would cheer her up. She felt a little silly, caring so much for the death of a man she had only ever seen from a distance and whose words she had only heard once, from the crowded pit of the groundlings.

'I was *saying*,' the woman said, 'I was *saying*, have you heard? That Christopher Marlowe's dead. You know, that playwright lad. No better than he should be, I daresay, but nobody deserves to die like that.'

Agnes forced a smile. 'I hadn't heard that,' she said. 'Die like what?' She had a feeling that perhaps she shouldn't share the information that Jenkins had already told her. His job as gatekeeper surely carried some responsibility of secrecy; he was, after all, all that stood between the world and the men who made it spin.

'Found on the foreshore just along there.' Dorcas gestured with a toss of her head. 'Drowned, they say. His ferryman overturned and him nor his boat has been found.'

'Dreadful,' Agnes muttered. Could it be that everyone had it wrong? But even if they had, the word was hissing along the line of women like the tide washing the shingle.

'Marlowe's dead.'

'Marlowe's dead.'

'Marlowe's dead.'

'You've got that wrong, Edmund.' Anthony à Wood closed his Bible. 'Who've you been talking to? I had it on the best of authorities.'

'Who?' Rudierde wanted to know.

'Uh-huh,' Wood wagged his finger at him. 'Walls have ears. You can't be too careful.'

'Well, what's your version, then?'

'It's not my *version*, Edmund,' Wood assured him, his nose in the air. 'It's the truth.'

'Your truth?'

'God's truth.'

'Ah.'

'This Marlowe was in love with … shall we say, a certain Woman?'

'Harlot?'

'Such people as Marlowe know no other kind.'

'Quite.'

'He and a bawdy-serving man …'

'Do you mean a pimp?'

Wood looked exasperated. 'Who's telling this story?' he asked.

'All right. Go on.'

'Marlowe and the bawdy-serving man fought each other over this trollop. The playwright tried to stab him and the other man turned his hand and stabbed him in the head. Since he was a playwright, of course, it missed his brain entirely but no amount of surgery could save him.'

'So … Marlowe's dead?'

'Marlowe's dead.'

The Winchester geese south of the river kept much the same hours as Jenkins the gatekeeper, but there was less snoring and next to no drooling. The darkened room was full of faint breathing and now and again a stifled cry as one of them remembered something from the night before which she would rather forget. Into this soft, skin-scented, down-filled dusk crept a figure who normally would have been among the sleepers but she had been kept busy by a well-paying gentleman who disliked breakfasting alone. Usually, she would have stayed as long as he would have her but this morning, his man had come in with news which had shocked her to the core and she had run for home, leaving him sitting there with the butter still melting into his crumpet.

She shook the nearest sleeper. 'Sister, sister, wake up. Awful news.'

The girl she had woken turned fretfully. 'Can't it wait?'

'No.' The breakfast companion stood upright and addressed the rest, some of whom were grunting their displeasure at the interruption of their sleep.

'Worrizit? one of them demanded. 'Spit it out and bugger off.'

'Marlowe's dead.' She would have dressed it up a bit, but she was tired too and hungry, having missed her breakfast.

'Marlowe? *Kit* Marlowe?'

'Yes. Is there another?'

And round the room, from every mouth, there came a

keening cry, for a man they all loved, the only man who had never so much as stroked a breast or cupped a buttock in his hand. They cried because now he never would.

Marlowe's dead.

'Francis Archer,' William Vaughan said, looking back at the eager faces crowding around him. 'That was the pimp's name. He and Marlowe had a history. They were at school together, sharing women as soon as they were out of their hanging sleeves.'

There were gasps of astonishment all round. Vaughan clapped his hands. 'Now, brethren, it's time for Meeting. Another member of the Ungodly has met his end. Let's all rejoice in that.'

'Surely,' said a voice from the back, 'it is wicked to rejoice in the death of any man. No man is an island.'

'Shut up, Donne,' Vaughan snapped. 'We will rejoice, as I have said. Marlowe is dead.'

It was dusk, Master Sackerson's favourite time of day, when the people stopped hanging over his wall, throwing all kinds of unspeakable things as well as insults. The bear's back was broad and his hide was thick but even so, a little of that kind of thing went a long way and he spent most of the daylight hours hunkered down resting against an old tree stump in the corner of his pit. Master Sackerson had not seen the world outside his pit since they had brought him here, more years ago than bear or man could remember. It wasn't a bad life, taken one way and another. When he was younger, he was with a travelling band and while it was good sometimes to have the company of a female bear when the moon was full and the season right, the people he could take or leave. He had been glad when he got too big and grumpy to be safe around small children with sticks and toys that squeaked and he came here, to his pit.

Since then, he had seen few people. Now and again, a whey-faced lad would come in through a secret door at the back, to retrieve lost hats and to clean the pit out with a bucket of water. The lad didn't have much to say, but he didn't seem to judge – even a polite and considerate bear has to shit somewhere and Master Sackerson was a private soul so gave no grave offence.

The bear had learned to read the mood of the crowd above his head. Sometimes, after the silence which came along like clockwork every evening, there would be a sudden upsurge of laughter and those were the nights when halves of soft manchet bread would be thrown into his pit, apples, yeast cake and honeyed buns. Sometimes, the air would be full of sobs and soft sniffs and then he would get nothing. He didn't know why this was, but he had learned to smell the happiness or the sadness and since the night before, sadness filled the air.

Things had been quiet lately anyway but for the last day and night, the air above had been heavy with an unspent grief which had communicated itself to Master Sackerson and he slouched now, his great moth-eaten shoulders leaning against his dead tree. He lifted his snout to the sky and blew out a breath which held the sadness of all creatures far from home and lonely. A movement against the darkling sky caught his attention and he looked up with a grunt of recognition. A head was outlined there, just briefly, so briefly that the bear wasn't even sure he saw it. And then, an apple soared through the air and landed at his feet. By the time he had snuffed it up and crunched it down, the juice running down his chin and into his fur, the figure had gone. But the sadness remained.

Marlowe's dead.

Marlowe's dead.

Marlowe is dead.

The usher cleared his throat and bounced the butt of his staff of office on the chamber floor. 'Inquisition at Deptford Strand in the County of Kent,' he barked, 'within the Verge, of the first day of June in the year of the reign of Elizabeth by the grace of God of England, France and Ireland, Queen, defender of the faith et cetera, thirty fifth.'

The court had come to order and the coroner stood up, magisterial in his robes of office, glittering with the heraldry of Her Majesty. 'In the presence of William Danby,' he intoned, 'Gentleman, Coroner of the household of our said Lady the Queen, upon view of the body of Christopher Morley …'

There was a cough from the usher.

'Er … Marlowe,' Danby corrected himself, 'there lying dead and slain …'

All eyes shifted to the corpse in its winding sheet, stretched out on a makeshift catafalque. Only the head was visible, the wild hair spread over a pillow, the mouth that once smiled and laughed closed now in quiet repose. Above the left eye was an ugly, jagged wound, dark with dried blood. Otherwise, all was peace.

'Upon the oath of …' the usher droned on and one by one, the jury, the great and good of Deptford, placed their right hands on the court's Bible and gave their names.

'Nicholas Draper.'

'Wolston Randall.'

'William Curry.'

The list went on. Each man was someone of substance; a shopkeeper; an innkeeper; a tallow manufacturer. The first two were gentlemen. They could be relied upon to lead the rest. One by one, they passed the body on the catafalque and looked down at it. Somewhere, in the bowels of the court where the public were allowed to stand, a woman was crying. None of the jurors was. Several of them were of the Puritan persuasion. They were all locals. London itself was four miles away, less than an hour's ride. They'd all heard of Kit Marlowe, he of the mighty line, the pure, elemental wit who had given them, via Philip Henslowe's stage, *Tamburlaine, The Jew of Malta* and *Dr Faustus*. The Puritans hated him for that. The rest loved him. Nobody was indifferent.

Yet that was exactly what Coroner Danby said they must be; English justice depended on it. 'Without fear or favour' was the verdict the law demanded. And Coroner Danby, the Queen's man, the friend of Lord Burghley, talked them through it.

Marlowe had gone to the house in Deptford Strand, an ordinary run by Eleanor Bull on Wednesday 30 May. He had dined and played at tables with three other guests – Nicholas Skeres, gentleman; Ingram Frizer, gentleman; and Robert Poley, gentleman.

From his place in the gallery, Nicholas Faunt watched the proceedings closely. He couldn't help but smile at Danby's whitewashing of the facts. Skeres and Frizer were actually *walking* gentlemen, extras in Henslowe's plays; they weren't gentlemen at all. And as for Robert Poley, gaolbird, spy and murderer, he was just a shit. But Sir William was in the chair and he soldiered on.

The other three guests were at tables and Marlowe was lying on a bed behind them. Faunt's heart skipped a beat. That wasn't what he had told Frizer to say. Men didn't play backgammon side by side; they faced each other. But nobody else seemed to notice and Danby was in full cry. There was some quarrel over the reckoning, the bill of fare for the day. Frizer said Marlowe should pay. Marlowe pointed at Skeres. A row broke out and Marlowe grabbed Frizer's dagger from the sheath at his back and bashed his head with the hilt. Good, thought Faunt, Frizer's agreed account was back to where it should be now, short diversion notwithstanding.

'This,' Danby held up the dagger, 'is the murder weapon. This is the deodand. What's it worth, Master Usher?'

'One shilling, my lord.'

Danby weighed it in his hand. Probably right. He'd never owned anything that cheap in his life. He'd take the man's word for it. 'In the struggle,' Danby told the court, 'Frizer and Marlowe grappled and the tip of the blade,' he held it up as a gasp rose from the crowd, 'went into his head above the eye-socket and entered his brain.'

'And he cursed and blasphemed,' a voice called from the crowd.

'Silence!' Danby roared. 'I'll not have my court turned into a bearpit. Guards – remove that man.'

There was a clattering of boots and steel as the Puritan was bundled through the doors. Nobody had ever handled Edmund Rudierde like that before; he was outraged. Danby waited until the court had settled again. Then he stood up.

'Upon your oaths,' he said to the jurymen, 'how say you?'

There was the briefest of whispered conversations. Then Nicholas Draper, as the foreman, stood up and cleared his throat. 'We find, sir, that the said Ingram Frizer slew Christopher Marlowe at Deptford Strand aforesaid and that he did so to save his own life.'

'So say you all?' Danby checked.

There was a collection of 'Ayes'.

The usher handed the coroner a parchment scroll and Danby pressed his ring into the still malleable wax. 'Given under our hand,' he said to all present, 'a recommendation to Her Majesty of mercy to the said Ingram Frizer in the matter of the justifiable homicide of Christopher Marlowe.'

Faunt smiled. All was well, it seemed, that ended well. Now, if he could just get to that body before …

'That was … that was …' For a supposed playwright, Will Shaxsper was having difficulty coming up with the words.

'Bollocks?' Tom Sledd was not a wordsmith but on this occasion had knocked the nail on the head.

Philip Henslowe didn't feel like chuckling, but he almost chuckled now. He had just been to the inquest on the biggest cash cow he had ever had on the farm and all he could see ahead was darkness, ruin and living in a hedgerow with Mrs Henslowe and all the little Henslowes, slowly starving to death.

'That will do, for now,' Shaxsper said, shaking his head gloomily. 'I always thought that a coroner's inquest was there to … I don't know. Apportion blame. Make sure that evil doesn't triumph, that kind of thing.'

Henslowe sighed. 'The only thing old Danby seemed interested in was the deodand.'

'The what?' Shaxsper was from Warwickshire and he didn't get out much.

'The value of the murder weapon,' Alleyn told him, 'vis a vis the worth of the murderer. Henslowe's right; it's all about money.'

'But I thought you said Ingram Frizer was the murderer.' Shaxsper was being forced to look hard at a world about which he knew next to nothing. 'He doesn't have any worth.'

'Now, now, Will,' Henslowe scolded like a much-tried schoolmaster, 'even walking gentlemen have their place, you know.'

'No, no,' Shaxsper flustered. 'I didn't mean that. I mean Ingram Frizer's poor as a church mouse … isn't he?'

Burbage snorted. 'He owns an inn in Kent,' he said, 'and that's an inn that you and I don't own, Will. How long have you lived in London?' Burbage leaned in and whispered in his ear.

'Erm … I'm not sure.' Shaxsper wasn't good at arithmetic.

'Too long.' Burbage's nemesis Ned Alleyn leaned in from the other side. 'I say, Will. Is that an earring I spy?'

Shaxsper fingered his lobe. 'Yes. I've had it ages.'

'No, you have not,' Tom Sledd said, crossly. 'It's still all red. Did you have it done down Slack Alley? By old Mistress Semple, with a needle and a drop of jenever to take the sting out?'

Shaxsper nodded slightly and grunted. He didn't like moving his head much at the moment.

'You must be more simple than you look,' Henslowe said. 'More people have lost their ears to Mistress Semple than I have had hot dinners. Why on earth …?'

He suddenly realised and shook his head ruefully.

'It takes more than an earring to make a playwright, Will,' he said. 'And, to be honest, we don't need any more plays just now. I have a whole season's-worth of Kit's to perform. A retrospective, I'm going to call it.' He waved an arm in the air; he could smell the ink of the posters now. 'Coming Shortly,' he declaimed, 'A Compleat Retrospective of the Works of the Late and Lamented Christopher Marlowe! Details to Follow!'

'Will people know what "retrospective" means?' Burbage asked, with a snide note to his voice. He had never held the groundlings in much regard for all they, by definition, looked up to him.

'Do *you* know what "retrospective" means?' Alleyn said

waspishly. 'Long words aren't really your thing, are they?'

Burbage flared his nostrils and took a deep breath. Tom Sledd caught Philip Henslowe's eye and they sloped off down Maiden Lane, trying to ignore the growing shouts from behind them. Even with the death of the greatest playwright in the world, those two hams were still trying to outdo each other.

'Not much of an end, is it?' Henslowe said, sadly. 'Some ghouls listening to an idiot pontificating on the death of one of the geniuses of the century. No one is going to be punished for this and Kit is going to go down in history as the victim of a brawl over the bill in a low drinking den. It's wrong, Tom. It's just *wrong.*'

After his lucky choice of words outside the inquest, Tom Sledd hadn't much to add. He had shed his tears. He had put out feelers for his next job because, retrospective or no retrospective, he couldn't see Henslowe's glory days seeing out the spring, let alone the rest of his life. There was nothing they could do to bring justice to his dead friend.

CHAPTER 2

Tom Sledd was barking orders the next day. Sir Edmund Tilney, Master of the Revels, had, in his wisdom, re-opened the theatres as the plague seemed to be abating. Sledd didn't know that there had been an unholy row between Tilney and Philip Henslowe over this very issue. The Rose's stage-manager had not been in the half-locked theatre on the day in question and had not heard the swearing match taking place in Henslowe's eyrie under the eaves.

'I was merely following the scientia, Master Henslowe,' the old humbug had said.

'Bollocks!' had been the impresario's thoughtful response. 'You're just a miserable old Puritan who can't bear the thought of people enjoying themselves.'

Tilney had turned purple. 'The pestilence is spread by the miasmic odours in the air. You can even catch it from jakes seats.'

'Again,' Henslowe had persisted, 'I have to say bollocks.'

But Tilney had sailed on regardless, in full flow. 'It's a scientific fact. And what with all the purse-snatching and placket-fingering that goes on, both among the groundlings and in the better seats, theatres are hell-holes of putrefaction.'

'Excellent,' Henslowe had shouted. 'I think I'll put that on my posters. That'll bring in the crowds.'

But somebody had leaned on Edmund Tilney.

Rumour had it that it was the queen herself, who liked nothing better than a bit of mumming enlivened with the tongs and bones. So, it was now official. The plague had gone and the theatres were open. And men like Tom Sledd had a job to do.

Henslowe watched him from the secret slats of his eyrie window, ordering the workmen about as they scurried this way and that to construct the set for Marlowe's *Tamburlaine*. Philip Henslowe had thought long and hard about this one. *Anything* by Kit Marlowe was pure gold now. That great elemental wit was no more, but it had to be said that these days, when walls had ears as well as eyes and daggers lurked in darkness, some of Kit's later stuff was a little too edgy. *Dr Faustus* was all about the devil – best not upset the Puritans with any of that. *Edward II* criticised governments – perhaps not one to put on for Her Majesty or the Cecils who *actually* ran the country. But *Tamburlaine* was safe enough. He was a shepherd, for God's sake and nobody had a clue where Scythia was anyway.

There was a tap on Henslowe's door and he opened it. The greatest living actor of the age (according to him) stood there, hands on his hips, smiling.

'Yes, Ned,' Henslowe sighed. 'You're playing Tamburlaine.'

'Of course I am,' Alleyn beamed, 'but that's not why I'm here. You know Adam Proud?'

A second figure stood a little behind, as befits anyone in the company of the greatest living actor. He half bowed and held out a hand. 'Master Henslowe; it's an honour.'

'I'm sure it is,' the impresario said and ushered the pair to seats. 'What can I do for you, gentlemen?'

'Adam,' Alleyn did the unthinkable and gave centre stage to somebody else.

Proud cleared his throat. He was a personable young man, a little younger than Alleyn and not remotely as good looking. 'I represent the Lord High Admiral,' he said.

'The Admiral's men,' Alleyn added. Henslowe thought he had been quiet for rather a long time.

'Ah, so that's what they're called now, is it?' the

impresario said. 'Only, yesterday they were the Earl of Nottingham's men.'

'His Lordship has many titles,' Proud said, smiling, 'but throughout, his passion for the drama has shone through. He is dedicated to the muse, Master Henslowe, and is keen to put on as many plays as possible, both to enrich the populace and to educate them.'

'Amen to that,' Henslowe said. 'So, you're the Admiral's man?'

'Oh, Adam's far more that that, Henslowe. He's an actor of some repute and a playwright of rare talent. He is already, I suspect, the next Marlowe.'

Proud held up his hand, his face grim. 'No, Ned, no, that's several steps too far.' There was a break in his voice. 'There will never be another Marlowe.'

'Oh, rare Kit Marlowe,' Alleyn declaimed, as though the groundlings were milling around his feet, adoring him.

'Quite,' Proud said. 'No. I merely dabble. But I am here with an offer from the Admiral.'

Offers, deals, arrangements – these words were music to Philip Henslowe's ears. 'Say on.'

'His lordship feels that he has neglected his troupe of late.'

'Sadly, true,' said Alleyn glumly.

'But he intends to make up for that by reigniting the torch of the drama now that the theatres are to re-open.'

'Excellent,' Henslowe nodded.

'But he hasn't got a theatre.'

'Ah,' said Henslowe.

'But you have,' Alleyn pointed at him, 'And from what I've seen of it over the last couple of days, the Rose could do with a lick of paint.'

Henslowe frowned. 'Let me see if I've got this straight. The Admiral wants his Men to take over the Rose and perform … whatever. And I'm to take early retirement. Is that it?'

'No, no,' Proud and Alleyn were both laughing. 'Not at all. You would continue to manage the Rose,' Proud went on, 'with the usual take on the gate. You would select the plays and the playwrights …'

'But I have a say in the leading actors,' Alleyn butted in.

'Surprise, surprise,' Henslowe chuckled.

'His Lordship is not contemplating a buyout,' Proud said, 'but he has authorized a payment to you to make the new arrangement acceptable.'

There it was again; that word 'arrangement'. Henslowe was used to cutting to the chase – 'How much are we talking about?'

Proud fumbled in his purse and pulled out a piece of parchment. He passed it to Henslowe. Alleyn had seen the impresario's face light up like that before, but only ever in the presence of large amounts of money. Henslowe looked at Proud.

'When do you want to move in?'

Will Shaxsper was feeling down. Like everyone else, he had always known that Kit Marlowe was always frying other fish, that there were people who had more say in his life than ever the assembled company of the Rose did and yet … he still felt that they would miss him more than anyone else in his world. As he mooched along Shoreditch to his lodgings, his fingers interlaced behind his back, his face turned to the ground, he thought about his future. Surely, now, Henslowe would have to put on his plays – *Henry V, both* parts. Once the retrospective was over, of course. And although he didn't mean to, he couldn't help writing himself a rather splendid leading role from time to time. Alleyn and Burbage always got them in Marlowe's stuff, because Marlowe hadn't wanted them for himself. But surely … he lurched a few steps sideways, one shoulder hunched up to his ear then flinched and changed sides. Perhaps they had been right about having his ear pierced by Mistress Semple in Slack Alley. But by the time he saw her wiping the bacon grease off her hands on the cat, it had been rather too late. It was rather tender, but perhaps it was early days. He had learned in school that Hunchback Dick had walked like that and he couldn't see Alleyn or Burbage being prepared to show themselves like that to their public. He sighed and unlatched the door to his rooms. It had come to a pretty pass when a man had to write a cripple as a hero, just so he could get to play him himself. But there it was, no choice if he wanted to be rich and famous. He'd given up on handsome years ago.

Shaxsper sniffed the air and counted on his fingers. It wasn't his day for having his room swept out, he was sure. And as he hadn't paid for the last three times, he was doubtful whether he would get it done again any time soon. Not that he was sorry. He was almost certain that the girl just shook her broom out and moved a few bits around to make it look as though she had dusted. His bed wasn't due for a change for another couple of months, so it couldn't be that and yet … there was a fresher smell to the room than he was expecting. Perhaps it was just that spring was here. Her fragrance was even reaching into his foetid little room under the thatch. He sniffed again and shook his head. He laced his fingers and pushed away from him, stretching the tendons till the knuckles cracked. Then he extended his neck, his enormous forehead gleaming as it turned to the ceiling, to the floor, to the right, to the left. He couldn't remember who, but he had read somewhere that a famous writer did this religiously every day before starting work and where was the harm? There was no one to see. Shoreditch kept itself to itself.

He pulled a clean piece of parchment towards him and squared it carefully with the edges of the battered table he had managed to squeeze in under the meagre window of his room. He looked closely at the tip of his quill then tested it against his lip. Frowning, he ran a thumbnail along its edges, then ferreted in an ancient pot on the desk and brought out a small blade embedded in a rough handle. He swept the edge of it along the feather, then rubbed the newly honed nib on the edge of the pot, to take the fine shavings off. Then, he dipped it delicately into the inkpot sunk into a hole at the edge of the table. His landlady didn't know about this yet, but so much ink had been spilled as Shaxsper flung his arms around in his frenzy of invention that he was happy to deal with that when the time came; even paying for the table, he would still be groats in on the deal.

He looked down at the virgin sheet and frowned. He turned it at fifteen degrees and then thirty to the edge of the table. He took the quill out of the fingers of his right hand with thumb and forefinger of his left and flexed his hand this way and that before taking up the quill again. He pursed his mouth and looked out of the window, reflecting. He needed something dramatic to start Act 1 Scene 4 with, but what? He could see them as plain as day, Brackenbury and the doomed Clarence in the darkness of the Tower, but getting them to say the right line was causing him some trouble. Brackenbury would probably ask how Clarence was doing, but then what?

Taking a deep breath, he wrote, 'Why looks your grace so heavily today?' He looked down at the line, mouthed it and nodded. Yes, that was iambic enough – the beat of Marlowe's mighty line. He dipped the quill again and poised his fingers … he looked up. What was that noise? Rats in the bloody thatch again. If he had asked once he had asked a hundred times … there it was again. How could a man work in this racket? And now it was clouding over, London turning a dismal shade of grey. He'd have to light a candle in a minute. Did the Fates think he was made of money? How was he going to write a masterpiece if …

'It needs work, Will.'

The voice from the corner almost made Shaxsper shit himself. He had always had a vivid imagination, but this was above and beyond anything he had ever imagined before. It was Kit Marlowe's voice to the life and not bringing news of the hereafter or anything else that ghosts brought. No warning. No chain rattling. Just the line he had heard from him a thousand times before. He pressed a trembling hand to his pounding heart and waited for it to still a little. He held the hand out in front of him and willed it to stop trembling. Finally, with a deep breath and slow exhalation, he gripped the quill again and dipped it anew in the ink.

'No, seriously, Will, stop. It really does need work.' From the corner, the wraith unfolded itself, the very live and spit of Kit Marlowe, his brow unbroken, his clothes unbesmottered with gouts of blood. His jaw did not hang agape. His fingers as they adjusted his cuff were not withered claws. All in all, he looked pretty much like the Kit Marlowe who had waved an airy goodbye to Shaxsper not that long before he had been foully murdered.

'I … I … begone, foul fiend,' Shaxsper managed, fending the creature off with his quill.

The phantasm took the quill and placed it firmly in the inkwell. Then it took Shaxsper's hand and placed it on its own chest, where the doublet was unlaced.

'Will, does a ghost have a heart? Are its hands warm as yours … although, to be fair, your hands are really cold. Are you well? Are you coming down with something?' The ghoul looked anxiously into Shaxsper's eyes. 'Mother of God, not the Pestilence?'

'I … I … shock.' It was all the man could come up with, at short notice.

'Sorry. I can see it would be a shock, but I couldn't announce myself exactly, could I? Does it give you any comfort to know that you are the first person to know of my survival? Well, almost the first. Obviously, I couldn't do this alone. But since the inquest, the very first.'

'So …' Shaxsper was getting so he could hear things over the thudding of his heart.

'I'm alive, yes. And thirsty. I'm afraid I have polished off your Rhenish. Here.' Marlowe foraged in his purse. 'Nip out and get some more, will you? Some decent stuff this time. And some bread. And cheese. Do you ever eat? There's nothing here at all.'

'I … So you didn't die, then?'

'Indeed not. Stout fellow. Now, don't mention this to a soul and when you get back, I'll explain it all to you.'

Shaxsper stood irresolute. The grin was beginning to take over his face and there were so many questions he needed to ask. But he also knew that the sooner he was gone, the sooner he would be back, as his old grammer used to say. So he showed a clean pair of heels and Marlowe watched him go out into the grey of Shoreditch.

Buying Rhenish, bread and cheese takes longer sometimes than others and when Shaxsper got back, Marlowe was stretched out on his bed, fast asleep. On the page he had left adorned with just one line on his table, he now read, 'O, I have pass'd a miserable night, So full of ugly sights, of ghastly dreams, That, as I am a Christian faithful man, I would not spend another such a night, Though 'twere to buy a world of happy days, So full of dismal terror was the time!'

He looked at the man on the bed and smiled fondly.

Marlowe was not dead.

CHAPTER 3

Michael Johns was rarely what other people would call happy. He didn't smile as a habit, although when he did, it was as if the sun had broken through. So solemn was his normal expression that even his closest friends – of which he had but few – would have found it hard to tell when he was immeasurably sad. And today he was, indeed, immeasurably sad.

Since he first clapped eyes on Christopher Marlowe when he had walked into his study at Corpus Christi, he had known he was special. His wit and charm were only part of the man's character but they were what most people saw. Johns had known at once that there were many more layers beneath the glossed exterior and he had slowly peeled them away and he knew that Marlowe himself would admit that he, Michael Johns, knew him as well as anyone in the world. He had come to love him as he loved no one else and the fact that he was in the world somewhere was enough for him once their paths had diverged. So now, the world was a darker place.

Marlowe was dead.

Johns had shaken the dust of Corpus Christi from his feet years ago, sometimes it felt like a lifetime. He lived and worked now in Lincoln's Inn and enjoyed the feeling that he could bestride his world like a colossus, taking only a few hundred steps. It was true that the Devil's disciple, Gabriel

Harvey, was on the floor below, but the pair studiously ignored each other. John's room was sparse and neat, with a frugal look, but it suited him in more ways than one. As far as he could be, Michael Johns had been content and he knew he would be again. He just needed to reset his world, to accept it was a world where Marlowe was not breathing. With a sigh, he turned back to marking the confused whitterings of one of his stupider scholars. One thing was sure – Lincoln's Inn did not have the spark of genius in its lads that Corpus Christi had had. That they would one day be lawyers and therefore more or less ruling the world sometimes made their emeritus professor wake up in the night with a small nerve-racked scream. He scratched through a particularly inane comment from the youngest scion of a mighty house and ran desperate fingers through his hair, making it stand up on end. But still, it was a living – he shook his head ruefully, and ameliorated the remark he was about to write in the margin. But oh, for a mighty line. Just one, just one.

The tap on the door was on the edge of hearing. In fact, it was more of a light scratch than a tap. Johns looked up, his head cocked, unsure whether he had actually heard anything at all. But there it was again. He balanced his quill across his inkpot and pushed back his chair. He didn't get many visitors and certainly not this late. The denizens of Lincoln's Inn did not keep late hours, the domini because they had no need to, the scholars because they were all but nailed down after sunset by the proctors. He leaned his head against the oak panels and murmured, 'Who is it?'

'It's me,' a ghost said. 'Let me in.'

Johns felt the hairs on the back of his neck rise and fall in waves. He had been sitting in silence for so long that his ears were fizzing gently and he told himself that that was what he had heard. 'Me?' he said, louder. 'That doesn't tell me much. Who are you?'

'*Me*,' the voice whispered. 'I can't say any more out here. This is Lincoln's Inn. The walls have ears and after all, I am meant to be dead.'

John's hand on the latch jerked and the door gave, just a threat.

'That's it,' the voice urged. 'Let me in.'

Johns had heard of this kind of thing, of demons who took the shape of loved ones. If you let them in when they asked, then they could stay and no power on earth could dislodge them. 'I … I don't want to,' he said, leaning his forehead on the door jamb, trying to steady himself.

''I'm not a demon …'

But surely, they all said that.

'Michael, for the love of all you hold most dear, let me *in*. Someone could come along at any moment. And this is the kind of place where I would be recognized in a heartbeat. The scholars here make up the swell of groundlings any day of the week.' The whisper became more urgent. 'I can hear footsteps. *Let me in*!'

And, against his better judgement, Michael Johns opened the door.

Will Shaxsper was a married man, a fact he kept up his sleeve for when any woman he shared his dubious charms with became a little too friendly for comfort but otherwise generally chose to forget. He hadn't lived in connubial bliss for … he chewed his lip and closed his eyes, counting on his fingers, but couldn't come up with a finite amount of time. He settled for 'never'. He had never lived in connubial bliss and the children were more of an accidental result of a bit of threshing in his second best bed than the mortar that held together his happy home. But one thing he had enjoyed a little when living with Anne, on the few occasions she shut up and let him get a word in edgewise, was that she was someone to talk to. Whether she listened or not was another thing and in retrospect, he doubted that this happened very often. But he could talk and he knew that there was someone in the room with ears, so who knew; perhaps his news was listened to, perhaps not. And now that he had the most momentous piece of news he had ever had, there was no one to tell. He pressed his face into the pillow where Marlowe's head had recently lain and whispered his news into it. The goosedown, he found, reacted in similar fashion to his abandoned wife and somehow, that didn't surprise him overmuch.

John's door had only opened a crack before Marlowe squeezed himself inside and shut it soundlessly behind him. He stood inside, his back to the wood and smiled at Johns, looking for a brief moment like the boy who had walked so unwillingly into the lecture room at Corpus Christi those few short years before. So much had happened, but for that minute it could have been yesterday. Michael Johns felt the questions rise in his throat, but realized as they took shape that every one made him sound like a hectoring mother or lover, when their beloved turned up after a night on the tiles. This was more, much more than that and so he opted for silence.

'You are quiet, Dr Johns,' Marlowe said, still pitching his voice low, as if the room were full of ears.

'I confess I am stuck for anything to say,' Johns replied. He was a man of few words at the best of times, but just now, he had none.

'I haven't seen many people since … well, since,' Marlowe told him. 'But those I have in the main have asked what happened. How it is that I am still in the land of the living.'

'And how do you answer them?' Johns asked, pragmatically.

Marlowe chuckled. 'I don't. I will, but for now, I can't. I need to speak to a few other people first, to find out who I can trust, if anyone.' He caught the look on Johns' face. 'You, of course, I know I can trust *you*. But it is still better – safer, I might almost say – for you to know as little as you can bear. But I wanted you to know I am alive.'

Johns dipped his head. It was like a dream and he looked back at his desk, half afraid to see himself sitting there, intent on marking his essays. But the desk was empty. He surreptitiously pinched himself and winced. No, this was happening, that much was certain.

'Well, tell me nothing, then,' he said, ushering his guest to a chair. 'Except perhaps to tell me what you intend to do next. Where you intend to go.'

Marlowe sat and stretched his legs out in front of him,

flexing his feet at the ankles. He was wearing hand-me-down shoes and they chafed somewhat across the instep. 'What I intend to do next will depend on a lot of things, but mainly on who it was who tried to have me killed.'

Johns raised an eyebrow. 'The gossip is that it was the men you were drinking with in a low tavern …'

Marlowe whistled low and long. 'Has that story become *the* story already?' he asked. 'I know it was all in the inquest, but still … Nicholas Faunt knows how to spin a tale so it has its own impetus.'

Johns tutted. He had never really approved of Nicholas Faunt. 'I might have known he would be in there somewhere.'

Marlowe patted his arm. 'Nicholas isn't as black as you paint him, Michael,' he said. 'In fact, were it not for him, I wouldn't be with you now. I really would be rotting quietly to myself in a cheap grave in Deptford.'

'How …?'

Marlowe held up his hand. 'Let's just say I had crossed some powerful people. Of late, accusations had been made against me. That I called Moses a conjuror, implied that Christ and John the Baptist were lovers …'

Johns crossed himself.

'Quite,' Marlowe smiled. 'All of it lies or, at the very least, taken out of context. I was accused and had to defend myself in front of the Star Chamber.'

'I'd heard nothing of this,' Johns frowned. As a dominus at one of the leading Inns of Court, there were not many cases that didn't pass by him.

'That's because it didn't happen. I was due to attend and had to report to them every day. In case, presumable, I skipped the country.'

'Deptford!' Johns clicked his fingers.

'Exactly, I was to sail on the *Marigold* with the next morning's tide. I knew my lodgings were being watched, so I needed some time and some space. I found an Ordinary run by a Mistress Bull. What I also found were some surprising fellow guests.'

'The men you were drinking with in a low tavern?'

'Precisely,' Marlowe said. 'You're a man of the law, Michael; you know how the truth slips sideways and once it slips, it's the devil's own job to get it back on the straight and narrow. Ingram Frizer and Nicholas Skeres I knew from the Rose; walking gentlemen and coney-catchers who'd fleece a man as good as look at him. What I hadn't realized – and I could kick myself for this – is that they'd also slit a man's throat for a groat. Sorry about the weak rhyme, by the way. It's an old one of Will Kemp's.'

Johns couldn't help chuckling. The old clown was dead now, but he had always found him hysterically funny; that bit with the dead sheep …

'The third man was Robert Poley.'

'Walsingham's man, wasn't he?' Michael Johns knew that Marlowe walked some strange corridors, those of the queen's spymaster among them.

'Among other people's,' Marlowe said. 'And that's the point. Frizer and Skeres are neither here nor there. A man has to make his way in the world as best he can. But Poley is in a different league altogether. He was the organizer.'

'Of …?'

'A plot to kill me. These men were paid to do the business. I just need to know by whom.'

'Tell me, Kit. Deptford; where were you going?'

'The Americas? Martin Frobisher's frozen north? Even, God help me, the court of the king of Scots? I don't know. It all seems unimportant now.'

Johns crossed himself again and Marlowe laughed.

'Skeres and Frizer, I could have handled,' the playwright said. 'Poley, probably. But all three – that was a trinity too far. That's where Faunt came in.'

'He was there?'

'At the last minute, yes. Apparently, he'd been following me since my arrest by the Star Chamber – "just in case", as he put it. We struck a deal. All of us would walk away but whoever the ultimate paymaster was would expect a body – mine.'

'How in God's name did that work?'

'Does the name John Penry mean anything to you?'

Johns shook his head. 'Should it?'

'Penry was involved in the Marprelate tracts. He was a Puritan criticizing the bishops.'

'One of many,' Johns nodded.

'They found him guilty of blasphemy and hanged him the day before I got to Deptford. At Thomas a Watering along the old road to Canterbury. Faunt, of course, knew all about that and pulled his usual strings to acquire the man's body. Penry was about my age and since none of the jurors at Deptford knew either him or me by sight, Faunt got away with it. He was there at the inquest and must have had a few anxious moments as the jury viewed the body. If they'd inched down the shroud, they'd have seen the rope burn around Penry's neck. Rumours were swirling that I'd been stabbed in the eye, with the usual roaring and cursing you'd expect from a heretic and atheist of course …'

'Of course,' Johns smiled.

'So at some point, Faunt made an obliging wound to the man's forehead.'

'Good God!'

'The ways of Faunt are strange, Michael. Trust me; there's a whole world out there of which you know nothing. Best to keep it that way.'

'And Poley? Skeres? Frizer?'

'Frizer … they drew lots for this … admitted to killing me in self-defence. He'll do a little time at Her Majesty's pleasure and then be released. Skeres is probably back at the Rose, carrying a spear in my *Tamburlaine* – Philip Henslowe is cashing in on my demise as only he can. As for Master Poley … well, he's a gentleman I need to talk to. I want to know who put the silver in his purse.'

'Kit, Kit,' Johns shook his head. 'Let it go. It's over. You were lucky this time; Nicholas Faunt might not be around next time.'

'That's a chance I'll have to take. But the main reason that I am here,' Marlowe ran his hands through his hair, 'is that I need to look a little less like myself. I have avoided people where I can in the past days, obviously, but I have nevertheless had two people tell me I look a lot like that whatisname, you know, the one what wrote them plays what got stabbed in the eye. And I had to agree that indeed I do, but I am an apothecary from the Isle of Dogs.'

Johns laughed. 'You could pass for an apothecary, at a pinch,' he said. 'But you do look much more like that whatisname what wrote them plays, I must agree.' He leaned back and half closed his eyes. 'It's the silhouette, the shape your hair makes against the light. You need to change that. And the beard. If that went you could pass as a scholar new up from Eton.'

Marlowe looked stricken. 'The beard? No, surely, that can stay, can't it? I've had that since I first grew a hair on my chin.'

John's raised an eyebrow. 'Indeed you have and, if I might say so without causing offence, you did look like a proper natural with about four hairs sprouting from your lip. But when they all joined up eventually, I'll grant it does suit you and stops you looking like a boy wet behind the ears at least.'

Marlowe went up to the window, dark now beyond the glass and examined his reflection, distorted as it was in the cheap plate. He fingered his face and pulled it this way and that. Then, he turned back to Johns. 'As you say, I need to lose the beard.' He sighed. 'Can I keep the moustache, perhaps?'

Johns shook his head.

'The earring, though.'

Again, that was a definite no.

'I will look like a common apprentice,' Marlowe wailed. 'With no hair, no beard, no earring.'

'Isn't that the point?' Johns said, crisply. 'I don't know how many apprentices London contains, but there seem to be as many as stars in the firmament. The best way to hide a grain of sand is to put it down on a beach. Now, the only question is, are you going to shave your head, or shall I do it for you?'

'*Shave* it? What, down to the skin?' Marlowe's eyes were always wide and watchful but now they were almost starting out of his head.

'No, we say "shave" but I believe it is achieved by some kind of clippers. We have a man here in the Inn who makes sure the scholars' heads are neat and louse free.'

'Lice? Is that something that …' Marlowe surreptitiously lifted his head away from the back of the chair.

'No. Because we have a man here in the Inn who …'

'Oh, I see. Prevention is better than cure. Well, I can't go to him, not really.'

'Don't worry. I will go down now and borrow his clippers. I'll say … I'll say … well, I'll think of something. Will you take something to drink while I am gone?'

Marlowe remembered that among his many good points, that Michael Johns had only a rudimentary knowledge of what made a wine fine and shook his head. 'I ate with … someone else, earlier.' Marlowe had been an intelligencer for all his adult years and only now was he realizing how hard it could be to balance lies and friendship. For now, he was keeping the list of who he visited close to his chest. Johns was secretly glad he said no – to his knowledge, all he had in his press was a long-opened bottle of Hippocras and half a macaron which he wasn't at all sure was unsullied by mouse nibbles.

'I'll go down now and get them, then. I'll get some hot water from the kitchen while I'm there. You will find a razor and some soap in that cupboard in the corner.'

Marlowe looked quizzical.

Johns rubbed his chin. 'For the beard. Now that *will* have to be a shave, I'm afraid. Clippers can only do so much.'

Marlowe was still hoping that the beard would be able to stay, but he could see he was fighting a losing battle. And Johns was right. Another apprentice among so many would disappear like no playwright could. While he waited, he removed his earring and, finding Johns' copy of Ovid's *Metamorphoses*; on every level, it seemed to be the right place and who knew, in years to come, when he really was dead, it might bring some comfort to his old mentor to find it there, the gold dimmed, the pages marked with a permanent circle to show where he had been, once.

Johns was soon back with the clippers, fearsome things

with a spring handle and two blades so sharp they seemed to cut time itself. Marlowe eyed them suspiciously.

'Do you know how to use those things,' he said, backing away despite himself.

'I've seen them used,' Johns hedged.

'But not actually *used* them,' Marlowe persisted.

'Not as such. But it can't be that hard, can it? I would imagine that all a person needs to do – that is, a person whose hair is being shorn – is to keep still.' He clicked the blades. 'Very still, probably. I have seen many haircuts and never any bloodshed.'

Marlowe tipped his head back and looked down his nose at his nemesis. 'Let's take it bit by bit, shall we?' he suggested. 'Cut the long bits first and then go nearer the skin if you – if *we* – feel inclined?'

Johns shrugged and walked over to the clothes press beside the bed and got out a linen nightshirt. 'Put this on, it will catch some of the hair. Then I have some clothes you can borrow for now. They are simpler than your usual and will serve you as an apprentice, I think.'

Marlowe stretched out his arms and looked at what he was wearing. 'Simple things indeed,' he said. 'But needs must, when the devil drives. Who knew that being dead would be so complicated.' With the air of a man going to the gallows, he flung the nightshirt over his head and sat down on a hard stool by the slumbering fire. 'Get on with it, quick now, before I change my mind. Better light another taper, perhaps, so you don't accidentally snip off an ear.'

And so, bit by bit and lock by lock, Marlowe's hair, every curl and tendril, fell to the floor around his feet. Michael Johns got into the rhythm after a while and began to see the solemn ritual as a calming catharsis of everything which had gone before, the worry, the longing, the love. Soon, instead of a wild playwright who was all things to all men, the Muses' darling, there sat before the fire a young apprentice, all eyes and downy cheek, his hair a close cropped whisper of corn and sunlight.

'How do I look?' Marlowe said. He had never been vain, but now he realized that perhaps he should have been.

He wondered if he would ever be able to look like himself again. He wandered over the to mirror of the window and looked at himself then through it to the dark shapes of Lincoln's Inn.

Johns watched him from the shadows. Kit Marlowe was indeed finally dead. Even the eyes, dark in the reflection, looked different, deeper, more brooding, were that even possible. A thought passed through his mind and he spoke it without thinking.

'What are you going to call yourself?' he said.

'That's a good point,' said the ghost in the window. 'Eventually, perhaps something like William Shaxsper. But for now, something more prosaic. I haven't decided but I will know it when I say it. And I will, of course, let you know as soon as I do.' He passed his hand across his newly shorn head. 'Thank you for this, Michael. And for everything.'

And with that, Michael Johns was satisfied.

Sir William Danby took his pleasures where he could. That didn't involve Lady Danby, who had the intellect and, these days, the skin of an old prune. A rather more voluptuous pleasure sat on the coroner's lap that morning, letting the old man's hands wander where they would. And Lizzie Wallace didn't come cheap. The most expensive of the Winchester geese who offered their services to gentlemen along the river's south bank, the Bishop of Winchester himself had often dipped his ecclesiastical wick and only rented Lizzie out to those he reckoned.

'Oho, careful, my dear,' Danby winced as the girl's attentions to him became too vigorous. 'This damask cost an arm and a leg.'

'Arms and legs are important, Willie,' Lizzie purred, 'but they're just a warm-up for the real thing, aren't they?'

And she straddled him, sliding the fabric of his cod piece to one side. Silly old duffer! Who wore a cod-piece these days?

'I can come back,' a voice from the door interrupted proceedings somewhat.

Danby nearly swallowed his goatee; even Lizzie lost

her rhythm. The coroner all but kicked the girl off his lap and pulled his robes around him. The man in the doorway had the close-cropped hair currently fashionable among London's Puritans, the same cut, as it happened, that the apprentices wore with their rough manners and appalling language. This man was clearly no apprentice, though. His doublet and Venetians were of cheap velvet, with a lawn collar at his throat and a dagger at his back.

'Er … that's all the dictation for today,' Danby said to the girl. 'We'll continue at some other time.'

The visitor waited until Lizzie had gone. As she passed him, she gave him an odd look. That face … it was so familiar, but the hair …

'Good morrow, mistress,' the visitor said. 'Robert Brackenbury.' He took her hand and kissed it. Lizzie blinked. Brackenbury. For all the world, he looked like Kit M … and she was gone, shoved gently but inexorably out of the door.

'Sir William.' The stranger crossed the room, giving the coroner time to ensure he was decent. 'Robert Brackenbury.' He bowed.

'Master Brackenbury.' Danby was still recovering his composure. He was getting too old for all this. 'Did my man not tell you I was indisposed?'

'Your man?' Brackenbury repeated. He must have been the slime at the outer door that he had paid off with a couple of groats. 'And, if I may say so, you seemed to be doing quite well for a man who is indisposed.'

Danby frowned. All in all, the morning was not going well.

'What do you want?' he asked.

Brackenbury threw himself down in the chair facing the coroner. 'The late Christopher Marlowe,' he said. 'Can we talk?'

'You went to see Danby?' Nicholas Faunt couldn't believe what he was hearing. 'Why, in God's name?'

Marlowe shrugged. 'To find out what he knew.'

'That could have taken you seconds or a lifetime, depending on how you approached him.'

'Well, there you are,' Marlowe said. 'I approached him in the way you taught me; you and Walsingham.'

'But the man is …'

'A crony of Burghley's, yes. And yet …'

'And yet?'

'He seemed to be as honest as the day is long, at least in the legal department. As to his private life, Lady Danby may be a little less than pleased.'

'How did you gain access to Her Majesty's coroner?' Faunt wanted to know.

'The usual way,' Marlowe said. 'Pieces of silver. I told him I was Christopher Marlowe's cousin once removed and that I had heard that the playwright was dead.'

'What did he say?'

'That was usual, too. He was very sorry for my loss, but he couldn't divulge. Individual cases. Client privilege. All the platitudes that men come out with when they're put on the spot.'

'So, you're no further forward?'

'No.' Marlowe sat down, throwing his hat onto the table. 'You were in court – at my inquest. How did Danby handle it?'

'Professionally, I thought. No obvious signs of fear nor favour. There again, he didn't call any witnesses, either.'

'No Poley? No Skeres? No Eleanor Bull?'

'Nobody.

For a while, the two men looked at each other. Then Faunt said, 'Look, Kit, I thought we agreed that you would take this Heaven-sent opportunity of your rebirth, as it were, to do what you said you intended to do, go north to the king of Scots.'

'No.' Marlowe shook his head, missing the bounce of curls on the back of his neck and absent-mindedly smoothed his shorn scalp. 'That was what *you* said I should do. I have unfinished business.'

'Oh?' Faunt raised an eyebrow. 'In the shape of …?'

'You know as well as I do. The four horsemen of the Apocalypse – the Cecils, father and son; Howard of Effingham; Lord Hunsdon.'

'The most powerful men in the country,' Faunt said, grimly.

'Who effectively signed my death warrant,' Marlowe reminded him.

'You don't know that for a fact,' Faunt defended them.

'No, I don't,' Marlowe concurred. 'That's why I must finish my business – to find proof, once and for all.'

Faunt looked into the dark eyes of the man he had trusted now for nearly a decade. 'If they *are* guilty, Kit,' he said, 'they won't fail next time. I won't be around for ever.'

Marlowe smiled. 'Yes, you will,' he said.

'They'll kill you, Kit.'

Marlowe nodded. 'They can try.'

CHAPTER 4

Tom Sledd had not always had an easy life although, were he to be queuing at the Pearly Gates, he would be able to tell St Peter that, by and large, it had been happy. He had been loved for most of it and if the love had shown itself in the early years by a cuff upside the ear from his mentor Ned Sledd, actor manager extraordinaire, it had also come in the shape of his lovely Meg and their little ones and of their love he had no doubt. And he had loved back in return, Ned, the force of nature, he had loved with all his heart and soul though showing it would have got him short shrift. Meg took all the love and kisses Tom knew how to give and smiled at it all. But Kit Marlowe had been in another league. Tom had had no brothers, but if he had, he would have wanted them made in the image of the playwright. Honest, clever, witty – and not bad company to have in the days when Tom would be out wenching. Although he had never seen Kit creeping up the back stairs to the loft with any of the many girls who threw themselves at him, petticoats, eyes and teeth all flashing white; a wise man standing at his shoulder could do quite well with the lush pickings of the rebound.

But his soul was torn. Here he was, stage manager of the Rose, right hand man to the great Philip Henslowe, rubbing shoulders with legends like Ned Alleyn and Richard Burbage, about to put on a dazzling retrospective of Kit

Marlowe's plays. All around him lay the half-carpentered props of the pampered jade of Asia, the backdrop for *Tamburlaine*. But the heart had gone. The genius who had made all this possible – the agonies of Dido of Carthage, the torment of Dr Faustus, the malevolence of the Jew of Malta – was no more. It was as though there were a trapdoor in the centre of the wooden O and there was no bottom to it.

Will Shaxsper couldn't read men's minds. He liked to think he could, but his reading of a situation was often woefully wide of the mark. Yet, on the sunlit stage of the Rose that morning, before the carpenters arrived with their saws and awls, he had rarely seen a man more miserable than Tom Sledd sitting there, idly twirling a spear in his hand. And for once, the seer, the yellow leaf, knew exactly why.

'Come on, Tom,' the Warwickshire man said. 'It can't be as bad as all that.'

'Piss off, Will,' Sledd growled. He was not in the mood for bonhomie this morning.

Shaxsper sat down alongside him, his mind spinning. It would only take four words to put the man out of his misery for ever. And yet he had been sworn to secrecy. All his life, Will Shaxsper had agonized over things. By the time he was five, he knew that his father, the glover, was the most hated man in Stratford. He wasn't that fond of school, either, dawdling on his way there with his satchel dragging in the mud. Then there was the nonsense with the deer in Charlecote Park – all an ugly rumour, of course, caused by people who hated his father and schoolfriends who were nothing of the sort. And then, there was Anne – dumpy, frumpy Anne who had seemed all right before he set eyes on the delights that London had to offer. She had her own cottage, of course, which helped. But all in all, she was not enough to keep him on the edge of the forest of Arden. And, so, London it was. He'd never believed that Whittington rubbish abut the streets being paved with gold, but the place had a lure of its own. There was no city like it in the world. And that made him feel guilty as well.

So, with all that in mind, as it flashed before him in an instant, he put a playwrightly arm around the stage manager and said, 'It's all right, Tom. Kit's not dead.'

Shaxsper had never quite believed the Bible's stories of thunderbolts and flashes of lightning on the Damascus road, but he saw one now, reflected in Tom Sledd's eyes. What emerged from Tom Sledd's lips was not so much a rejoinder as an animal roar. The sound echoed around the Rose and as it ended with a sort of query, Shaxsper felt an explanation was in order.

'It's true, Tom,' he said. 'I saw him last night, fit as a fiddle. Of course, I can't divulge …'

Sledd had so many questions that wanted to come tumbling out of his mouth, that in the end he just sat there with said mouth wide open. Shaxsper grabbed the man's cheeks and forced him to focus. 'Tom,' he said gravely. 'This is between us. Do you understand? On no account can you tell anyone.'

'Marlowe's alive?' Ben Sharpe repeated. He'd been hammering nails into the Rose's woodwork for so long now that he had a permanent ringing in his ears and he wasn't quite sure what Sledd had just told him.

'As I live and breathe,' the stage manager said. 'Which is what he does too.'

'What …?' The carpenter was as full of questions as Sledd had been, but the stage manager held up his hand.

'You didn't hear this from me,' Sledd said. 'Mum's the word.' And he beetled off to bully his workforce, joyously happy that there was, after all, a God and that He sat in His heaven.

'What was that?' Jack Semple bent Sharpe's ear, which was what Jack's old mum did for people south of the river. He had been a little out of earshot and what with the paint filling his nostrils, his hearing was a little out of whack too. A doctor of physick he met once in an inn had told him that it was all about the mercury, but he might have got that wrong. Because surely, the lead would counteract any harm the mercury could do? He'd have to ask his mum.

'Marlowe,' Sharp murmured out of the side of his mouth. 'Alive.'

'I heard he'd jumped from St Paul's steeple.' Will Clegg couldn't help but join in. 'That's a bloody miracle, that's what that is, right there.' He caught sight of a new arrival, hauling off his cloak. 'Master Proud, Master Proud.'

The playwright looked askance. He was a university wit, for God's sake, a man of letters and substance, well known and liked in the establishment of Lord Howard of Effingham, the hero of the Armada. Very much alive though Proud was, he already sat at God's right hand. 'What?' was the only word he could spare that morning.

'Kit Marlowe's alive,' Clegg blurted out. The man smelt of tar and timber, things of which Proud knew nothing.

'Alive?'

'Incredible, isn't it?'

'What's incredible?' Ned Alleyn clicked his fingers and a lackey took his cloak and sword.

'Marlowe's alive,' Proud said.

'I knew it!' Alleyn laughed. 'I've never believed the prattle of South Londoners. Men of Marlowe's calibre don't die over a quarrel about a bill. It isn't seemly.'

'What isn't seemly?' Richard Burbage clicked his fingers too, but nobody was quick enough to take the cloak and he threw it over one of Sharpe's truncated columns.

'Marlowe,' Alleyn told him. 'Rumours of his death have been much exaggerated.'

'Of course they have.' Burbage sat down on some newly planed steps. 'All that's very well, Alleyn, but I've just heard an uglier rumour still.'

'Oh? What's that?' The world's greatest actor squatted several times and turned his upper body, hands on hips. Grace of movement – that was what acting was all about and you didn't achieve that without work.

Burbage looked at him with undisguised contempt. 'That you're playing Tamburlaine.'

'Of course I am, dear boy.' Alleyn stood up, adopted a new pose and limped across the stage. 'Look, I've got the legs for it.'

'Yes,' Burbage conceded. 'Shame about the rest of you. I'm going to see Henslowe about this.'

'You do that,' Alleyn began gargling from a goblet one of the women had provided for him. 'Adam and I have things to discuss.' He beckoned Proud to him. 'How are things progressing with the Lord Admiral's Men?' he asked loudly.

Philip Henslowe was sitting in his eyrie that morning, dipping his quill idly into the ink and planning what to write on his latest playbill. Perhaps he should edge it in black to mark the passing of the legend that was Kit Marlowe. Perhaps …

'Alleyn's playing Tamburlaine?' Burbage had made louder entries on the stage, but this one rattled the rafters.

Henslowe's face fell. One moment, he was in a transcendental frame of mind, musing with the Muse's Darling and now, the harsh reality of the theatre world had brought him howling back to the here and the now. 'You've heard,' he said.

'Did you think I wouldn't?' Burbage snarled, flinging himself into a chair. 'Look, Henslowe, you and I go back aways.'

'We do,' the impresario acknowledged.

'And I believe I have always given satisfaction with my performances.'

'You have,' Henslowe sighed.

'Then why, in God's name, have you set me aside now? Oh, Alleyn will make a reasonable actor one day, but until then … especially since your Retrospective is dead in the water.'

Henslowe blinked. 'What do you mean?'

'Well, Henslowe,' Burnage was confused. 'How can you have a Retrospective when the man's alive?'

Henslowe dropped his quill. 'Marlowe's alive?'

'Of course,' Burbage said. 'Really, Henslowe, as a theatre owner of some repute, I'd have thought you'd have known all about it.'

'I know *nothing* about it,' Henslowe growled. 'As always, I'm the last to know.'

'Yes,' Burbage chuckled. 'You probably are. Certainly, when I arrived a few minutes ago, everybody was talking about it. Not that it will get beyond the Rose, of course.'

'No,' Henslowe shouted. 'No, it can't. Call the company, Burbage. Everybody down to the lowliest hautboy player. I want this one scotched. Immediately.'

'What's your problem?' Burbage asked. 'I thought you'd be delighted that your golden goose can continue to lay eggs. My God, how the money rolls in. And frankly, I don't see how you can stop them talking.'

Henslowe raised an eyebrow and hooded his eyes. 'Tell me, Richard,' he said, smoothly. 'How long could you live if I stopped paying you?'

Burbage shrugged. 'I don't do this for the money, Philip.'

'Naturally not. But just give me a round figure. A week? A month? For ever?'

Burbage thought of the women, most of them elderly, all of them ugly as the Devil's arse, who kept him in frills and furbelows. No one – least of all Richard Burbage – thought they loved him for his well-turned calf. Once he wasn't famous any more, they would move on to whoever was. His shrug was now less confident. 'A while.'

'Well, the carpenters could probably go a week. The musicians – lucky to get past the next meal. Plus the accidental crushing of a finger here or there tends to keep mouths shut, I find. We'll keep them quiet, never you fret. But ...' Henslowe gnawed his lip, trying to take it all in. This was better than a play and twice as complicated. 'Yes,' he said. 'to go back to your rather hackneyed goose analogy, long term, you're probably right. But it'll ruin the Retrospective. Better to keep the idea that Marlowe's dead, make a killing with *Tamburlaine* and then announce his miraculous renaissance.' He caught the look on Burbage's face. 'Come on,' he said. 'It happens all the time. Green children in Suffolk, missing for years, turn up again unharmed if a little, er, green. Then there was that scone in Wolverhampton with the face of John the Baptist on it. And the eighty year old woman from Boscastle who gave birth to triplets. People *love* miracles. Yes, yes; it'll work. But for now,' he leaned forward, his eyes burning into Burbage's, 'Marlowe must remain dead.'

The actor shook his head. 'Your capacity to make money out of disasters never ceases to amaze me, Henslowe,' he said. 'And, just think, you can do this again and again, can't you? You'll just have to kill Marlowe a second time.'

'If you could leave your dagger with me, sir?' The gatekeeper of the Marshalsea was politeness itself.

'If I could do that, turnkey, the world would be a better place than it is.' Nicolas Faunt had never suffered lackeys gracefully.

'It *is* for your own protection, sir.' The gatekeeper was nothing if not persistent.

'No, turnkey,' Faunt smiled. 'My dagger is for my protection. I'll take my chances.'

'As you wish, sir. It's just that there are some rough people in this house.'

'Aren't there, though,' Faunt agreed. 'You should see the House of Commons.'

Since the gatekeeper had only ever seen the Commons from the outside, he had to take Faunt's word for that. 'What name again?' He was trying to read his ledger by the guttering flame of a candle in the wind of the lodge and it wasn't easy.

'Frizer,' Faunt said. 'Ingram Frizer.'

'Oh, him,' the gatekeeper grunted. 'Murderer, that one.'

'Judge not, turnkey,' Faunt wagged a finger at him, 'lest ye be judged.' Nicholas Faunt could quote scripture with the best of them if push came to shove. And in the darkness of the Marshalsea, push *always* came to shove.

'This way, sir.'

'Not the Hole,' Faunt said. 'I want to see Frizer on his own. Just the two of us.'

The gatekeeper raised an eyebrow. He had no idea who this man was, except for the colour of his gold. And all sorts of people turned up at his lodge with all sorts of reasons for seeing prisoners. Some came to poke the lunatics with sticks. Others to make them turn to God. He wasn't sure which was worse.

'Follow me,' he said, and Faunt did.

The candlelight gave way to torches in iron braziers that threw macabre shadows onto the rough stones. Faunt followed the man up a tight spiral staircase and across a walkway. In the dimly lit room below, he saw a scene from Hell. Half naked wretches lay there, or squatted in corners, the felons that time forgot. Time had no meaning here. Day and night blended into each other and the thickness of the prison walls blocked out the sound of striking clocks and church bells. Outside was the largest city in the world, hustling with noise and life, but on the ground floor of the Marshalsea was the Hole, aptly named for the desperate space between life and death, where men and women had lost all hope.

The odd scream and cackle of laughter broke the monstrous mumbling. Two or three of the wretches looked up at Faunt passing above them, in his Spanish boots and velvet Venetians. One or two of the two or three spat, adding to the slime on the straw-strewn floor.

''Ello, your worship,' a girl called up to him. She was standing in the middle of a circle of men, lifting up her dress for Faunt's benefit and waggling her breasts at him. Otherwise she was naked.

The gatekeeper paused and caught Faunt's eye. 'Er … I don't suppose …' and he jerked his head towards the girl.

'Frizer,' Faunt reminded him.

'Right,' the gatekeeper marched on, the keys jangling at his belt. Clearly, this rich visitor swung the other way, although the gatekeeper had to concede that Annie wasn't to everybody's taste, even after a bath to disguise the smell.

The gatekeeper reached a low, oak door studded with nails and unlocked it. He ushered Faunt into a small windowless room which had a table and one chair. He lit another candle and waited until Faunt had sat down.

'I'll just get him, sir,' he said, and Faunt heard the door slam and the lock turn, no doubt, he mused, for his own protection. He could hear the rhythmic chanting from the Hole outside. Annie was clearly in fine form tonight.

Around the walls, he read the scrawled testimony of

the damned, a prayer here, a curse there. All of them innocent, of course, all of them wronged.

The key grated in the lock and Ingram Frizer was pushed into the room. His hair was a stranger to a comb and his beard was already wild and lawless. Chains rattled from the bracelets on his wrists and he smelt like a jakes. Even so, his face lit up at the sight of his visitor.

'Master Faunt …'

But Faunt held up a finger and he stopped. 'Thank you, turnkey,' he said. 'I'll take it from here.'

'But, sir …'

'Thank you.'

'This man is under indictment for murder, sir,' the gatekeeper persisted. He didn't want to be responsible for what might happen; not on his watch.

'Master Frizer and I are old friends,' Faunt lied. 'I'll knock when I need you.'

The gatekeeper hesitated; he'd had unpleasantnesses before and the Master of the Marshalsea took, if everyone excused the pun, no prisoners. He backed out and locked the door again.

Frizer had nowhere to sit. The bracelets chafed his wrists and his Venetians were caked in shit, one of the little by-products of the Marshalsea fare.

'Master Faunt!' he blurted out. 'What's going on? I've been here for days. You said …'

'Don't presume to tell me what I said, Frizer,' Faunt snapped. 'One word from me and you'll be looking at a rope's end.'

'But … we had an arrangement.'

'Attempted murder is a felony in this great country of ours,' Faunt reminded him. 'You will admit that you intended to take the life of one Christopher Marlowe, of the parish of St George's, Canterbury, on Wednesday last, thirtieth of May?'

'Well, I …'

'We've had this conversation, Frizer. You, Skeres and Poley were caught red-handed, with daggers drawn in a little room in Eleanor Bull's house in Deptford. Specifically, by me.' Faunt paused. 'Do you remember any of this, Frizer? Or has the Hole dimmed your senses?'

Frizer snapped, 'Of course I remember. And we had an agreement. I would confess to killing Marlowe in exchange for a certain sum and a pardon. Well, I haven't seen anything yet.'

Faunt looked up at him. 'Frizer,' he said quietly, 'I am a patient man, which is why I am not leaving here to have a little chat with Master Topcliffe.'

'Topcliffe?' Frizer swallowed hard.

'Yes, you know, Her Majesty's rackmaster, a gentleman who knows more ways to kill a man exquisitely slowly than you have had the shits over the last week. Yes, we had an arrangement as you put it, but you drew the short straw at Mistress Bull's. It could have been Robyn Poley. It could have been Richard Skeres, but as bad luck would have it, it was you. Master Marlowe had his own reasons, bizarrely enough, for wanting to stay alive, so I dreamt up this little subterfuge. He could be useful to me in the future. You, however,' Faunt leaned forward, 'are not.' He leaned back. 'The wheels of justice grind slow, Frizer,' he said. 'We cannot arouse suspicion by granting you a pardon too quickly. You *will* receive one. It will say that you killed Marlowe in self-defence. And it will be signed by Her Majesty – *such* an elegant hand. But you'll wait until she and I are good and ready. Do I make myself clear?'

'Perfectly.' Frizer knew when the game was up and he felt his old trouble coming on as his stomach growled and rebelled.

'I really came to make sure that you keep your mouth shut,' Faunt said. 'You and I both know that the Marshalsea leaks like a sieve. There are all sorts of malignant busybodies in here with ears like elephants.'

'What?' It was easy to confuse a man like Ingram Frizer.

'Never mind. My point is that your fellow reprobates can smell opportunity at every passing breeze. Your "certain sum" as you put it – and your pardon – are wholly dependent on your keeping mum. For ever. Do we understand each other?'

'We do,' Frizer grunted.

'Good.' Faunt stood up and crossed the room, hammering on the door with the pommel of his dagger. 'I'll see myself out,' he said to Frizer. Then he bellowed to the guard, 'On the gate!'

All in all, Sir Edmund Tilney didn't have much of a choice. From the Rose and halfway down St Mary Overy, he was half-carried on the one side by Ned Alleyn and on the other by Richard Burbage. At the butter cross, because neither man liked being a supporting actor, they passed the burden to two of the company's carpenters. Because that was the case, Tilney's feet were now further from the ground than they had been and the chippies were impervious to the Master of the Revels' muttered complaints.

'No, really.' He was craning his neck, trying to keep up a running commentary with the trio behind him. 'I'm not sure …'

'Come on, Tilney.' Philip Henslowe walked between Alleyn and Burbage. 'This is a celebration. The theatres are open again, thanks (eventually) to your good offices and all's well that ends well.'

Will Shaxsper's ears pricked up. He was ever a picker-up of other peoples' trifles.

'Not exactly, Master Henslowe,' Tom Sledd called from the mob behind. 'We're also having a wake for Kit Marlowe.'

There was a chorus of 'ayes' interspersed with sniggers which left Tilney more bemused than ever.

'Here we are,' Burbage announced. 'The Actor and Groundling.'

'Master Burbage's idea of a joke, Sir Edmund,' Alleyn said. 'It's actually the Golden Boy. And by the way, Richard – isn't it your shout?'

'Go to Hell, pizzle,' Burbage grunted; he'd rather cut his own throat than buy a round for Ned Alleyn.

'I'll get the first one,' Adam Proud was making his way to the bar as the merry band slapped him on the back.

'Mine's a Raspis, Master Proud,' Henslowe called. 'Large, before you ask.'

The Golden Boy was one of the many watering holes of the theatre crowd along the south bank. The profits from the place all went into the coffers of the Bishop of Winchester, whose geese were out in force tonight. Music struck up in the smoke-laden half darkness, shawms, drums and viols arguing with each other in a cacophony that would not have been out of place in the seventh circle of Hell.

'Isn't that Machiavel?' Tilney asked, desperately looking around for a friendly soul who might get him out of there. He was, after all, a celebrity, as Master of the Rolls.

Burbage and Alleyn glanced across. A slender figure stood silhouetted against the candlelight of the bar, his hair a wild tangle, an expensive dagger glinting in the sheath in the small of his back.

'Oh, no, of course not. Silly of me.'

'Nobody's called Kit Marlowe Machiavel for a while, Sir Edmund,' Alleyn said. 'And anyway, he's dead. Ah, the ale.'

A tray of foaming beer appeared on the sticky oak of the trestle table, held in the hands of a goose whose breasts threatened to drop into the cups themselves. Burbage groped the nearest nipple. 'Come and see me later, my dear. I'm at my best after midnight.'

'Who *is* that?' Alleyn was still looking at the drinker at the bar. 'He's Marlowe to a T from the back.'

'I'm not really an ale person,' Tilney was saying, looking with horror at the foaming cups and trying not to stare at the naked breasts that swayed above them.

'Of course you're not.' Henslowe had found a stool from somewhere and was waiting for his wine. 'Put that girl down, Burbage.' He pulled her towards him. 'A bottle of your finest Raspis, darling. See that man over there?' He pointed to Adam Proud. 'He's a personal friend of the Lord Admiral.'

'Coo,' the girl said, having no idea who the Lord Admiral was.

'And he's paying. Now, Tilney,' he raised the Master

of the Revels' cup of ale. Like Tilney he wasn't an ale man, but he needed something to fill the gap until the wine arrived. 'Here's to your very good health, Sir Edmund.' He closed in to his man. 'And if you close the theatres again, they'll find you bobbing in the river.'

Tilney looked aghast, but by this time another girl was in Ned Alleyn's lap and Burbage was downing his quart in one. The Master of the Revels wanted to die and considered how much worse it would be to accept Henslowe's offer and roll in the comforting waters of the Thames.

Lizzie Wallace wasn't having any nonsense tonight. She was the queen of the geese, in charge of the whole flock and she made sure that everyone knew it. She had rouged her nipples just so and loosened her plackets enough for furtive fingers to find their mark under her gown. But *she* would choose the hands those fingers belonged to and that would not be Richard Skeres, who was shambling towards her now.

'Kiss my arse, pizzle,' she snapped.

Skeres was stopped in his tracks. 'Now there's an offer I can rarely refuse,' he said. 'Fancy a dick, Lizzie?'

'Not for ready money,' she said. 'Does Mistress Skeres know you're out?'

Skeres' lower lip quivered. 'She's gone, Lizzie,' he said. 'Went of the pestilence last month. Wednesday, it was.'

'No, it wasn't, Dick. And it wasn't the pestilence neither. Alison did a runner with that ferryman from the Black Deeps. Hung like a mule he is, or so they tell me.'

'Oh, have a heart, Lizzie.'

She tapped him on his Venetians, not unkindly. 'If I had a heart, Dickie, I wouldn't be in this business. Look, that's surely Kit over there, Kit Marlowe,' and she vanished into the crowd. She didn't see Skeres' face grow pale and she didn't see him make for the door with a turn of speed he didn't know he could manage, not with his old trouble.

'Nice night for it, Lizzie.' Tom Sledd winked at her as she barged past him.

'Always is, Tom,' she smiled. 'Always is. How's little Willie?'

They both had an image of a bonny little boy in their

minds, all eyes and curls. 'He's well, thanks, Lizzie. Got two teeth now.'

'Aw.'

By the time she'd reached the bar, her quarry had gone and she looked around for him in vain. These bloody actors were out in force tonight. There was Henslowe, rich as God; those stuck up bastards Alleyn and Burbage. Who that little runt between them was she didn't know, but he didn't look any too happy. Angie and Hannah were all over them; she'd have to make sure she got her cut of their takings later. Although if one of them ended up with the runt, she would probably leave that alone – she would have earned her money, trying to get a rise out of him.

Suddenly, she saw him again. He was standing near the door and she made a beeline for him, colliding briefly with Adam Proud, decidedly lighter of purse than he had been. They exchanged apologies while Lizzie briefly toyed with lifting what cash the man had left. But he had a kind face, so she left it where it was.

'Kit!' she shouted and the man half-turned. But it wasn't Kit. Now that she could see him in the light, he was half a head taller. The hair was the same and the beard, but the eyes were smaller, more pig than angel and he didn't *quite* have the swagger of the Muse's Darling.

'Oh,' she said.

'Evening,' he smiled at her. 'What's a nice girl like you etcetera, etcetera?'

Lizzie was glad that he didn't bother to finish the sentence because she had heard that line before. In fact, she'd heard *all* the lines before, even Kit Marlowe's, though his tended to be rather more thoughtfully turned and poetic than the rest.

'Did you take me for somebody else?' he asked her.

'I thought …' she began; then, 'No, just a trick of the light.'

The man smiled. 'Tricky things, lights,' he said. Now that *did* sound like Kit Marlowe. The lawn collar, the flash doublet with the slashed sleeves, the broad back. It was uncanny.

'I'd buy you a drink,' he said, 'but …' and he finished his cup, 'I must be away.' He took her hand and kissed it. *That* was Kit Marlowe, too. She stood there for a long time, watching his shadow melt into the darkness along Maiden Lane.

'Mind how you go, Machiavel,' she murmured. Then she felt a hand on her backside and half turned her head. 'Unless you want to lose those fingers – and, as a lute player, I know you don't – I'd let go if I were you.' She turned to face the man. 'And anyway, you couldn't afford me. Come to think of it, neither could the whole bloody orchestra of the Rose, not if they had whip rounds every night for a year.'

The shame-faced musician shambled away, shaking his head at the group of his colleagues clustered in a corner. They all shrugged sadly and turned back to their ale.

Raspis Sir Edmund Tilney could handle. Ale he rarely touched. But the combination of the two was proving to be too much. He had no idea that both Ned Alleyn and Richard Burbage had doubles and it struck him as odd that all four men should be sitting at Tilney's table in the Golden Boy that night.

'Of course,' he was slurring to the four of them and the Henslowe twins, tapping his forefinger on the table for emphasis. His attention was taken by the glints of candlelight in the puddles of ale against the grain of the wood and he turned his head this way and that. He pointed. 'Pretty,' he told them.

All six men nodded and smiled.

'Of course, Her Majesty and I are like that.' He tried to hold his fingers crossed over each other, but it was a tricky manoeuvre and he was fighting a losing battle. 'Only the other night, she said to me, "Tiddly," she said …'

'Tiddly?' Alleyn checked, nudging his doppelganger.

'What?' Tilney was confused. He had thought he was the only person there who was sometimes called Tiddly.

'You said "Tiddly",' the Burbages cut in. 'Or is that what you are?'

'No, it's what the queen calls me when … when we're

… you know …' He tried a knowing mime but even in his cups realised it was far from clear and giggled helplessly, leaving his fingers wiggling unnoticed.

Since everybody around that table knew that Her Majesty was older than Methuselah, with a scrawny chest, sparse hair and only one tooth, the prospect of Gloriana and the Master of the Revels cavorting under the eiderdown made them all shudder.

Alleyn was in his element. 'Tell me, Tiddly, is it true that …?'

But he never finished his sentence because there was an ear-shattering scream even above the cacophony of the Golden Boy. All eyes turned to the side door and one of the geese stood there, pale and trembling.

'Quick,' she was shouting, steadying herself against the doorframe. 'Come quick. Master Sackerson's eaten a man!'

CHAPTER 5

Philip Henslowe led the surge of humanity up the hill to the Bear Pit. He knew it was impossible for Master Sackerson to eat anyone. These days, he even needed his cabbages shredded. When Henslowe had installed the bear in the pit below the theatre, it had been with the idea of perhaps entertaining the crowds for a week or two before the creature succumbed to one of the ills bear flesh seemed to be heir to – advanced alopecia, followed by the shudders, followed by head banging, pacing and death. But Master Sackerson had lived on. And on. And on. He was the mildest of bears, allowing the boy who went in weekly to clean out his den to tickle him on the nape of his neck. He liked nothing better than some sweet apples and if he found those apples thrown by Kit Marlowe to be the sweetest of all, he was not alone there. Henslowe had often hung over the low wall that bordered the pit at street level and told the animal his deepest thoughts and dreams. And there was something in those rheumy eyes that seemed to understand. So Philip Henslowe was going to defend his bear, with every breathe in his …

'My God, Alleyn,' he burst out. 'Master Sackerson has eaten somebody.'

Ned Alleyn looked down and his eyes almost popped out of his head. 'It … it's Kit,' he murmured.

'That's rubbish,' a female voice snapped in his ear. 'That bear loved the man. He wouldn't harm a hair on his head. Anywhere, Kit's already …'

Alleyn swung round and almost suffocated himself in Lizzie's opulence. 'What do you know about it?' he said, meeting snap for snap.

Lizzie looked at him with contempt. 'I know because not all men treat women like you do, Ned.' She flicked him away with a practised hand. 'We often spent a moment or two here, talking to Master Sackerson, feeding him treats. He would listen while Kit talked.' She looked down, remembering. 'And he wasn't the only one. So, if that is Kit down there, Master Sackerson isn't to blame.'

'And anyway,' Tom Sledd pushed through to the front and peered down. 'How on earth could Master Sackerson have dragged him into his pit? With the twelve foot arms he keeps crossed behind his back? The poor soul fell in, that's what happened. And if you ask me, Master Sackerson is as shocked as any of us. Look.'

Everyone who could reach looked down and had to agree that the stage manager was right on the money. Master Sackerson had climbed up to the highest rock in his Pit and was hunkered down, looking sadly on the remains of the human lying with his head skewed at an impossible angle in the sand. He, like many people, had had a frisson of joy when he saw a familiar silhouette appear over his wall. But his nostrils soon told him it wasn't his friend and he had lost interest. His short-sighted eyes couldn't tell what was happening up above and his muffled ears couldn't tell what was said, but his nose was as sharp as ever and he knew there were two men up there, one in his cups, but only slightly, and the other sour with anger. And then, suddenly, there was a dead man in his sand and the bear had clambered out of harm's way. He sat there still, his head sunk on his chest. Had he but known it, he had a lot in common with John Donne, the Puritan – this man's death diminished him, but also worried him; nothing good could come of it.

The mood of the crowd changed slowly but in the end, even the most voluble and blood thirsty had to agree that the bear was clearly not the murderer in this instance. The general consensus seemed to be that that Kit Marlowe what wrote the plays and what everyone said was dead, really was dead now, dead as a nit in the Bear Pit and no surprise. Drinking and carousing till all hours. The fact that nine tenths of the crowd were three sheets in the wind escaped their notice.

Pulling himself together, Henslowe turned and addressed the growing mob. 'Move along there, now, ladies and gentlemen. Nothing to see here. Move along.' He waved his arms and nodded to Tom Sledd and Will Shaxsper who had just wandered along from the other direction, the scent of a Winchester goose lingering on his tongue. They copied their leader and slowly, reluctantly, the crowd dispersed, leaving the bear alone with the body.

Sir Edmund Tilney, finding himself suddenly alone in the Golden Boy, sat for a moment, trying to remember how to walk. When he worked it out, he wandered up the hill and leaned over the wall of the Bear Pit. In the fitful light of the moon, he saw something which surprised him more than somewhat. Those damned bears had eaten the Marlowe twins. Outrageous! He had always known that no good would come of reopening the theatres. He put an admonitory finger in the air and after a moment or two looked at it, puzzled. Then he shrugged and wandered away.

They carried the dead man through the black streets of Southwark. Rumour followed his makeshift bier; the bear had half-eaten him; he was having unnatural relations with the bear; he was a Spanish spy; he worked undercover for the papacy. Men died all the time south of the river, for the price of a harlot or the price of a pint, but there was something different about this one. For a start, he looked remarkably like Kit Marlowe. But everybody except the company of the Rose and Michael Johns knew that Kit Marlowe was dead already. They carried Master Sackerson's snack into the wash house behind the Rose. Women who did, shaking off the effects of the finest the Golden Boy's host could provide, stripped the body and laid him out. He *was* a handsome one, no doubt about that. And well hung, too. The only oddity about him was that his head was no longer quite in line with his body;

someone or something had broken his neck.

Most men in the England of Gloriana, the virgin queen, spent at least a portion of their lives standing outside the houses of great men, waiting. Tom Sledd was no exception. It was well past dawn and the early light was creeping over the flint face of Lambeth Palace by the time the place so much as stirred. Not for the first time, Tom Sledd felt himself put out. His back ached and his feet were killing him. Were it not for the statue of St Jerome, behind which he'd had a pee, his bladder would have been giving him trouble too.

He knew perfectly well that Lambeth Palace, across the river from the queen's bower at Whitehall, belonged to the Archbishop of Canterbury, but the old bastard was hardly ever there, so he rented it out, at primates' rates, of course, to the Bishop of Winchester.

'My lord,' the stage manager bowed as low as he could for a man with a stiff back, once he was ushered into the presence.

'Do I know you?' The Bishop of Winchester peered out over his spectacles.

'No, my lord. I am Thomas Sledd, stage manager at the Rose.'

Thomas Cooper was a conflicted soul. Getting too old for this job as he was, the religious mood of the moment was pushing him into the Puritan camp. But at heart he was a writer and occasionally removed alb, surplice and mitre and joined the gentlemen and their gay ladies who had the best seats in Henslowe's emporium at the edge of the stage. Only a few months ago he had a *very* interesting close-up of Helen of Troy in Kit Marlowe's *Faustus*, only to discover that she was a strapping lad from Bermondsey. His Grace knew the law, of course, but he *had* raised the idea that this was very nearly the seventeenth century with Edmund Tilney and wasn't it about time that women on stage were actually *played* by women. Tilney had had to have a lie down at the mere suggestion.

'It is very early, Master Sledd,' his Grace said. 'I have yet to partake of my breakfast.'

'I'm sorry, my Lord.' Sledd was fumbling with his

picadil, 'but a man has been found dead. Murdered, we believe.'

'And this is interfering with my breaking my fast for what reason?'

'Well, my Lord … it happened in Southwark.' Sledd hoped that would be enough. Surely this old man, still in his nightshirt and hankering for his manchet bread and new laid eggs, knew how much of London he was responsible for? He didn't seem to do much else to fill his time.

'Southwark is large enough,' the archbishop barked. 'It's not *all* mine, you know.' He crossed himself lightly. That might well be a lie, but if it were, it was only because he had lost track.

'The body was found in the bear pit, my Lord. The one by the Rose. Near St Mary Overy.'

The bishop perked up. He knew where they were talking about now. 'Not Master Sackerson, surely? He seems to be the gentlest of God's creations.' The bishop found it a good plan to use God's name from time to time, just to remind everyone who he worked for.

'We believe him to be innocent, my Lord.'

'I'm sure he is. It's been some time since we put God's lesser creatures on trial for crimes that only man commits – but that, of course, was the Papist church for you.'

'I merely thought, my Lord,' Sledd went on, 'as Southwark is your jurisdiction …'

The bishop chewed his lip. Mrs Branscome boiled a fine egg and she had said just ten minutes ago when she had hopped out of his bed and into her working attire that she was going to be putting the water on momentarily. So he had … he realised with surprise he had no idea how long it took to boil an egg. Was it a minute? Ten? Sixty? He shook his head to clear it. However long it took, his breakfast would be ready soon and the man was already dead, when all was said and done.

'The Watch will know about the death by now,' Sledd happened to mention. 'And if the Under-Sheriff …'

'Hiddlestone?' The bishop snapped, his egg forgotten. 'Where did you say this body was?'

'Behind the Rose, my Lord. In the wash house. By St Mary Overy.'

'Sacristan!' Cooper bellowed. 'Get my robes. Full fig. And saddle the donkey. A man is dead in my jurisdiction.'

Walter Hiddlestone circled the corpse in the Rose's wash house. His constables of the Watch had woken him at daybreak and here he was, conducting his enquiries.

'Who found him?' he asked without looking up from the body.

'I did, sir.' A scrawny girl bobbed before him. She was barely more than a child, but the rouge on her cheeks, streaked with tears, told a different story. She was a Winchester goose, no better than she should be. He looked at her arms and her narrow shoulders. The man's neck had been broken. No mere girl could do that.

Hiddlestone ripped the rough shroud from the corpse, watching the girl's reaction. He liked to shock, did Master Hiddlestone, and sometimes it got results. But the girl merely trembled along with her lip and she crossed herself. Papist, certainly, but no doubt she's seen naked men before.

'For God's sake, cover him up!' a voice bellowed at the doorway.

'My lord bishop.' Hiddlestone did little more than nod.

'Under-Sheriff,' the bishop acknowledged.

Tom Sledd, standing behind Bishop Cooper, had not moved fast enough and for all the venerable churchman had prodded the donkey, the beast was far too plodding to beat the forces of the secular arm.

One of the women who did hauled the cloth back over the body.

'It was the bear,' Hiddlestone said, hands on hips.

'Don't be ridiculous!' Cooper snapped. 'When I looked last, the floor of the bear pit was a good eight feet below ground, probably more. When you take into account the wall around it, you seem to be suggesting that Master Sackerson leapt fifteen feet or so and dragged him in.'

'The deceased may well have been under the 'fluence,' Hiddlestone acknowledged, 'We know he was drinking in the

Golden Boy and probably other places prior to his demise. He probably fell in, pirouetting on the wall to impress the ladies or some such nonsense.' He shot a withering glance at the girl.

'Come here, my child,' the bishop beckoned her over. 'You found the body?'

'Yes, sir.' She bobbed again.

'What is your name, child?' he asked.

'Mary Goodenough,' Hiddlestone growled. 'She's known to us.'

'As are all God's creatures,' the bishop said. 'Tell me, Mary, were you with this gentleman last night?'

The clash and carry of *Tamburlaine* was in full flow that afternoon, with carpenters and painters jostling to make the Rose's O presentable. The cobwebs of Edmund Tilney's lockdown had become thick and tangled and the river rats had made the place their own, but brooms and wax polish worked wonders and the Rose was blooming again.

Philip Henslowe watched it all from his eyrie. The Marlowe retrospective would bring in everybody, from the great and good in their gilded carriages to the grumbling groundlings after free ale and a little tumble in the hay. True, the impresario had a dead body in the wash-house and he hoped that one of the bickering authorities would do something about that – and soon. But that was a trifle in the scheme of things and then the Admiral's Men could move in and add untold riches to a man already richer than God.

'Habeas corpus,' a voice whispered in Henslowe's ear so that he dropped his abacus and was secretly glad he was wearing his brown Venetians that afternoon. He spun to see a darkly handsome man of the Puritan persuasion, all cropped hair and grey fustian. The Puritan rightly translated Henslowe's dropped jaw and popping eyes as a sign that he hadn't quite grasped the gist.

'You have the body,' the man helpfully translated.

'Kit!' Henslowe shouted, then instantly regretted it. 'Thank God!' The whispered last part of the sentence said it all. Marlowe was a golden goose all right, but was he more golden dead than alive? It wasn't likely that the pope would make the playwright a saint any time soon, but nobody in the country was supposed to care what *he* did anyway. London, on the other hand and cobbled Canterbury and scholastic Cambridge would applaud from the rooftops and the theatre-goers would throng to anything by the Muse's darling … as long as the darling was dead.

'Rumours of my death have been exaggerated,' Marlowe said.

'Well,' Henslowe grinned, his teeth gritted, his mind a turmoil of confusion. 'Well …'

'I met Tom Sledd on my way in,' Marlowe said. 'He told me there's a dead man in the wash-house.'

'That's right,' Henslowe said. There was supposed to be a dead man in Deptford too, but things hadn't quite turned out that way.

'Murdered, they say.'

'Hmm.'

'Philip,' Marlowe closed to his man. 'Tom tells me that he looks extraordinarily like me.'

'Well, I suppose … in a poor light. Out of the corner of your eye. Just a coincidence, surely?'

'May I see him?'

'Er … yes. Yes of course.'

And the playwright turned to go.

'Um … Kit. Look, I won't beat about the bush. Delighted though I am to find you still walking about, this is a *threat* awkward.'

'What is?'

'Well … this.' He waved his arm vaguely in the air. 'You see, we're putting on *Tamburlaine* in your honour. Alleyn's playing the lead, of course.'

'Of course,' Marlowe smiled. 'I'm sure he wouldn't have it any other way.'

'But, well, not to put too fine a point on it, I rather thought …'

'… that you would capitalize on my demise. Yes, that's …'

'Oh, despicable, I know, I know,' Henslowe cut in.

'And I despise myself for it.'

Marlowe chuckled. 'I was going to say it was good business, Philip. And I was going to thank you for keeping the rumours of my death going. Because, for reasons of my own, I would rather be dead just at the moment. But, if you'd rather chastise yourself, well …'

'No, no,' Henslowe laughed. 'If you're happy, I'm happy.'

'Joy,' smiled Marlowe and made for the stairs on his way to the wash house. 'It's grand to be bloody well dead.'

'As you see, Kit,' Tom Sledd was saying, 'broken neck.'

'Tell me again,' Marlowe circled the dead man exactly as Walter Hiddlestone had done earlier in the day.

'We were holding your wake – sorry about that – at the Golden Boy. Anybody who was anybody was there. A good time was being had by all, despite, of course, the solemnity of the occasion.'

'Of course.'

'Tilney was well away. At one point, he put his arm around me and said – and I quote – "What's a pretty little thing like you doing in a place like this?" I heard similar questions being asked all over the place that night; it's just I had never been asked it personally before. And never by the Master of the Rolls.'

'Oh, I don't know … There was that time in …'

'I was playing the Queen of Sheba at the time as you well know.' Sledd looked above Marlowe's head, into the past. 'I was very convincing in those days, you can't deny.'

The playwright smiled. 'There hasn't been a lad to touch you since, Tom. The day your voice went was a sad day for us all.' He looked up and smiled. 'Except for you, presumably.'

The stage manager blushed despite himself.

'Anyway,' Marlowe continued. 'Tilney never met a cliché he didn't like. I expect he was saying that to all the girls.'

Sledd ignored it. He had started out in this business with a walk on part as Nell the Village Maiden and now he more or less ran the Rose. So he hadn't done so badly. He decided to move the conversation forward at a trot. 'So, after I got away from Tilney, I bumped into our friend here. I don't mind telling you, it gave me quite a shock. Shaxsper had told me you were alive, of course.'

'Did he, now?' Marlowe raised an eyebrow.

'I didn't tell a soul, of course.'

'Of course not,' Marlowe nodded. He reminded himself of the old saying that three men could keep a secret as long as two of them were dead.

'Then I realised it wasn't you, but I realised I had seen the bloke before. Not a regular at the Rose, really, but an occasional punter. Middling seats, if I remember it right.'

Marlowe took a step back. He knew Tom Sledd was a man of many parts, but remembering every groundling that came through the Rose's doors was a bit beyond the usual. 'Do you really remember faces that well? We must set you up as a magic turn in the interval. Here's a question; was he alone, on those occasional punts?'

'Ah, now that I couldn't be sure of.' Before Marlowe had time to be crestfallen, Sledd stuck his finger in the air. 'No, no, no … wait a minute. One time, he came with a girl on his arm. Not a goose from round here, but clearly a lady of the night. Another time, he came with a crowd just like him – overdressed but cheap, gaudy. *Faustus* it was.'

'Did you see him again at my wake?' Marlowe was a wordsmith but never imagined he would hear himself say that.

'Briefly. He was chatting up a couple of geese, but then he left. Maybe he'd run out of money. Oh, no, that can't be right. He had his purse on him when he was found; quite a bit of silver.'

'So he wasn't robbed?'

'No. There are his clothes over there.'

Marlowe crossed to the pile. This was ridiculous. The dead man not only looked like him, but his doublet and Venetians were scarlet and black, not unlike the playwright's usual attire in what he must now call his old life. Except that the slashes in the sleeves and chest were roughly done, the hanging threads snipped with scissors, not interlined as any decent tailor worth his salt would do. The cambric of his singlet passed muster at first glance, but just by picking it up, Marlowe could tell it was wool, not silk. The man wasn't a reflection in a mirror, he was a blurred image in a puddle.

'Was he armed?' he asked Sledd.

'This is Southwark, Kit,' Sledd reminded him. 'He had a knife … ah, well, he did have. What with the washer-women, the Under-Sheriff and the Bishop, someone will have had that away. Worth a few groats.'

'The deodand,' Marlowe said.

'As you say.'

'And a goose found him?'

'Yes. Mary. She was giving somebody a quick one … well, when I say *giving* …'

Marlowe nodded with a chuckle. Geese didn't give much away for nothing. From some, even a kind word had a price on it.

'Anyway, she was along the inappropriately named Maiden Lane when they heard a noise. She reckoned it was the sound of this one's neck being snapped, though I puzzle to know how she might know that. Then, she said, there was a thud.'

'The dead man hitting Master Sackerson's pit floor.'

'I'd say so, yes. They dashed over there, their … how do the lawyers put it? … their coitus being definitely interruptus. And there he was, being sniffed at by Master Sackerson.'

'What a way to go,' Marlowe murmured. He went back to the body, looking at the grey skin, the purple mottling where the blood had sunk to his back and legs. Then something caught his eye. He held up first the right hand, then the left, feeling the cold clamminess of death. And he smiled.

'What is it, Kit?' Sledd asked.

'The hands always tell their story,' Marlowe said. 'Look at yours.'

Sledd did.

'Splinters, bruises where the hammer slipped. Broken

nails. You're a builder, Tom, a carpenter. Look at my index finger and, God help us, Shaxsper's and you'll find the black of the ink. Writers to a man.'

'So, what was he, then?'

'Look at those finger ends,' Marlowe said. 'Worn smooth over the years. Bruising on the balls of the thumbs. This man pressed books for a living, Tom. We'll find out who he was in Paul's churchyard.'

They kept odd hours in the stationers' enclave in the alleys that ran around St Paul's. In the shadow of the largest cathedral in the world, the evening sun gilding the spire shattered by lightning before Kit Marlowe was born, the playwright, born again and looking for answers, browsed every shop. He took in the smell of paper and ink, the indescribable feel of old books. He chatted casually to men he vaguely knew and was gratified to find that they didn't seem to know him at all.

But in terms of his immediate enquiries, he was getting nowhere. He had been offered more Aristotles than he knew what to do with, umpteen volumes of Ramus. One rather furtive bookseller had wondered whether Ovid was to his taste. Since Marlowe had been translating the old Roman pervert since his university days, he was less than tempted. What about, the bookseller asked him, a one-off, never to be repeated account of an adventurer's travels in the brothels of Abyssinia, complete with illustrations? Since neither Marlowe nor the bookseller could make out exactly what the illustrations showed, no matter which way they turned the book, the playwright declined yet again.

He couldn't help smiling, however, at the display in the window of the Gun at the end of Amen Alley, just before it widened onto Ludgate Hill. He smiled because, as far as he knew, the works he saw there had not been published yet. And because all of them had been written by him. He went in.

There was a little man behind the Gun's counter, older than the cathedral behind him and he peered at Marlowe through thick spectacles. 'How may I help you, sir?' he asked.

'I see you have works by Christopher Marlowe in your window.'

'Yes. Yes, indeed. Very popular just now, on the grounds that he is no longer with us, you know.'

'He isn't?'

'No, no.' The bookseller leaned forward, conspiratorial. 'Murdered, they say.' He looked left and right. 'In a tavern brawl.'

'Never!' Marlowe was suitably horrified.

'Indeed. And not far from here, either. In an alley behind the Harlot and Banker.'

Marlowe knew it well.

'Would you like to peruse one, sir?' the bookseller asked. '*Faustus, Tamburlaine. The Jew. Dido.* Even *Edward II* – I have them all. And his latest, of course – *The Blasphemer's Tragedy.* Master Philp Henslowe is putting on *Tamburlaine* at the Rose in Southwark. I shall have a modest stall, in the entranceway.'

'And a modest stall in some dark corner of the Marshalsea,' Marlowe smiled.

'I beg your pardon?'

'Master stationer.' Marlowe rested his elbows on a pile of books and looked the man in the face. 'You and I both know that these works are … what's the word? Purloined? No works of Marlowe have been published to date. They belong to the writer or, assuming the rumours of his death are to be believed, his estate. At the very least, they are under the legal control of the Master Henslowe you just mentioned.'

'Well, I …' the bookseller was clearly flustered. He pulled off his spectacles that had unaccountably steamed up and wondered whether this customer might not be some sort of spy, an intelligencer for the Master of the Revels or Her Majesty's Stationery Office. Such people did not mess around; hands had been lost.

'Let me see *The Blasphemer's Tragedy*,' Marlowe said. 'I confess I've never heard of that one.'

The bookseller obliged, rummaging in his window display and Marlowe flicked open the cover. There was a prologue, spoken by a man named Machiavel, who admitted, in perfect iambic pentameter, that he believed that God did not exist and that Christ and all the saints were merely inventions of the Church, an institution set up to fleece the masses and terrify them into submission by tales of Hellfire and Damnation. It was exactly what a blasphemer might believe. It was exactly what Kit Marlowe believed. But Kit Marlowe hadn't written a word of this.

'Intriguing,' Marlowe said. 'Where did you get this, Master Stationer?'

'Ah.' The man replaced his spectacles. 'For that you'd need to talk to my partner, Jack Willoughby.'

'Is he here?'

'No, I'm afraid not. But he's a *huge* follower of Christopher Marlowe – hence the books.'

'Is he?'

'He even looks like him,' the bookseller said. 'Dresses the same, too. It's a bit of a joke around here. Funnily enough, since the playwright died, Jack's been making even more of the resemblance. He goes to wherever Marlowe used to be seen. Oh, the theatres were closed, of course, on account of the pestilence.' The bookseller spat on the floor for good luck. 'But he found the man's lodgings in Norton Folgate and was asking questions in Southwark. He intended to go to Cambridge, of course …'

'He went to Southwark?' Marlowe asked.

'Of course. That's where the Rose theatre is. Are you a stranger round here, sir?'

Marlowe chuckled. 'It appears that I am,' he said. 'Tell me, Master Stationer, when did you see Master Willoughby last?'

'Ooh, let me see. Two days ago, I think. He'd been to Southwark – that's where he got the *Blasphemer* copy. He had to go back to meet someone.'

'And you don't know who?'

'No, I'm afraid not. Er … about these play copies, sir and the legality thereof …'

'Your secret's safe with me, Stationer,' Marlowe said. 'In fact, I'll take a copy of *Blasphemer* … if you can just tell me where Master Willoughby lives.'

CHAPTER 6

National treasures like the Lord Admiral didn't come to Southwark often. After all, the place was a stews and many were the kings of England who had tried to close it down. That was one reason why the Bishop of Winchester had been granted its swampy murkiness in the first place, to clean up the morality of the place. Unfortunately, successive Bishops of Winchester seemed to be totally blind to the goings-on and everything went on much as before.

So when national treasures arrived, everybody knew about it. The outriders came first, clattering past St Mary Overy in the morning sun, the banners of Effingham flapping at their staff-heads. Clarions and drums followed, because the Lord Admiral never went anywhere without a band. Behind them came the coach itself – the Lord Admiral could ride, of course, but he was so rich he didn't have to – all gilded flounces and tassels. The great man nodded and waved to the crowd that had suddenly appeared from nowhere. Most of the geese weren't up yet at that time of the morning, so the serving men, the shit shovellers, the pie makers and cordwainers jostled at the road's side to catch a glimpse of the man who had destroyed the Spanish Armada.

'God bless you, sir,' they shouted as their caps came off. 'You gave the Dagos what for!'

Howard of Effingham was ever the realist. He knew perfectly well that it was the Channel weather that had seen off the Spaniards, with a little help from Drake, Ralegh, Hawkins and Frobisher, but he was equally happy to bask in adulation.

'Good God!' Philip Henslowe was peering out of his eyrie window at the cacophony in the street. He briefly heard Master Sackerson howling his indignation and incomprehension at the row thundering past his pit. 'That's Howard heraldry,' the impresario shouted to the girl still wrapped up in the covers of his bed. 'Matilda. Get some clothes on and make yourself scarce.'

'Oh, Philly,' the girl whined

'Just do it!' Henslowe was hauling on his shirt and trying to find his Venetians. In the courtyard below, Tom Sledd still had his mouth full of breakfast and was spraying his people with breadcrumbs and ale.

The gates of the Rose were hauled open with squeals of iron on iron and the entourage came to a halt, dust rising to the heavens. A lackey opened the Admiral's door and released the steps as the horses stood quiet, scenting the air. Their quiet didn't last for long as their nostrils picked up the alien whiff of Master Sackerson and they shifted in their hames and snorted. The coachman steadied them with soothing words and Howard of Effingham, in all his scarlet finery, set foot in the Rose's precincts for the first time.

'Welcome, my lord.' Henslowe dropped to one knee, realising to his horror that his Ventians were still undone. 'Philip Henslowe, my lord, owner of this humble abode of the Muse.'

'Yes.' Howard let the man kiss his hand as he looked around the walls and porticos. 'it needs work, Henslowe.' And he swept towards the entrance. 'That's why I'm here. You'll excuse the unfashionable hour, but there's much to be done. You know Proud.'

The playwright had travelled in a smaller coach behind the Admiral's and he nodded at Henslowe.

'He tells me you're putting on some of Marlowe's rubbish,' Howard said, as Henslowe's lackeys scurried ahead to open doors for him.

'He is ... was ... the greatest of our playwrights, my

lord,' Henslowe reminded him.

'Yes. Yes, of course.'

Suddenly, they were standing in the wooden O, the sunlight streaming in through the open roof. The entourage of heavies who had followed Howard formed a rough circle around him, leaning on halberds and bristling with weapons. The galleries were suddenly full of every hanger-on in the world, shiny, gawping faces of people Henslowe realised he probably paid to do … whatever it was they did.

'This set,' Howard pointed to the half-built Persian palace. 'That's the word, isn't it? Set?'

'Indeed, my lord,' Henslowe said. 'And this is Thomas Sledd, the man who built it.' The stage manager was hauled into the arena and bowed low to his lordship.

'Fascinating,' Howard said flatly, barely acknowledging the man at all. 'What play is this, Henslowe?'

'*Tamburlaine*, my lord. We're having a retrospective for Marlowe, the late lamented.'

'Hmm. Take it down.'

'My lord?' Henslowe thought he must have misheard.

'We're not doing this. I have my own plans.'

'My lord,' Philip Henslowe was as much of an arse-licker as anyone else in Gloriana's England, but he was also an impresario. This was *his* theatre. *And* he had a deal. 'I understood we had a deal, my lord.'

Howard narrowed his eyes. 'A deal, Henslowe?'

'Perhaps we could discuss it in my chamber?' Henslowe suggested, pointing to the stairs rising at the back of the auditorium.

Howard looked the stairs up and down and made a small moue of distaste. 'I don't really do … rickety,' he said. 'We'll discuss it here.' He looked around for a chair. Usually, there was a chair.

Tom Sledd read the great man's mind and an elaborate throne appeared from nowhere. Howard plonked himself down. 'So,' he said. 'What's this about a deal?'

Henslowe took a deep breath. 'I understood from Master Proud here that you wished the Admiral's Men to have the use of the Rose but that I would continue to select the plays.'

'Well, yes,' Howard said, 'but ...'

'With Christopher Marlowe's demise,' Henslowe was in full flow now, 'he is the hottest property in London. If you'll excuse the pun, we'll make a killing.'

Howard looked up at him.

'May I suggest a compromise, my lord?' Adam Proud stepped forward.

Howard of Effingham didn't usually do compromise, but he realised at once that everybody in this ghastly building was Henslowe's creature and collectively, they could make or break plays and theatre companies. He wasn't about to give any edge to the Lord Chamberlain's men. 'What?' he asked.

'This, my lord.' Proud produced a thick sheaf of paper from his satchel. 'It's Marlowe, but it's brand new. Never been performed. Everybody knows the great man's works, but this one will have your Lordship's imprimatur. And what a coup for you, eh, Master Henslowe? A new Marlowe. And from the pen of a man who will write no more.' Proud risked the subtlest of winks in Henslowe's direction.

The impresario took the script. '*The Blasphemer's Tragedy*,' he read aloud. 'Never heard of it. How do we know it's genuine?'

'I'm not as familiar with Kit's hand as you are, Master Henslowe, but look for yourself. I do remember reading some of his poetry at Corpus Christi.'

'You were at Corpus Christi?' Henslowe checked.

'A year or two below Kit. I was about to begin the Quadrivium when he went down. Look, there, on the title page. Ch. Ma. That's his signature, isn't it?'

'Yes,' Henslowe said. 'Yes, it is.' He flicked through the pages. The mighty line was there, the thundering pentameter, the sort of thing Will Shaxsper was trying so hard to copy. 'If I may take some time to read this, my lord?'

'You don't have any time, Henslowe. Young Proud here knows Marlowe's work and can vouch for it. And the pestilence hasn't gone away, you know. We must get this out before that moron Tilney closes the theatres again. Master of the Revels, my arse.'

'A double compromise, my lord,' Henslowe suggested. 'Ned Alleyn is immersing himself in the *Tamburlaine* again and it will take him a while to con the *Blasphemer*. Burbage wouldn't be right for it. How about a week's run of the Scythian shepherd, *followed* by the new stuff?'

Everybody looked at each other. 'Proud?' Howard spoke first.

'I am an executant, merely, my lord. This decision must be yours.'

'And mine,' Henslowe reminded everybody.

'So be it.' Howard stood up. '*Tamburlaine* and *Blasphemer* – a double bill. I shall invite Her Majesty. Now … er … Henslowe, some breakfast, I think. Do you have an Ordinary nearby, somewhere where I won't catch anything nasty? Oysters, I think, manchet bread. I've brought my own wine, of course. Oh,' and he took Henslowe aside, 'A little female companionship, perhaps; brunette for preference, redhead at a pinch.'

Lurking in the background, the blonde Matilda pushed out her breasts and went off in search of one of the Rose's more convincing wigs.

Rachel Willoughby had not seen her brother for several weeks. But she saw him now, a dead, pale face in the outhouse of the Rose, a charnel house that was already a crypt. No one had entered, out of respect, even though Tom Sledd kept his paint there. His set was still unfinished and *Tamburlaine* was due to open a week on Thursday.

Marlowe had found the woman in the precincts of Paul's and talked to her gently about the man in the outhouse. All London was talking about the ghastly murder of a poor soul eaten by a bear. Time, the Puritans railed, for somebody to *do* something; close down the bear pits. *And* the brothels. *And* the inns. It was outrageous that such bestiality went on in land belonging to the Bishop of Winchester. But then, scoffed the Presbyterians, that was Bishops for you!

Rachel Willoughby was a difficult woman to read. She had lived all her life in the shadow of the greatest cathedral in the world, had tottered her first steps in time to the solemn tolling of its bells. She had no memory of the terrible night that God, in His fury, had thrown a thunderbolt to hit the steeple, bringing tons of masonry crashing to the ground. But she had grown up with such stories. It wasn't God, it was the Devil. More prosaically, it was the Spaniards, the French, the southern Dutch – Papists, certainly – who had never been able to come to terms with the fact that their church no longer existed in England.

And now, a man she'd never seen had knocked at her door to tell her that he believed her brother was dead. 'I must see for myself, Master Brackenbury,' she had said.

Marlowe didn't think that was a good idea. To take the woman to the Rose, where his identity was known, was courting disaster. But the weather was with him. Spring it may have been, but London was hit by a downpour that Tuesday that saw giant raindrops bouncing off flagstones and puddles appearing where there seemed to be no dip in the ground. Both Marlowe and Rachel wore their hoods pulled low and a wink from Marlowe to the Rose's gatekeeper got them inside.

The rain was thudding with a steady rhythm on the outhouse roof as Marlowe pulled back the shroud. He heard the woman gasp and saw her pull back her hood. Tears filled her eyes and she reached out to touch the cold, dead cheek. 'Jack,' she whispered. 'Oh, Jack.'

For a moment, Marlowe thought she might faint. She sagged, her eyelids fluttering. Then she took a deep breath and steadied herself. 'I'm sorry,' he said. 'I'd hoped …'

When she turned to him, her voice was hard. 'Why your interest, Master Brackenbury?' she asked. 'Why have you brought me here?'

'I told you,' he said. 'A friend of mine is the bearward here in Southwark. Rumour has it that your brother was killed by a bear. In the interests of justice …'

'It's all Kit Marlowe's fault,' Rachel told him.

For the most fleeting of seconds, Marlowe was rattled. 'Who?' he asked.

'Marlowe,' she said. 'The playwright.'

'I thought he was dead,' Marlowe said.

'So he is.' She turned away from the body. 'And that's when this nonsense really started.'

'Nonsense?'

'The fact that you knew Jack was here, Master Brackenbury – you know the Rose.'

'I dabble,' he said. 'I'm not a regular.'

'I suspect that Jack was. He was a stationer by calling but he had become obsessed of late with Christopher Marlowe. He printed copies of his plays.'

'Illegally,' Marlowe muttered, despite himself.

'Really?'

'Most of Marlowe's plays have yet to be published. Now that he's dead, of course …'

'However that may be,' she said, 'Jack's obsession went further than that. He'd obviously met this Marlowe or at least knew what he looked like. He started wearing flash clothes, despite the Sumptuary Laws and recently, or so I am told, took to carrying a dagger. I don't pretend to understand it, Master Brackenbury, but it's almost as if Jack was trying to *become* Kit Marlowe.'

'I see,' Marlowe nodded, 'and can you think, Mistress Willoughby, of anyone who wanted to see your brother dead?'

Rachel frowned, 'But, the bear …'

'… is as innocent as the day is long. The only bear left in Southwark now is Master Sackerson. He wouldn't hurt a fly. Some of his best friends are humans. No, I'm afraid your brother was stabbed to death, Mistress.'

Rachel breathed in sharply.

'The Under Sheriff of Southwark is carrying out his enquiries, but I wouldn't hold your breath.'

She raised an eyebrow. 'Do you have no faith in the wheels of justice, Master Brackenbury?'

'If you know as many of the cogs as I do, Madam,' he said, 'you wouldn't either.'

'Jack was an easy-going man. He liked a drink.' Her face darkened. 'He liked the ladies. I suppose he might have crossed someone. A rival? A cuckolded husband? Who knows?'

'Who indeed?' Marlowe echoed. Having found Rachel Willoughby, he had hoped that she could have been more helpful.

'But, of course ...' she began, but her voice trickled away. 'What if this has nothing to do with Jack at all?'

'Meaning?'

'What if,' she turned back to the body again, 'what if someone believed that he really *was* Kit Marlowe? Marlowe, if the rumours are true, had enemies galore.'

'Oh, he did,' Marlowe smiled.

'You knew him?' she asked.

'After a fashion,' Marlowe said.

Rachel walked back to the silent witness on the bier and looked down at the pale, still face. 'Jack never used to wear his hair like that – and he was clean shaven. You don't think ... oh, no, it's too preposterous ...'

'Go on,' he urged her, because he was thinking along the same lines.

'You don't think that someone killed him because he believed Jack to be Marlowe? That Marlowe isn't dead, after all?'

Marlowe smiled. 'As you say, Mistress Willoughby, too preposterous.'

Marlowe was a gentleman, so he made sure that he stopped a passing call-boy who had been hoping for a quiet life while the Rose was just in rehearsal to take the grieving sister home. He had enjoyed being dead, but it was different when it was a two-way street. Being dead like Jack Willoughby looked very unappetising and Marlowe had found his sister's disbelief and then distress quite dispiriting and so thought he would go back into the theatre and quietly watch for a while. Ned Alleyn losing his lines for the umpteenth time in *Tamburlaine* was always something to make a person smile, even when the person involved had written every golden syllable. He slipped round behind a flat and peeped out, but there was no one on stage but an old woman wielding a balding broom. Marlowe tutted to himself. He had taken too long with Mistress Willoughby and had missed all the fun. He squeezed back out from between the scenery, disentangling himself from a protruding nail, and went in search of someone to gossip with. The dead are like that; they do love a gossip.

In the Rose's gallery, Will Shaxsper was still tinkering with his *Richard III*. White Surrey, he thought to himself; strange name for a horse. Still, it was in Holinshed and there was no finer chronicler and historian in the world. He wrote it down. 'Saddle White Surrey for the field tomorrow.'

He glanced out beyond the wooden O and watched the Heavens still opening on Tom Sledd's stage. Tamburlaine's palace, getting a soaking. Across the yard outside, he saw two figures, huddled against the rain making for a waiting carriage. One he knew, despite the cloak and hood and the disguise, was Kit Marlowe. The other … he didn't know. When it came to Kit's private life, perhaps it was better he didn't know. Shaxsper dipped his quill into the ink again and another thought occurred to him. It had nothing to do with Richard III but everything to do with Jack Willoughby and the recent bizarre events in Southwark. His nib scratched out the words, 'Exit, pursued by a bear.'

The room was green. Sets were always a problem for a stage manager. They had to be light and moveable, but not so light that a passing walking gentleman would knock them over. And they had to be realistic. And that, he had to admit, was where Tom Sledd kept his fingers crossed. He was fairly confident that no one, from the Lord Admiral to the most grounded of the groundlings, would know the topography of Scythia from their left elbow. In fact, many of them would be under the distinct impression that Scythia was that whore with the big nose who plied her trade down by the fish dock. But with all that said and done, it had to be exotic, not anything that the average Billingsgate porter would have seen in the Vintry. And of course, anybody working along the Queen's wharves would have seen all sorts of foreign knick-knacks arriving from Elsewhere. Peacocks, apes, ivory, all worth a king's ransom, gleaming and chattering in the rat-infested holds along with barrels of sweet white wine.

So it was that Nicholas Skeres was standing in the wooden shrubbery with a wooden pomegranate tree over his head, doing his best with Marlowe's mighty line.

'Madam, your father and th'Arabian king,
The first affecter of your excellence,
Comes now as Turnus 'gainst Aeneas did,
Armed with lance into th'Egyptian fields,
Ready for battle gainst the lord the king.'

Hmm. Not bad. Not bad. Perhaps if he stood like this … Skeres threw out his left leg, folded his arms and tried the line again. He'd seen Ned Alleyn do that a hundred times. Usually when he'd forgotten his lines. Perhaps … Skeres twisted sideways and placed his hands on his hips. Hmm. Maybe. He delivered his line again.

'Are you going to do it like that?' A voice from a palace doorway made Skeres jump and drop his script.

A Puritan wandered into the light, grim in black and white.

'Who are you?' Skeres wanted to know, annoyed that his private rehearsal had been interrupted.

'I'm the man whose lines you're butchering,' Marlowe said.

Skeres wasn't sure what noise came out of his throat next, but it wasn't human. He dropped his script again and dodged backwards as Marlowe slowly drew the dagger from its sheath up his sleeve.

'Kit. Er … Master Marlowe. I didn't expect …'

'No one ever does,' Marlowe smiled. 'But surely you knew that one reckoning wouldn't be enough?'

'Look, I mean … I thought that Master Faunt had …'

'Taken away your guilt, Nicholas?' The playwright finished the man's sentence for him. 'Absolved you of your sins? Nicholas Faunt may be many things, but a priest is not one of them. It's a funny old world, isn't it?' Marlowe was throwing his dagger in the air and passing it casually from hand to hand. 'Here you are, working on *Tamburlaine* without a care in the world and the last time I saw you, you, Frizer and Poley were about to cut my throat.'

'No, no, Master Marlowe.' Skeres was abject. 'Frighten

you, that's all. That's all we were trying to do. Ing and I, that's what we do, you know. Put the frighteners on people. Catch the odd coney. Fleece the gullible. We don't want no trouble.'

Marlowe held the knife steady in his right hand. 'But that's where it's all gone so wrong, isn't it, Nick, me old walking gentleman? Ingram Frizer's rotting in the Hole; there's no sign of Master Poley. And yet, here you are. Just you. Now, let's look at some different odds. Last time, it was three to one. Let's see how it goes with just the two of us.' Marlowe pointed his blade forward, level with Skeres' face.

'I'm not armed,' Skeres babbled.

'Yes, you are, Nicholas,' Marlowe said. 'That sneaky little placket in the right leg of your Venetians; it holds a blade. Worth about a shilling, of course, unless I miss my guess. You wouldn't go to the jakes without that.'

Marlowe took a step forward and Skeres whipped out his dagger from its hiding place. He didn't take his eyes off Marlowe's blade, slowly circling in air as he moved forward, one deadly step at a time. When he did take his eyes off the dagger, it was to look Marlowe in the face and what he saw there made him drop the knife and crumple to his knees.

'Can't we ...? Isn't there something ...?'

'Unluckily for you, Skeres, there is no Nicholas Faunt hovering at your elbow. And I don't see much sign of your God intervening on your behalf. Unless, of course ...'

'What? What?' Skeres would accept any crumb of comfort about now.

Marlowe smiled. 'We go back a while,' he said. 'You've walked through all the works of the great Kit Marlowe.'

'I've done my best,' Skeres almost sobbed. It sounded as if the playwright were reading the walking gentleman's obituary.

'Of course you have.' No one condescended like Kit Marlowe. 'And because of that, if you tell me who paid you boys, we'll call it quits. I might even tell you how to deliver your line.'

'Ingram,' Skeres shouted. 'It was Ingram, Master

Marlowe. I hate to rat on a friend, but it was all his idea. I didn't want to go along with it. I told him, I said, Ing, I said. Master Marlowe's a saint, I said, a saint, he is. Salt of the earth. His immortal words have put clothes on our backs and food in our bellies, I said. But I was weak, Master Marlowe. Weak. And I hated myself for it. I let Frizer talk me into it. On my mother's life, *he's* the one you should be talking to.'

Marlowe happened to know that Skeres' mother had died of the pox years before, an occupational hazard, but he was too much of a gentleman to bring it up. He smiled again, reversed the dagger in his hand and sheathed it.

'Right,' he said. 'Ingram Frizer it is.'

'He's in the Hole, remember.' Skeres could feel the cold hand of death relaxing its grip on him.

'How could I forget?' Marlowe said and turned to go. At the gateway of the pampered jades of Asia, he stopped. 'Oh, and Nicholas.'

'Yes, Master Marlowe?'

'If I don't like Ingram's answers, I *will* be back.'

And for the second time that day, Nicholas Skeres let out a strangled cry. He thought it was a laugh, but it wasn't. and after that, he didn't have the nerve to ask Marlowe how to deliver his lines.

Lord Howard of Effingham liked to describe himself as a man of the people. He had never gone to the trouble of defining quite what he had in mind when thinking of 'people' but had he been asked, he would have vaguely waved a hand at people like him. So the Ordinary in Overy Lane came as quite a serious shock to his system. Straw on the floor he could just about live with. True, it was sodden with the sludge dragged in on his own pattens and everybody else's now that Noah's flood had descended on London from the heavens. But he was, after all, first and foremost a sailor and had suffered the rigours of life at sea, although even then he had silken sheets on his cot and a well-stocked larder. But he had heard things; weevils, water in the wine and worse things too bad to repeat. It was when the straw moved about that he began to get squeamish. When it stared back at him, he lifted his beautifully shod feet onto the next chair and hoped the food would arrive quickly.

When it came, it was surprisingly good. Fresh, soft bread, new laid eggs and some perfectly cured ham. The brunette provided by Henslowe proved to be the perfect breakfast companion – Matilda somebody? All he needed at his age was a nice warm bosom to lean against and this she provided willingly. She didn't keep grabbing at things. He did so hate drabs who grabbed. When he wanted something grabbed, he would let them know. Henslowe was amusing company, and if he was surprised to be given the reckoning at the end, he hid it well.

So, all in all, Lord Howard of Effingham, High Admiral of England and favourite of Gloriana, was feeling very pleased with himself as he returned to his carriage, now facing back in the direction of his home on the river. The rain had given him another soaking and his coachman, high on his perch, was already trembling with the ague, dripping the while. The footman helped his lordship on board. He settled back in his padded seat and prepared to be jolted back to his house, where he could probably squeeze in another breakfast before he had to begin going through the papers that would have certainly been delivered by now from the Admiralty. He had a suite of offices there, of course, but generally he worked from home.

He tapped on the roof of the carriage as the wheels hissed through the deluge and he heard the coachman cluck to his horses and the reassuring clop and whinny that told him they were underway. He leaned back and closed his eyes, thinking of the soft breasts and flowing chestnut locks of the lovely … what was her name again? It began with an M … Lord Howard of Effingham began to doze.

The tap on his knee was not a hard one, but somehow in its gentleness it was more disconcerting, melding seamlessly as it did with his dream of Matilda. Matilda, that was definitely it. His eyes flew open and he stared frantically around for a moment while they focussed.

He had known all along that it couldn't be Matilda, but even so the Puritan sitting across from him came as a surprise. The man was dressed so plainly as to be almost an offence in this sumptuous interior, he stood out as a crow would in a flock of parrots, his soaking hood thrown back. Howard licked his lips.

'Who in Hell's name are you?' he croaked. 'And how did you get in here?'

'I will tell you who I am all in good time,' the Puritan said, in a voice Howard seemed to recognize. 'Getting in was rather easy, my lord, and were I you, I would think seriously about how loyal your men are.'

'Loyal?' Effingham was outraged. 'Loyal? I'll have you know that my men would happily die for me!'

'Hmm.' The Puritan sat back and looked at the admiral, a smile on his lips. 'Perhaps once upon a time you had men who would die for you, and did, in their hundreds, as you let them rot of scurvy in the holds of their own ships. But your coachman is not one of them. A few minute's dalliance with the lovely Mattie and the coast was clear for long enough for me to ensconce myself quite comfortably in this dark corner. The coachman even lent me his cloak, just to make me blend into the shadows.'

Effingham was spluttering now. It had taken him a moment to equate Matilda and Mattie and that somehow made it worse. He struggled to get the words out, so furious was he. He had nestled into her soft delights just minutes after she had .. had ... He spluttered some more.

'I daresay what you are getting round to saying is that he will be dismissed forthwith?'

The admiral nodded and gestured.

'With a good flogging first? Well, that seems a little draconian. Perhaps we can ask the Lady Catherine what she thinks? She will probably have other views ...'

The Lord Admiral pulled himself together at the invocation of his wife. She was usually a sobering influence. As a lady-in-waiting to the Queen, she could do him a world of damage; and her right hook was no laughing matter. He thought quickly, not normally his strong suit. And anyway, this man was probably just here for some kind of donation to his church, something like that. He coughed and checked his laces. There had been no grabbing, but still …

'As you wish,' he said finally to the enigmatic stranger, now sitting at his ease, legs crossed. Although his clothes were plain, he wore them well, like a gentleman. 'He can keep his position … for now. But now we come to my other question. Who are you? I don't know you and yet … your voice …'

The Puritan smiled. 'I did think of disguising it,' he said. 'I prefer not to tread the boards but I have done it, when needs must. So if I wanted to, I could change how I sound.' He dropped his voice half an octave and assumed a slight Devon burr. 'But I can't keep it up, to be frank with you. And Devon is about all I can manage without sounding deranged.' He reverted to his gentle Cambridge tones with just a background hint of Kent. 'So I didn't bother. Can you really not tell who I am?'

The Admiral squinted his long-sighted eyes and looked again. 'Can you turn to the light?'

The Puritan obligingly did so, then changed sides.

'It's on the tip of my tongue …'

Marlowe sighed and gave up. This game got old very quickly and he knew it was only going to get worse. 'My lord. I never intended this to be a guessing game. Longer hair. Curls, even. Little goatee …' he waved his hand vaguely in front of his face. 'Brown eyes. They're still there, can't do much about them …'

His companion leaned back, then forward. 'Marlowe? Christopher Marlowe? But … you're dead, aren't you?' Like most sailors, Howard of Effingham was a superstitious man. 'I say, Marlowe. We're not *both* dead are we, doomed to spend eternity rattling over cobbles in a seedy part of London with water trickling down my neck?'

Marlowe laughed. He had always considered Howard of Effingham to be among the best of a dodgy crowd. 'No. We're not both dead. My death was … well, exaggerations were made, I suppose I could say.'

Effingham wasn't quick, but when he got the drift of anything, he was like a terrier. 'I'm assuming, from your visit, that you suspected I was complicit in the attempt.' A sudden thought struck him. 'Assuming there was an attempt. Or is it all a fabrication?' Another thought struck him, more forcibly. 'It's that damned rogue Henslowe, I'll be bound. Doing it for the publicity!'

'No, no, my lord. By no means. Although I admit that Master Henslowe did begin plans for my retrospective with what one might almost call unseemly haste, he had nothing to do with it. And it was a very real attempt. At odds of three to one, I think we might call it real, might we not?'

Effingham was horrified. 'Three to one? We're not looking at a gentleman, then. No gentleman would use odds like those. One to one. Misty morning. Seconds. Jousting, even.' He looked beyond Marlowe to the altercations of his youth. 'Oh, yes. Any of that. But three to one! I'm saddened you thought it could be me, Marlowe. Saddened indeed.'

For a man who had been almost killed, Marlowe was feeling surprisingly guilty. He almost apologized and then stopped himself. If Howard of Effingham was a gent, he certainly mixed with many who weren't.

'But, tell me.' The admiral was back again in the here and now. 'Three to one. However did you escape?' He leaned forward, his eyes alight. He did love a good tale, although he preferred it to be after a huge dinner and several bottles of decent Rhenish. 'Did you kill them all single handed? Maim two, kill one? What?'

Marlowe hardly liked to burst his bubble. 'I'm sorry, my lord. It was rather prosaic, actually. Nicholas Faunt paid them off.'

Howard slumped back in his seat. 'Oh. That's very boring, Marlowe. And how like Faunt. To sink that low. Paid them off. Well ...'

'One *is* in prison, my lord.'

Effingham flapped a hand. 'Prison. What's that these days? Not like when I was a lad. Rats the size of horses in some of the lower levels. Might as well not bother these days. Soft. That's what our judiciary is. Soft.'

Marlowe didn't like to argue. As Effingham could have anyone he wanted imprisoned or let free with the stroke of a pen, his words rang rather hollow. 'I know who they are, my lord. So, in time, who knows ...?'

Howard's eyes lit up again. 'That's the spirit. But, to get back to your … well, your demise, I suppose. Do you know who is behind it all? Any ideas? Except me, of course.' He let out what he hoped was a salty seadog, bluff and honest laugh.

'I'm still looking at all the people who it might be.'

Effingham snorted. 'Take you a long time, that, won't it?'

Marlowe inclined his head graciously. He knew better than most how long the list of his enemies was.

'Why did you think it was me, though? I've always liked you, lad. I wouldn't try to kill you. If it had been me, no one I sent would be paid off by Nicholas Faunt or anyone else.' He chose to forget his coachman for a while.

'I did call you – and others – atheists.'

'True. But sticks and stones will break my bones, but words will never hurt me. You should write that down, you could use it in a play. By the way, I like that latest thing of yours.'

'*The Massacre at Paris*?' Marlowe asked the question with his best innocent expression firmly fixed, but he knew what the answer would be.

'No, no, not that. Although I do like that. No, I mean this *Blasphemer* thing. I saw the script today. It's among your best work, I would say.'

'Hmm. Oh, that.'

'Don't dismiss it just like that. Henslowe's putting it on as soon as Ned Alleyn has learned his lines.'

'It'll be a cold day in Hell when that happens, but I catch your drift.' Marlowe thought he would be polite and put a nautical reference in. He reached up and tapped on the roof of the carriage and the horses whinnied and slowed as the coachman pulled on the reins. 'Well, this is me.'

'Where are we?' Effingham looked vaguely out of the window, seeing nothing but rain.

'I have no idea,' Marlowe said, reaching out and undoing the door.

'Then how do you know this is where you want to be?' The admiral genuinely wanted to know. This Machiavel was full of surprises.

Marlowe shrugged and jumped down landing, unsurprisingly, in a puddle. 'All the world's a stage, or so I believe,' he said through the window. 'So anywhere is as good as anywhere else to me. Now, don't forget, my lord. Not a word to your confederates. Let's keep this a secret between us, shall we? Remember Matilda.'

'Always,' the coachman said, from above him.

'Yes, well,' Howard said, craning out of the window. 'You've got more to remember than I have. We'll talk about this later. And as for you, Master …'

But Marlowe had gone.

Lord Howard of Effingham was a man who liked things to be pleasant. He had a pleasant wife and a pleasant house and if he sometimes dallied pleasantly with complaisant women, that was just a little peccadillo he kept to himself. As he alighted from his carriage, he tossed a couple of gold coins into the air over his shoulder and his coachman deftly caught them and drove off smiling. Despite the rain, it was turning out to be a pleasant day all round.

Later though, ensconced in his room above the gatehouse, he began to mull things over. The Matilda issue was fixed; his coachman might be a roue and a rogue, but the coins in his pouch would ensure his loyalty. But Marlowe. What of him? Effingham didn't deny that a little thrill of relief had run through him when he had heard the man was dead. His money was on one of the Cecils, as nasty a pair as walked the earth. Robert in particular, seemed to embody sliminess and malevolence and pound for pound was as unpleasant a creature as a man could meet in a day's march. And yet the Queen seemed to reckon him a man worth her time. Effingham tutted to the wolfhound spread out at its leisure in front of the small, springtime fire in the grate and the animal looked at him quizzically.

'You may well look askance, Gellert.' Effingham's daughter was an avid reader of books of the more romantic sort. 'But I don't think even the Queen's Elf would arrange to kill Marlowe without meeting with the rest of us first. Unless

...' he pulled at his beard pensively, 'do you think the others met, perhaps, without me?'

The dog muttered in its throat as dogs will and chewed aimlessly on a foreleg.

Effingham closed his eyes. He could feel himself getting testy and that rarely ended well. He picked up a small pewter bell from the table beside him and gave it a shake. Almost before the clapper had stopped moving, his steward was at his side. Effingham looked up.

'Ambrose,' he said. 'Could you fetch me a nice bottle of ...'

The man placed a bottle of Rhenish and a goblet on the table.

'Ah. Yes. And a few small plain ...'

A plate of biscuits, still warm and pliable from the oven materialised alongside the wine.

'And if you could order the ...'

The faint sound of hoofbeats and the rumble of wheels rose from the courtyard below.

'Ambrose?' Effingham was determined to catch the man off guard.

'My Lord?'

'I don't pay you enough. Er. How much do I pay you?'

Ambrose shifted uncomfortably and looked suspiciously at the dog. He bent down and whispered in his lord's ear.

Effingham looked startled. 'Really? Do I?' He did some rudimentary reckoning on his fingers. Where was Thomas Heriot when a man needed him? 'That's enough. But in any event, thank you. Tell the coachman I will be down shortly and we need to go to the Palace of Westminster. I have urgent business with Sir Robert Cecil.'

'My Lord,' Ambrose murmured and withdrew.

He stuck his head out of the door and whistled to the coachman, who hopped down from his perch and ambled over. Good God, the rain had stopped.

'Yer?'

'Yer, Master Ambrose,' Ambrose corrected him. 'His lordship's on the Rhenish. He'll be hours yet. So if you have anything to do, I suggest you go and do it.'

The coachman chuckled. He had coins in his purse and an hour or two at leisure. And he knew where Matilda lived, or if not lived, where she plied her trade. He jingled the coins in one hand and his balls in the other as he walked out onto the highway. 'Yer,' he said, over his shoulder at the closing door. 'Yer.'

CHAPTER 7

Nicholas Skeres had finally stopped shaking but he was still prone to jumping in his skin at loud noises. He finally realised that if he could be with other people, he would perhaps feel safer; as long as the other people did not include Kit Marlowe. Skeres was not the brightest of men. In a room of two or in a room of a hundred, he was likely to be in the stupidest one per cent. But he was personable and pleasant enough and when he had money in his pocket, he wasn't averse to spending it. So when he turned up at the Golden Boy, where the walking gentlemen and other theatrical types tended to gather, he was welcomed in the time honoured way.

'Ho, there,' someone shouted. 'Everybody budge up and make room for Nicholas.'

He nodded his thanks and sat down in the one buttocked pose reserved for latecomers. A goblet came his way, passed hand to hand down the table and he drank from it greedily.

'You look a little green around the gills, Skeres. Not sickening for something, I trust.' Tom Sledd had never really taken to Skeres but he had a line now and so needed to be taken care of. What with Ned Alleyn making it up half the time and the queen's maid's voice having broken halfway through his only scene just that morning, he really didn't need grief from a walking gentleman going down with something.

Nicholas Skeres had never really taken to Tom Sledd. He and Marlowe clearly had a history that went way back, back to when Skeres was just a humble pickpocket down the docks, rolling sailors for their pay when they were too drunk to fight back. But Skeres was a man on the edge and he knew that if anyone knew what Marlowe had in mind, it would be Sledd, so he leaned in and said, 'You know Marlowe's alive, right?'

Sledd raised an eyebrow. Surely, this must be the worst kept secret in London. Even so, his reply was quiet.

'Yes.'

'Well, I knew, right from the start, see, and he's been to see me. And he thinks I know who … well …' Skeres was close to tears. He felt that he was speaking in a foreign language, or one where certain words were banned. His sisters had played some stupid thing like it when they were children and he had never really understood the rules. He didn't understand them now.

Sledd looked at him encouragingly. As long as the man had nothing communicable, he hardly cared. He didn't often come out with the lads. He had a wife and what seemed to be an endlessly increasing number of children at home and usually that was where he went. But what with Alleyn and the lad with the suddenly enormous Adam's apple, he felt he needed a small break in his day before going home. He took another sip from his goblet and waited. In what was beginning to seem like an endless lifetime of dealing with actors and their sudden emotional explosions, he had found that waiting often did the trick. That, and a quick smack upside the head with a piece of timber, though it had rarely come to that.

Skeres' voice, when it came, was a little more controlled. 'He thinks I know who paid to have him killed.'

That got Sledd's attention. Since he had heard of Marlowe's death and certainly since he had heard of his still being alive, he, along with everyone else in on the secret, had wondered who could have wanted to do such a heinous thing as to cut off the Muse's darling in his prime. And he had to admit, the list was endless. He loved Kit Marlowe with all his heart, but he had to admit that on his best day he was annoying and on his worst dangerous. It was an opportunity to learn more and he grabbed it, while trying to sound disinterested. 'And *do* you?'

'Of course I don't.' Skeres was outraged. 'Look, Sledd, you know me. When did you ever know me take the initiative in anything? How many times have you had to poke me in the back with a stick just to get me to walk on on cue? Do you really imagine I could orchestrate someone's death? Yes, I grant, I was there. Everyone knows that. But I didn't *do* anything! I didn't *plan* anything. It was as much of a surprise to me as to anyone else when things went the way they did. Frizer might know. Poley. But not me.' He took a huge swig of his ale and sighed. 'I always get the blame.' He looked at Sledd and was so miserable that for a moment the stage manager felt almost sorry for him. 'I'm just a walking gentleman. That's all.'

Sledd had had enough of company, especially this Company. He got up, swinging his leg over the bench and everyone slid over gratefully to take advantage of the extra room. He raised his voice. 'That's me for now, lads. See you all bright and early tomorrow morning. Act Two and we'll be auditioning for the maid, if any of you know of a likely lad whose balls aren't ready to drop for a week or two.'

A wave of laughter went down the table. Puberty was always hanging over their heads, like a sword of Damocles.

He put a friendly hand on Skeres' shoulder and patted it. Bending down, he said in his ear, 'Don't worry about it, Nick. Just concentrate on your line and it'll all seem better in the morning.'

Skeres clamped a hand over his. He was at the point that a kind word might well tip him over the edge. 'Thank you, Tom,' he managed, his voice thick with unshed tears. ''Preciate it.'

Sledd extricated himself with another pat. 'You're welcome,' he said and with a wave in everyone's general direction, he made for the door.

Never let it be said that Sir Robert Cecil was a vain man.

True, his doublet and Venetians were of the finest cloth and he rouged his cheeks because it was fashionable at court. Oh, and of course, his pattens and even his ordinary heels were three inches higher than anyone else's, which was necessary when the Queen calls you her 'elf' and her 'pygmy'. She didn't mean to be unkind, of course, but God, Gloriana was a bitch!

His nurse had dropped him as a child, something half the Court wanted to do now he was an adult, so he had to put up with the crooked back and the splayed feet. He was sitting on his specially padded chair in the oak lined chamber in the palace of Whitehall that he had made his own. He toyed with the dice in his hand, casting them against the inkwell on his desk. The portrait of his Lizzie caught his eye and he found himself chuckling. She was silent, true and chaste, which was just as well because Lord Burghley, her father-in-law, rarely shut up.

The documents spread out before him never went away and he felt as if they were burning into his soul. Supplies; relief for the poor, the many-headed monster. And always, although there was no documentation for it, was that irritating business about Marlowe. Cecil had met the man, of course, shortly before his alleged death in Deptford. He had interrogated him himself in the Star Chamber. *And* he liked the man's plays, except that last one, *Edward II.* Set in an earlier century it might have been, but it was patently an attack on the Queen herself and on the Imp himself and his father. That was why the four most powerful men in the realm, a quarter of whom was rolling his dice idly now, had decided to silence the blasphemer, the atheist. Atheist! Cecil found himself chuckling again.

There was a knock on the door and the Secretary's secretary walked in. 'I'm sorry to bother you, sir, with such a trifling matter, but Francis Bacon is without.'

'Isn't he, though?' Cecil quipped. 'What does he want this time, Underwood, the Attorney-Generalship?'

Ralph Underwood was one of the few men who could read Cecil like a book. 'I believe he mentioned it, sir. Will you grant him an audience?'

'No, Underwood, I will not. He's got viper's eyes, has Bacon. I wouldn't trust him further than I could throw him. Was there anything else?'

'If not Bacon, sir, how about Baron Hunsdon?'

Cecil sighed. 'I'm not sure that's any better,' he said. 'Oh, all right, show him in. Tell Bacon I'm at Hatfield and I'll get back to him.'

'Very good, sir.' And the man bowed and left.

Henry Carey looked like shit. He'd got the poppy eyes that all his family had and now that he was putting on weight, it didn't suit him.

'God, Henry, you look like shit,' Cecill observed. Before he had a chance to offer the man a chair, hr had all but collapsed into it.

'Buggered if I ride all the way from Berwick again,' the old man wheezed. 'It's a ship for me next time.'

'How are the Marches?' Cecil thought it polite to enquire.

'Bugger the Marches, Cecil! I'm here about Marlowe.'

'Ah.' Cecil poured them both a large Muscadine. 'Say on.'

'He was about to come north,' Hunsdon said, 'going over, they say, to that malformed abomination the king of Scots.'

'Henry,' Cecil savoured the wine. 'This is all so last month. Marlowe has been dead …'

'Is he dead?' Hunsdon was sitting forward on the edge of his seat. 'I know there were rumours here in London, but they've reached Berwick now. I had a deputation from the king of Scots, some insufferable oafs in skirts who could barely speak English. I *think* they wanted to know why a man who had been stabbed to death in Deptford should be sailing to the court of King James.'

Cecil put his dice away and leaned back in the chair. 'Shall we start at the beginning? You remember the Marprelate tracts?'

'The what?' Hunsdon was confused.

'Libels that appeared all over the Dutch church here in the city, attacking the bishops.'

'Oh, that,' Hunsdon shrugged. 'Yes, of course. Everyday event, isn't it?'

'Quite so,' Cecil humoured him. 'Now, do you remember Marlowe's latest offering – *Edward II*?'

'No. Well, yes, although I haven't seen it, of course. Apart from striding around the battlements in Berwick, I don't get out much.'

'No, of course not. It's about …'

'Oh, I know what it's about, Cecil. I'm as familiar with this country's history as the next man. Edward II was a pederast, a catamite. Died with a poker up his   '

'Allegedly,' Cecil nodded.

'What's that got to do with the Marprelate tracts?'

'It may have escaped your notice, Henry,' Cecil purred, 'that we in the Privy Council are not exactly, how shall I put it? Popular. The Queen has been excommunicated. We're taxing everybody to death. And rumours are that another Armada is on its way.'

'Good God … Um, yes, I know all that.'

'Marlowe's play is actually an attack on us – me, father, you and Effingham in particular. And you know how the hoi-polloi flock to anything written by Marlowe. He's the Muse's darling and he's the people's too. If he tells them, albeit through his iambic rubbish, that their government is corrupt, that there is something rotten in the state of England, they'll do something about it.'

'You mean, rebellion?' Baron Hunsdon was not Warden of the Marches for nothing.

'Exactly. And can I remind you, too, that we have no police force worthy of the name, just decayed old idiots of the Watch. Our army, such as it is, doesn't add up to the Duke of Parma's personal bodyguard. The last battle fought on English soil was Stoke, over a century ago. Believe me, Carey, if the great unwashed take to the streets, we're finished.'

'Well, yes, but they wouldn't, would they? They have no leader for a start.'

'Don't they? Have you looked sideways at Ralegh lately? Essex? And don't get me started on Ireland.'

'So Marlowe's the … what do you call it, catalyst for

all this. That's a new word, by the way, catalyst. My son George introduced me to it.'

'Yes,' Cecil scowled. 'George is a member of the School of Night, isn't he? Sorcerers. Magicians. Alchemists … Devil worshippers.'

'Oh, I say,' Hunsdon frowned. 'Steady on.'

'Marlowe is a member of the School of Night, too, as is Ralegh. Do you see a pattern here, Henry?'

Hunsdon blinked and found himself reaching for more wine. 'Wait a minute. Are you saying that my son is a traitor, a devil-worshipper bent on rebellion?' The man had turned purple.

'No, of course not. I'm saying that Marlowe is a projector, an agent, a spy if you will. He worked for Walsingham and now he's working for us.'

'Well, if he's working for us, how can he be a threat?'

Cecil stopped in mid-sentence. He rang the bell that stood on his desk and his secretary appeared. His arrival was so sudden that Hunsdon – who preferred the more melodramatic type of entertainment – would not have been surprised to see the smoke and sparks that usually accompanied the entrance of the Demon King.

'Ah, Underwood. Be so good as to ask my father to join us, would you? I have Baron Hunsdon here and we have urgent affairs of state to discuss.'

'Very good, sir.'

Robert Cecil was only too aware that he was still in the shadow of the Queen's Treasurer, the most powerful man in England, but this was too important to let pride get in the way. For what seemed eternity, both men waited in silence, Hunsdon trying to ease the pain in his left buttock that the saddle had caused him.

'Lord Burghley,' he stood up as the great man entered. It had been less than three weeks since Hunsdon had seen him last, but he'd aged years. Below the white eyebrows, however, the eyes were as sharp and cold as ever.

'Henry,' the Lord Treasurer never smiled unless he absolutely had to and the fact that his favourite boy had sent for him meant that there was trouble in the wind.

They all sat down and Burghley declined Cecil's offer of a glass.

'Marlowe,' Cecil said.

'Ah.' That seemed to be everybody's comment.

'Is he dead or isn't he?' Hunsdon shouted. 'I thought we'd agreed …'

'We agreed that he was too dangerous to keep alive,' Burghley said calmly. 'He *did* accuse us of being atheists.'

'Oh, that.' Hunsdon dismissed it.

'No, Henry,' Burghley pursued it. 'Let's have this out.' He looked levelly at the man. 'Or do you believe in God?'

Another confused look flashed across Hunsdon's face. 'Er …'

'Let me clarify,' the Treasurer went on. '*I* don't believe in God. Robert here does not believe in God. And from what I know of you, you don't either.'

Hunsdon thought rapidly, drumming his fingers on the arm of his chair. What he said next could cost him his life. 'Between these walls, I don't.' His voice was barely a whisper.

'Say that in the street, Hunsdon,' the Treasurer said, 'and they'll burn you. Established family, member of Her Majesty's Privy Council. Warden of the Marches. And all the dozens of other little titles you've picked up. None of that would matter. First, they'd set up a little meeting for you with Master Topcliffe. I hear he's just had a new rack installed in the Tower. He'll go for your fingers first, then your elbow joints. Skeffington's Gyves are a little old hat nowadays, but there are other little gadgets that crush bones and tear flesh. Then they'll pick a day – it'll be sunny and blue-skied at this time of year – when they'll tie you to a stake and light the brushwood.'

'All right, Burghley,' Hunsdon snapped. 'I get the picture.'

'Marlowe was shooting off his mouth. He'd found out our beliefs – we four, we happy four – and he was going to shout it from the rooftops. You, Effingham, Robert, me – we'd all have gone to the fire. And that would have meant the collapse of government as surely as if someone had planted barrels of gunpowder under the vaults of the Parliament

House.'

'Don't be ridiculous,' Hunsdon laughed, but the Cecils weren't joining him.

'Then, of course,' Burghley went on, pouring a glass of wine for himself, 'we relented.'

There was a crash as the door swung wide and Howard of Effingham, the hero of the Armada, stood there, fuming.

'Ah, here he is,' Burghley said. 'The fourth horseman of the Apocalypse.'

'What's that supposed to mean?' Effingham bellowed. He never liked it when his colleagues of the Privy Council met without him. What were they plotting? What with the Rhenish and the sudden appearance of a dazzling sun, his temper was not what it might have been.

'A little thing called the Bible,' Burghley said. 'Look it up.'

'Marlowe,' Effingham ignored the man.

'Ah,' the others chorused.

'The blackguard was in my coach!'

'When was this?' Cecil asked.

'A few hours ago. He dresses as a Puritan these days, but those eyes … dammit, Burghley! He could have killed me!'

'He could kill any of us,' Cecil nodded.

'Not me.' Hunsdon was on his feet. 'I'm going back to Berwick.'

'I hear they have witches bobbing about in the sea up there,' Burghley smiled. 'Take care that one of them isn't Machiavel, in yet another disguise.'

'Cecil.' Effingham tried to focus on the little man, but he'd downed a few and the biscuits hadn't soaked much up. 'If I remember rightly after Marlowe's last reporting to us, it was you who decided how the deed should be done.'

'It was,' Cecil agreed. 'But that was before we relented.'

'Yes,' Effingham growled. 'I'm not sure that was the right move. Oh, I like Marlowe well enough – I told him so – but I wouldn't turn my back on him. Who did you select?'

'That hardly matters now,' Burghley said. 'Suffice it to say that we agreed to call the man off. We'd take our chances with Marlowe. If need be, we could set it all up again.'

'But somebody didn't get the message, did they?' Effingham pursued it. 'If I remember the court papers aright, didn't your old mucker Danby hold an inquest on him?'

'He did,' Burghley nodded. 'At Deptford Strand.'

'Well, forgive me,' Effingham said, 'but to have an inquest, you have to have a body, don't you?'

'Corpus delicti,' Cecil said.

'Whatever. In that Christopher Marlowe was alive and well in my carriage earlier, who the hell was under the shroud at Deptford?'

'And who,' Hunsdon followed it up, 'did they bury in St Nicholas churchyard?'

There was a silence.

'The ways of the Lord are strange,' Burghley said and they all laughed, although there was no mirth in it.

'And so, it seems,' Cecil said, 'are the ways of Marlowe.'

Another silence.

'Gentlemen,' the Lord Treasurer pulled them all together. 'Let us admit that we have had something of a shock. Let us also admit that our secrets belong exclusively in this room. Whoever attempted to kill Kit Marlowe, it wasn't one of us.'

The next morning dawned dreary, with a hint of sunshine to come. After the torrential rain on the previous day, anything short of a shower of frogs had to be a good thing and Tom Sledd was light of foot as he hopped over the puddles on his way to the Rose. He had had a good night, one way and another. These days, he realised with a rueful smile, a good night was a night in which only one child at a time was awake and this had been achieved for once. So he was looking forward, in an odd sort of way, to auditioning talentless lads for the role of the maid and putting the finishing touches to the scenery. The play was almost ready. And Kit Marlowe was alive. All was right with Tom Sledd's world. He stopped by the bear pit to throw Master Sackerson a cabbage he had bought from a cart on the way. The bear grunted his thanks and even he seemed to be relishing the rain-washed air of a perfect June morning. Tom was still smiling as he executed a perfect one heeled turn around the corner of the main building of the Rose.

Suddenly, his life was in turmoil. Frantic fists had his doublet tightly held and he was being shaken to and fro like a rag doll. He opened his mouth to protest and all that happened was that he bit his tongue. He clapped one hand to his mouth, and with the other tried to fend his assailant off. Tom Sledd was not tall but he was powerful, with all the carpentry, climbing, carrying and general physical work he did in an average day. The man who was currently trying to tear his clothes off his body was a little taller, but slight and the stage manager could feel his grip weakening already. He weaseled his hand in between them and pushed hard on the man's chest. With a cry, he lost his grip and fell back into a muddy patch in the yard.

He looked down. Adam Proud lay there, his arms still up, his fists still clenched. He drummed his heels in anger, splashing mud and last night's rain up his own legs. Sledd grabbed a wrist and pulled the man to his feet. He was never a man of many words but now he could feel quite a few choice ones rising to his lips.

'Proud! What in God's …?'

Proud flung himself at him again, pulling at his sleeve this time, seemingly oblivious to the mud and the fact that his whole back was sopping wet. 'Quick! Quick! I think he's dead.'

'In that case, what's the rush?'

Proud stopped in his tracks. 'That's a bit harsh,' he said. 'I only *think* he's dead. I could be wrong.' He looked Sledd up and down. 'I didn't have you down for a cynic, Tom.'

'I'm not,' Sledd said. 'But I am willing to bet that I have seen more dead men than you have and they lose their ability to shock after a while. Who is it, do you know?' He ushered Proud ahead and the man half trotted, half sidled ahead of him, wanting to get to the scene quickly, yet still tell the dread tale.

'I don't know who it is. It's a man. He's ... well, follow me and you'll see. This way,' he dashed on ahead. 'This way.' He led the way through the maze of corridors which led to the Groundlings' pit.

They turned a corner and the wooden O opened before them. Although it was his everyday environment, Tom Sledd could never quite overcome the little thrill that the space gave him. He sometimes sat quietly, talking to the shade of his mentor and – to all intents and purposes – father, Ned Sledd, actor manager extraordinaire, to use the man's own phrase. He could only dream of a place like this. Ned Sledd's wooden O was a stand of trees behind a flattish piece of meadow, a market square, the inner courtyard of an indulgent rich man's house. And yet Sledd Snr had created magic, brought plays to life in ways that Philip Henslowe could only dream of.

The last thing that Tom Sledd had seen the previous afternoon was an old man sweeping. Now, right in the centre of the O was a deep puddle and, alongside it, a man, spreadeagled on the sawdust scattered boards.

The two men broke into a run, Proud breathlessly filling Sledd in on the details.

'I came in early, you see, to see if anything needed to be done that I had missed yesterday. What with the maid and all that, I wanted it to go as smoothly as possible. And there he was. Face down in the puddle. I pulled him out, in case he had just fainted or something. Then ... well, almost straight away I bumped into you.'

'So you found him when? Five minutes ago? Ten?'

'Something like that. Ten. Yes, ten.'

By now they were alongside the man and Sledd already had a sinking feeling in the pit of his stomach. He thought he knew the back of that head. It was flat, without much brain in it, but it didn't hold much real malice either. He took him under one armpit and rolled him over. The leading arm swung and the knuckles fell with a crack on the boards. Nicholas Skeres' head lolled sideways, his eyes slitted and seeming to look down at his own shoulder. He was clearly dead.

'Skeres!' Proud stepped back, his hand to his mouth. 'But … what …?'

Sledd walked over to the curtain of the stage and snatched a cloth from a piece of unfinished scenery. He covered Skeres' dead face with it and led Proud away. It was bad enough that the man was dead, without Proud being sick all over him.

He sat Proud down on a seat with what the management euphemistically called 'limited view', in other words, behind an enormous pillar. Sledd completed the isolation by standing in front of the man until he gathered himself together. He waited in silence until finally, with a shake, Proud brought up his head and spoke, albeit quietly.

'I've never seen a dead man before.'

'Really?' Sledd was frankly amazed. He seemed to have spent his life seeing dead people, in gutters, in beds, on gibbets. Proud must have been extremely sheltered to have missed that stage of growing up.

'I was brought up very quietly,' Proud said. 'I suppose you could say I was coddled. I know now, looking back, that my mother spoiled me. I slept in her bedroom until I was fifteen.' He looked up at Sledd at that point. He was used to the reaction that statement usually got. 'Nothing untoward, I assure you. My father had … gone … by the time I was out of swaddling bands and she just wanted to know I was well, not ailing, you know. Nurses can be so thoughtless, as I'm sure you know.'

Sledd had no idea of how thoughtless nursemaids could be. His first memory was of looking up at the boards on the underside of a travelling show cart and nursemaids had never been a feature of his life. Except that one in Daventry that time … but that was something else altogether.

'She didn't want me to come to London.' He chuckled, looking down at his hands, the fingers lacing and interlacing constantly. 'She thought it was a den of iniquity.'

Sledd did a double take. 'It *is* a den of iniquity,' he pointed out.

Proud shrugged. 'I suppose it is. I just never seem to be in the wrong place at the right time.' He looked up with a wry smile. 'I might just as well still be sleeping in my mother's bedchamber.'

'Really?' Sledd was feeling that this conversation was not taking the direction it should, 'Is this anything to do with poor Skeres out there?' He gestured to the stage.

'In a way. I didn't come in early to check on things. I came in early because ...' the fingers twirled even more madly 'because sometimes, early, you see a couple of geese about and if they haven't made enough for their rent, well, they'll let you ... I don't want to give myself, you see, until marriage. That's very important to me, mother impressed that on me from an early age. But sometimes, the girls, they'll let you ...'

'Yes, yes.' Sledd put a stop to Proud's maudlin pre-pubescent maunderings. 'I need to fetch the Watch. We can't just leave bodies all over the shop. And Nicholas didn't just keel over in that puddle.'

'He *was* drinking,' Proud said, somewhat sententiously. 'After you left, he really did get rather drunk.'

'That's hardly a surprise,' Sledd said. 'He had had a bit of a shock. But even drunk men don't just lie face down in puddles. And even if they do, they try not to break their necks as they fall. Stay here. Keep people away. I'll not be long.'

Proud made to grab Sledd's sleeve then thought better of it. Straightening his shoulders, he got up and walked with the stage manager to the door. 'I'll make sure no one comes in. Nicholas deserves some dignity, don't you think?'

'There, now,' Sledd said, glad to be away. 'That's the spirit. I'll be back soon. Stand here in the door, so you don't have to look at him. He's not going anywhere.' And he went off in search of the Watch. And another Walking Gentleman who could learn five lines by Friday.

Ingram Frizer had never seen sun like it. He'd been in the Marshalsea before. And the Whit. And the Compter. It was always a pleasure to breathe God's fresh air again, especially on an early summer's day such as this. The bell of St Mary

Overy tolled the hour and Frizer's new-found freedom told him – and the world (should the world care) – that there was a God after all. All right, 'God' in this instance came in the form of Her Majesty's signature at the bottom of a piece of parchment. And Nicholas Faunt, the devious bastard, must have had a hand in there somewhere. Ingram Frizer was not to know that this was the fastest pardon ever granted by Her Majesty in all the long years of her reign.

'It's been a delight, Master Keeper,' Frizer beamed to the man on the gate, dangling as he was with keys and menace.

'Wait until the next time,' the oaf grunted.

'Oh, no,' Frizer assured him. 'You won't be seeing me again. I told you people all along that I was innocent. You wouldn't listen. Her Majesty, now – Gloriana – she knew a wronged man when she heard of one. And I …' he held up his scroll, 'have a royal pardon to prove it.'

'A man's still dead, though, isn't he?' the turnkey called after him.

Frizer didn't look back. He just chuckled to himself. 'Is he?' he said softly. 'Is he really?'

So, what now? A flagon or two of good ale at the Actor and Groundling, certainly. Some oysters, not *too* long raised from their beds. A little Winchester goose … he smelled his armpits … perhaps a bath first. His last one was before Christmas, so it was probably time. 'Did I just say *a* Winchester goose?' he muttered to himself. 'Make it a gaggle, Ing, old boy. You owe it to yourself to live a little.'

He turned into the cobbled street beyond the prison's precincts and breathed in. Had the river *ever* smelt so good? The tanneries? He could even catch a whiff from the public jakes on London bridge. Who, he wondered, would be on hand to welcome his liberty? Not the Queen, of course. He was *far* too humble a subject to merit that. Nicholas Faunt? Probably not. The man was a snob with more side than the Bank. He'd only turned up in the Marshalsea to threaten him.

No, it would be the lads from the Rose, that was certain. His old mate Nick Skeres, glad to be on the road with him again. Tom Sledd, the stage woman turned stage manager. Will Shaxsper would be there, begging him to take the lead in whatever drivel he was trying to write now. Ned Alleyn wouldn't be there. Nobody bitched like Ned Alleyn. And now Ingram Frizer was back on the boards, the stuck-up bastard would never get a part again. It wasn't likely, but just possible, that Philip Henslowe would make an appearance, welcoming Frizer's freedom. Maybe even Sir Edmund Tilney, the Master of the Revels. Kit Marlowe …

The name had just flashed into Frizer's brain when he felt a strong pair of hands swing him sideways and hurl him face forward against a wall.

'Hello, Kit,' sounded decidedly odd against the brickwork and what with the swollen lip. 'Kit? Is that you?'

Marlowe had spun him round to face him and the liberty man couldn't believe what he saw. The ringlets and the earring were gone, as was the velvet and the silk. What had not gone were the smouldering eyes. What had not gone was the dagger blade glinting in the summer sunshine at Frizer's throat.

'Remind me, Ingram,' Marlowe said. 'How was it in Deptford? You were to my left, knife in hand. Skeres was to my right. Poley was in the centre. And what was that little thing you had in common? Oh, that's right. I remember now. You were all trying to kill me.'

'Kit, Kit,' Frizer was gabbling for his life. 'That was all a misunderstanding. We'd never hurt you, Nick and me. We go back years.'

'Indeed we do.' The blade tip was still at Frizer's throat.

'There was no need for Master Faunt to involve himself. We were just about to burst out laughing when he came in.'

'And misunderstood.'

'Exactly. Just three old mates larking about. We've all done it dozens of times at the Rose. Remember that time when …'

'Who paid you?'

'What?'

'Who paid you and Skeres to "lark about" in Deptford? And don't tell me it was Skeres; I've asked him already.' The blade pressed against Frizer's skin and he felt it break and he felt the blood trickling down onto his shirt.

'Poley!' Frizer rasped. 'It was Poley.'

Marlowe's eyes had never left Frizer's. Then, as suddenly as the meeting had begun, it ended. The playwright tossed his dagger in the air and caught it, slipping it into the sleeve of his doublet.

'Somehow,' he said, 'I knew it would be. And where can I find Master Poley?'

Frizer shrugged and puffed at the same time. If his life still depended on his answer, then his time was up. 'No idea,' he said. Then, a thought occurred. 'I thought you knew him. In the Ordinary, you said you'd promised to kill him if your paths crossed again.'

'And thanks to Nicholas Faunt, I didn't,' Marlowe said. 'But I'm being unkind. You. Skeres. Poley. One by one, that would be fine. But all together?' he chuckled. 'I'm not that good. I owe Faunt my life. And you, Ingram, owe me yours. Not to mention the debt you owe Faunt for getting you out of the Hole. And whatever Poley paid you, for the job you didn't do.'

He turned and walked away. Without looking back, he shouted, 'I'd be very worried about that if I were you. Sweet Robyn Poley doesn't like to be cheated. Whatever arrangement he came to with Faunt, he'll hold you and Skeres responsible for baulking him of his prey. Count on it.'

CHAPTER 8

Walter Hiddlestone was not best pleased to have to fight his way through a throng of theatricals that morning. For one thing, most of them were in disguise, dressed in outlandish costumes with wigs and *far* too much makeup. Two or three of the younger men were wearing gowns and skirts, but the Under-Sheriff of Southwark didn't judge.

'Who's in charge here?' he barked.

'I am,' at least four voices chorused.

Hiddlestone spun to the first. 'Name?'

The tall, good-looking actor bridled. 'Surely you know, Master Sheriff. I am Tamburlaine. I am Dr Faustus. I am Piers Gaveston.'

'Are you trying to be funny?' Hiddlestone snapped. He wasn't a Puritan as such; he just didn't like theatres.

The man of many parts sighed. 'I would have thought it would have been obvious. I am Edward Alleyn, principal actor of the Rose, the Curtain and several wayside inns.'

'Don't listen to him, Sheriff,' another of those-in-charge chimed in. 'Richard Burbage, of Henslowe's Company, the Lord Admiral's Men, the Lord Chamberlain's Men.'

Alleyn scoffed. 'Jack of all Companies,' he hissed. 'Master of none.'

'This is my stage,' a third stepped forward. Hiddleston looked at him. He was a head shorter than the last two and lacked their hauteur. Even so, he had the air of a man who knew what he was talking about. 'I am Thomas Sledd, stage manager. I sent you a messenger.'

'You found the body?'

'No, I …'

'Hiddleston, what the Hell is going on?' Another face had joined the throng. 'Why are you pestering my people?'

'Ah, Master Henslowe. At last someone I recognize.'

Alleyn and Burbage both bridled.

'I was informed that there has been a death here today.'

'And he hasn't seen you perform yet, Burbage,' Alleyn hissed in the man's ear.

'Sledd' Henslowe rounded on his stage manager. 'Why wasn't I told?'

'We couldn't find you, Master Henslowe. I sent Dickon with the news. And Willie to find the Sheriff.'

'*Under* Sheriff,' Henslowe corrected him. It was Hiddlestone's turn to bridle. Technically, of course, the impresario was correct, but why was it always the *Sheriff* who attended the banquets and the masques where the wine flowed like water and the women were laid wall to wall? Why was he, the Under-Sheriff, always up to his armpits in somebody's gruesome end?

'Well, who is it?' Henslowe asked. 'And where, cliché though it is, away?'

'I want this crowd cleared, Master Henslowe,' Hiddlestone said. He was only too well aware that, if this was murder, any one of the theatricals might be responsible, but that was a chance he would have to take. He needed them all out from under his feet. 'Miller. McNeil.' His lackeys snapped to attention. 'Keep a record of their names.' He sneered at Alleyn. 'Their *real* names, mind you. And a place where they can be reached.' He then addressed the crowd. 'Nobody leaves this theatre without he – or she – passes my men first. Is that understood?'

'Wouldn't make much of a Prologue, would he?' Burbage muttered to Alleyn. For a rare moment, the two greatest actors in the world were in complete agreement.

'This way, gentlemen.' Tom Sledd led Henslowe and Hiddlestone through a labyrinth of passages, dimly lit even in the summer sun, and out onto the wooden O, dressed, as it was, for *Tamburlaine.*

There were two men centre stage. One was lying on his back, dead as a nit. The other was squatting alongside him, like a Puritan priest giving him the last rites.

'Who are you?' Hiddlestone wanted to know.

The man stood up, thrusting out a hand. 'Robert Brackenbury, Office of the Revels.'

'The what?' Hiddlestone asked.

'Tilney,' Henslowe murmured out of the corner of his mouth.

'Oh,' the Under-Sheriff sneered. 'Can I remind you, Master … er … Brackenbury, that this is a crime scene? A man is dead.'

'Indeed he is,' Marlowe said. 'And Sir Edmund, as Master of the Queen's Revels, wants to know what you are doing about it.'

'Oh, he does, does he?' Hiddlestone was beyond furious, his jaw and fists clenching in unison.

'You've checked the body?' Marlowe went on. 'Wounds? Signs of violence? You'd probably get all those people back here.'

'Why?' the Under-Sheriff asked.

Marlowe rolled his eyes. 'I don't think it's my job, as Deputy Master of the Revels, to explain basic procedure to you, Under-Sheriff.'

Hiddlestone's jaw dropped. He'd often known people who hindered the office of constable in their enquiries, but never *quite* as badly as this.

'It's because,' Marlowe was in full flow, 'it is well known that a fresh corpse will bleed anew in the presence of its murderer. Really!' Marlowe threw his arms wide. 'What *is* the world coming to?'

Hiddleston ignored him and turned to Henslowe. 'Sir, could I ask you to escort this gentleman elsewhere? Your stage-manager can stay with me, but otherwise I need to examine this body alone. Would that be possible?'

Henslowe flashed a glance at Marlowe who nodded imperceptibly. 'Of course,' he said. 'Master Brackenbury, in view of these tragic events, you and I have a great deal of paperwork to fill in. Shall we?' And he led the righteous Reveller off the stage.

With a practised flick of his fingers that made no noise, Philip Henslowe eased open the wooden shutter in his eyrie under the eaves, the one that looked down onto the stage. Onto the scene of a murder. Sound carried oddly up here. Henslowe and Marlowe could whisper until the cows came home and no one would be any the wiser. The Under-Sheriff and the stage manager, however, were a different matter. If one of them so much as farted, it would echo all the way to the rafters, horrifying the swallows by day, the bats by night.

'Robert Brackenbury?' Henslowe muttered. 'Officer of the Revels? What the Hell, Kit?'

'Just a little bit of theatre for you, Philip,' Marlowe smiled. 'I'm not sure Kit Marlowe is quite ready to rise from his grave just yet. As for the Revels thing, I had to give Hiddlestone a reason for my being next to a body at all. He's not the brightest apple in the barrel, but he *is* an apple.'

'But isn't that Nicholas Skeres down there? One of my very own walking gentlemen?'

Marlowe nodded. 'He'll walk no more, I fear.'

'Did you just happen to be passing?' Henslowe was confused.

'No,' Marlowe chuckled. 'Tom sent Dickon to find you, Willie to the sheriff. And Dan Greenlees to get me. Naturally, dear old Tom left out that last bit.'

'So what happened? Do you know?'

'I know that Skeres' neck was broken.'

'Good God! Here in the Rose?'

'Where you see him.'

'Well, if it isn't too sick, it's where he'd have wanted to go.' Henslowe looked at Marlowe. 'We *are* talking murder here, aren't we? I mean, it couldn't have been an accident?'

Marlowe shook his head. 'No,' he said. 'The only *accidental* injury I can think of is a fall from the roof. And look, there's nothing above poor old Skeres but the sky.'

'If I were of the Puritan persuasion,' Henslowe said, 'I'd have put it down to God's thunderbolts against sinners.'

Marlowe smiled. 'Yes, but in the real world ...'

'Quite. Look, Kit, I hate to admit this, but I barely knew the man. Did he have anybody? Wife? Children?'

'Ingram Frizer,' Marlowe said.

'Oh, yes, of course. Joined at the hip, those two, weren't they? He'll be miffed.'

Far below them. Tom Sledd was sent to find the First Finder while Hiddleston circled the body, unaware that Marlowe already had. When they came back, Marlowe couldn't believe it. 'Who's that?' he asked.

'Er ... that's Adam Proud, of the Lord Admiral's Men. He's a playwright too. But surely, you know him. He told me he was at Cambridge with you.'

'So he was,' Marlowe chuckled. 'A couple of years down from me. There's such snobbery in Cambridge, Philip. It's not just Town versus Gown, it's Quadrivium versus Trivium. The Trivs run errands for the Quads who treat them like the shit on your pattens. I suppose I did that to Proud; I can't really remember. So, he's a writer now?'

'So he says. Goes in awe of you, of course.'

'Of course,' Marlowe laughed.

'So you found the body?' Hiddlestone was facing Proud.

'I did, yes.'

'When was this?'

'Er ... I don't know. Three or four hours ago. It's all been rather a shock.'

'Of course. How did it happen?'

'I don't know.'

Hiddlestone looked at the man. What was it with all these theatricals? If it didn't have lipstick and rouge, it wasn't happening. 'No, I mean, how did you find it? Er ... him?'

'Oh, I see. Well, in my position as the Lord Admiral's amanuensis ...'

'His what?' Hiddlestone asked.

'Dogsbody,' Henslowe and Marlowe whispered

simultaneously and had to stifle their giggles despite the grimness of the scene below them. They didn't hear Proud's explanation. He went on, 'I'd checked the rigging, the sets to the left. Then I made my way around the back. I was just coming onto the stage – enter stage left – when I … saw him. I had no idea who he was. He looked … Tom, could I trouble you for some water?'

'Of course, Master Proud,' and the stage manager went off to manage.

'I wasn't sure whether he was dead or not. I ran, I can't remember in which direction. The first person I bumped into was Tom …'

And pat, on cue, the stage manager returned, a cup of water in his hand. Proud snatched it gratefully.

'Is that right, Sledd?'

'It is, sir.' He was shaking his head. 'This kind of thing doesn't happen at the Rose.'

'Oh, yes it does,' Hiddlestone growled. 'I was here only the other day with reports of a bear attack. There was a body in one of your outhouses as stiff as a bishop's tadger. *And* there was that shooting in this very theatre not so long ago.'

'Oh, *that!*' Sledd chuckled. 'That was all a misunderstanding. Will Shaxsper …' and he clammed up, suddenly aware that the Rose's walls had ears.

'Did you know the dead man, now that you've had a chance to see him properly?' the Under-Sheriff asked.

'No,' Proud said. 'I'd never seen him before … earlier.'

'You Cambridge boys,' Henslowe tutted. 'No offence, Kit, but your old alumnus is about as useful as a colander in a shipwreck.'

Marlowe smiled. 'As I remember,' he said, 'Scenes of crime weren't on the curriculum at Corpus Christi. There is one thing, however, that the ever-perspicacious Under-Sheriff has yet to realize.'

'What's that?'

'Nicholas Skeres and Jack Willoughby were killed in the same way. Their necks were broken.'

Christopher Marlowe had more or less had enough of death,

both his own and other people's. His Puritan clothes were itchy and tight where they should be loose, loose where they should be tight. He really couldn't be doing with shaving every day but even with his colouring, more than 24 hours between the laborious task and he looked anything but Puritan, veering to the louche. He was in a slough of despond … he made a mental note to remember that alluring allegory. He might find a use for it one day, it was too good to waste. He slouched out of the Rose, hands behind his back, eyes on the ground. He leaned over Master Sackerson's pit but the bear was fast asleep on his nice sun warmed rock after the rain and only his snores came as reply when he softly called his name.

Pushing himself off the wall, he ambled down Gaunt Street, idly kicking a pebble. It was hard for a dead man to find any amusement in London these days. Where could he go? He mooched a little further when it suddenly struck him. Doctor John Dee spent most of his life in a hinterland between the living and the dead, so who would welcome him more? Marlowe was also not sure whether Dee knew that the news of his passing was somewhat exaggerated, so it would be good to let him know in person, as it were. The reactions from Michael Johns and Will Shaxsper had taught him that not everyone was that welcoming to a ghost, but he knew that Dee would welcome him with open arms, shade or living. He took a sharp left and headed for Shadwell Stair, where the boatmen gathered.

'His neck was broken?' Ingram Frizer was sitting in a niche in the Golden Boy's wall, nursing an ale big enough for a man to drown in.

'That's what Kit reckons.' Tom Sledd sat alongside him as the great and not very good of Southwark swirled around them. In the noise of the Boy all conversations were as secret as if no one was there; nothing could be heard, anyway.

'Kit?' Frizer's grip tightened on his cup. He'd heard that well enough.

'Look, Ing,' Sledd closed to the man. 'I don't pretend

to know the ins and outs of what exactly happened at Deptford. Suffice it to say that Christopher Marlowe is not only very much alive, as you know only too well, but is looking to settle a score. As, I might add, would I, given his circumstances.'

Frizer's eyes flashed left and right. 'Well, that's just it, Tom,' he growled, swigging hard. 'What if … what if this is the start of it?'

'The start of what?'

Frizer rolled his eyes. How this man had risen to be stage manager of the Rose he couldn't imagine. 'The start of his settling the score. For reasons which, I must say, I find a little harsh, he seems to hold me, dear old Nicholas and Robyn Poley responsible for what was almost his demise. *Almost*, mind you. No playwrights were actually hurt at Deptford.'

'Come on, Ingram.' Sledd leaned back, smiling. 'That's not Kit's style and you know it. How long have you been out now?'

'Of the Marshalsea? Two days.'

'Well, there you are.' Sledd threw his arms wide. 'You've already had forty-eight hours more of life than you would have done if Kit Marlowe had it in for you. And the broken neck thing … that's not Marlowe either. He'd use his razor-sharp wit first to make you feel as small as possible. Then, if he had to, a knife or sword.'

Frizer was nodding. 'You're right,' he said. Then another thought occurred to him. 'But that's even worse.'

'What is?'

'As long as I've only got Marlowe to fear, I can watch my back; keep away from him. But if it's somebody else …' He couldn't help noticing the biceps on Tom Sledd; the man built cities of wood for a living. A little thing like a neck wouldn't faze him.

Sledd had a different take. 'And if it's not Marlowe, why would you be a target at all? You knew Nick Skeres better than anybody. Who'd want to see him dead?'

Marlowe tapped one of the watermen on the shoulder as he

took his ease on the damp stones of the Stair.

'Help you?' the man said, squinting up into the sun. He wasn't pleased by what he thought he saw. One of those damned tight-arsed Puritans, unless he missed his guess. He had ferried the buggers the length and breadth of the Thames and the only tip he had ever got out of them was on how to avoid the fires of Damnation by piety and clean-living. That wasn't even a tip – everyone knew that. It was whether you could be bothered to do it that was the sticking place.

'I want to go to Mortlake,' Marlowe told him, thoughtfully leaning over a few degrees to give him some shade.

'You're a rare one,' the waterman said. 'Don't get many as *wants* to go to Mortlake. *Has* to go, now, we get some of those. *Need* to go. Not *wants* to go.' He cocked his head and waited. Any clever dick stuff from this one and he would fold his oars until he had gone away.

'I'm visiting a friend,' Marlowe said, reasonably. 'And he lives in Mortlake. So I suppose you could say I need to go to Mortlake because I want to visit Dr John Dee.'

'Why didn't you say so at the start?' The waterman jumped up and ushered Marlowe towards his waiting skiff. 'Get a lot of business from Dr Dee. Got that many children, you're up and down the river like a rat. Nice wife, an'all.' The man's eyes grew misty. '*Very* nice.' He settled in his seat, facing Marlowe. 'Know the missus, do ya? Mistress Dee?'

'I do know Jane, yes,' Marlowe said. 'She is a lovely woman indeed. Very kind.'

The waterman's eyelids fluttered. 'Kind, yes, that as well. Kind.' He bent to his oars. 'In an 'urry, are ya?'

'Not particularly.' Marlowe lay back and prepared to watch the world go by. 'They're not expecting me.'

'Har har,' the waterman chuckled. 'They say as how the doctor has a mirror he scries the whole world with. He'll be expecting you, all right. Nah, the reason I ask is, it's different price, innit, fast or usual.'

Marlowe flicked a coin at him. 'I'll buy fast, but the usual will do me. I've got a lot to think about.'

The waterman narrowed his eyes and bit the coin

suspiciously. A Puritan free with his money. The world was turned upside down, for sure. 'Well,' he said. 'Let me know if the pace suits ya. D'you want me to wait for you?'

Marlowe considered it. 'Why not. Yes, if you would. Same price?'

'Same speed?'

Marlowe laughed. 'Same speed, waterman. Same speed.' And he turned his face up to the June sun he should not be alive to see and let the gentle bob of the river take him.

Howard of Effingham didn't like to be kept waiting, especially by a cypher like Edmund Tynsley. But Edmund Tynsley was the Queen's Master of the Revels and Effingham knew that he needed the idiot's authority for what he was about to undertake.

'My lord,' Tynsley half-bowed as he bustled along the passageway and threw his chain of office to an underling. 'How can I ever apologize for keeping you waiting?'

'How indeed?' Effingham sighed.

'McKellen,' Tynsley barked to the underling, 'Have you pandered to His Lordship's every whim? Wine? Cakes? Ale?'

Before the man could answer, the greatest sailor in England interrupted. 'For all I care, Tynsley, there will be no more cakes and ale. All I need is your signature on my request to transfer my Men to the Rose. Back in the day, such trivia was irrelevant but now, it seems, every tee must be crossed and all eyes dotted. I would have sent my under-secretary but the man borders on the imbecilic and I don't have all season. Now that you've opened the theatres … Er, you *have* opened the theatres …'

'Indeed, sir,' Tynsley smarmed. 'Although, of course, we must be wary lest the plague return.'

'Yes, yes,' Effingham dismissed it, making for the door. 'I shall expect the necessary paperwork by … shall we say … this time tomorrow?'

'Very good, my lord.'

In the doorway, a shifty-looking lackey stood there. He was wearing a chain of office too.'

'Do I know you?' Tynsley asked. Visits from the Lord Admiral were rare; they always rattled him and now here was somebody else who, no doubt, wanted something.

'Walter Hiddlestone,' Hiddlestone said, 'Under Sheriff of Southwark.

'I had nothing to do with that wretched woman playing a woman at the Curtain. She appeared to be wearing a codpiece for all I knew. And anyway, what's the Curtain got to do with you? It isn't in Southwark.'

'I haven't the faintest idea what you're talking about. I am here about your man Brackenbury.'

Tynsley blinked. 'I don't have a man Brackenbury,' he said.

'But he's your Deputy,' the Under Sheriff said. 'From this very office.'

'The subject of Deputy is a sore point with me,' Tynsley snapped. 'I don't have one. Despite frequent requests.'

'Then, who's Brackenbury?' Hiddlestone wanted to know.

'I haven't the faintest idea,' Tynsley all but screamed, 'or why you're wasting my time with all this.'

The Under Sheriff pulled himself up to his full height and marshalled his thoughts. These airy fairy theatre types were so over-emotional. Hiddlestone couldn't be doing with emotions. 'A man has been found dead at the Rose,' he said. 'One of the theatres under your jurisdiction, Master of the Revels. A second man was found nearby and taken to the Rose for investigation. The second man, I have discovered, was a walking gentleman employed by the theatre and the first was a man passing himself off in a peculiar way as the late Christopher Marlowe.'

'Marlowe?'

'The same. This fellow Brackenbury claimed to be from this office, which I now realize is not the case.' He closed to his man. 'I come across some pretty rum people in my line of work, Master Tynsley; people who are not all they seem.'

'Actors, you mean?'

'I mean murderers, sir. This Brackenbury was clearly lying through his teeth as to his identity and to his reason for being at the Rose in the first place. It is more than a possibility that I have been talking with a killer.'

Mortlake didn't change. Marlowe hadn't been there for a long time, but he could have sworn that the same old woman, sitting on the same corner, was selling the exactly same bunch of lavender she had tried to press on him the last time. The trees were in full leaf and some were still clinging on to their blossom and it was altogether a glorious day to be alive. The rain had washed the air and the bricks clean, there was a sparkle in the air; not a huge surprise when Dr John Dee was in the vicinity. Marlowe had seen with his own eyes an eagle swoop down from the ceiling of the Rose and land on the man's shoulder. He smiled to himself as he walked along. He had missed his old friend, his wife and his growing brood of children. He shrugged off the burden of being the newly-undead and swung in through the gate of Dee's house, a fragment of a Tallis plainsong unexpectedly on his lips.

He looked up at the house. He noticed that the thatch was patched and in places non-existent, rough boards roped down in the bald spots. Two windows were also boarded up, another two patched with small pieces of wood, held together with a bolt to stop them falling out. The door was ajar, so someone was home – or was it simply that it wouldn't shut any more, the jamb having been split at some time with an axe, if Marlowe was any judge. He knocked anyway. Just because a man was dead didn't mean he couldn't also be polite.

After a moment, the sound of brisk footsteps sounded in the hall and the door was flung open. Jane Dee stood there, a baby on her hip. Marlowe had nothing against children in principle, but he would be the first to admit that one looked pretty much like another to anyone but their parents. So he smiled generally in its direction and then looked at Jane. She was a beautiful woman these days. She had been an ethereal, incandescently pretty girl of eighteen when, to everyone's surprise including his, she had married John Dee. She was now a lovely matron, pearly of skin and soft of eye. When she saw who had come calling, her face broke into her usual angelic smile of welcome.

'Kit!' She looked around helplessly for somewhere to put the child, so she could hug him properly, as a visitor from the past should be hugged. 'Martha! Martha!'

A little maidservant appeared from nowhere and took the baby, who clung to her as she had clung to her mother. Jane Dee's children were as placid and loving as she was, happy with anyone with whom they could share a smile and a cuddle.

Jane grabbed the playwright around the neck and hugged him till his pips squeaked. 'Oh, Kit,' she murmured in his ear, 'we were so sad when we heard you were dead. But John said, no, he's not dead. If he was dead, he would be here to tell me so.' She suddenly let go and held Marlowe at arm's length. 'You're not here to tell him so, are you?' She pinched his cheek and ran a hand over his cropped head.

'No, Jane, I'm not here to tell you that. I'm .. alive.' He smiled. 'I've got a little tired, telling people that.'

'Well, you'll need none of that nonsense here.' She looked into his eyes, turned him this way and that. Jane Dee was everyone's mother. 'You're thin. Are you eating? Where are you living? And who, in the name of all that's holy, cut your hair?'

Marlowe laughed aloud. He had never felt the imperative to marry, but if and when he did, it would be to a woman as exactly like Jane Dee as he could manage. 'I'm not thin,' he said. 'I don't eat much in any case. Here and there. And,' he also ran a hand over his head, 'you chose your words well, my hair was cut by Michael Johns, as holy a man as you would ever want to meet.' He bent to see his reflection in her eyes. 'I'm quite getting to like it.'

'Are you?' She raised an eyebrow. 'Well, let's see what John thinks. Let me just tell Martha …' She stuck her head round a door off the hall. Marlowe remembered that it led to a scullery where the family always seemed to congregate, spurning the other, more splendid rooms. 'Martha?'

There was an answering call from within.

'Martha, I'm just taking Master Marlowe to see the Master. I'll be back shortly.'

The maidservant gave some kind of reply, Marlowe didn't know what.

'I don't know why I tell her where I'm going,' Jane said, kirtling up her skirts to go down the precipitous steps to Dee's inner sanctum. 'Ever since the mob, we've really only got this room, the scullery and a bedroom. Some, mind, say it's crowded, but I prefer to say it's cosy.'

'You say "mob" so calmly, Jane,' Marlowe said, stepping behind her with care. Stairs were never to be taken for granted in Dr Dee's house.

'I'm calm now,' she said, with only a small wobble in her voice. 'It was frightening at the time, of course. John said that we would be safe, and of course, as you see, we *were* safe, but even so … the children are so little and mobs can be so cruel. They seem to feed off each other, the hatred was almost palpable. Madinia can't sleep most nights, she wakes up screaming.'

Marlowe had thought that that was normal with small children but smiled wisely and said nothing. 'She seems a sweet little soul,' he remarked, for something to say.

'No, no,' Jane laughed. 'The one you met just now is Frances. I like to call her Fran, but her father doesn't like it, so no slip ups if you please.' She patted her belly. 'This one, please God, will be with us by Epiphany and we will call her Margaret, I think.'

Marlowe wasn't all that au fait with childbirth, nor arithmetic for that matter, but even so, he had to ask. 'How … um … how do you know … um?'

Jane turned on the stair, making Marlowe reach out instinctively to catch her but her balance was perfect. 'Kit, you are in the house of Dr John Dee, the Queen's magus. Everything is known here, both what has been and what is to come.'

The voice of an angry toddler wafted down the stairwell and Jane Dee looked up, a mother tiger at bay.

'I'm sorry, Kit, to be so skittish. But since … well, I must go these days when my children call.'

'I understand,' Marlowe said, pressing himself against the slightly clammy stone wall of the stair so she could squeeze past. 'Off you go. I know the way.'

Jane Dee sprang up the stairs as if she hadn't a care in the world. She had every care, but she chose to wear them lightly and Marlowe bowed his head for a moment, in awe of her and just a little bit in love. As he stood there, the door at the bottom of the stair opened and John Dee stuck his head out. He looked at Marlowe and a slow smiled filled the sweep of his beard.

'Kit, there you are,' he said, as if it were the most natural thing in the world that a friend believed dead should be on his threshold. 'I was wondering when you'd come. Look at this, I know you will be fascinated …' and without further ado, he turned and disappeared into the permanent murk of his laboratory.

Marlowe watched his old friend go, then shook his head with a chuckle, and jumped down three stairs at once to follow him. It was true what he had thought when he had left his boatman. Mortlake doesn't change.

CHAPTER 9

T he *Terra Nova* rocked at anchor in the harbour at Lynn. Beyond it, the land that was the county of Norfolk lay flat and soulless, a grim fog blurring the levels for all that, elsewhere, it was June. The gulls wheeled and dipped, scouring the wharves below them for any scrap of food. It was richer pickings there than the foam and fury of the high seas.

In the darkness below decks, two men sat facing each other, their features lit by a solitary candle. The timbers creaked and groaned all around them and the hold reeked of tar.

'A passing good Rhenish,' the younger man said, sampling the contents of his goblet.

'There'll be more when I return,' the other said.

'Where is it you're going, again?'

'Vlissingen – not that it's any of your business.'

'Where?'

The older man chuckled. 'You probably know it as Flushing. Pretty place when it's not being bombarded by the Spanish.'

'Do a good Rhenish there, do they?'

The older man's smile had vanished. 'You're altogether too inquisitive, sirrah,' he said. 'My business in Vlissingen s my business. It has nothing to do with you.'

'Indeed not, Master Poley, indeed not. And it's not

why I'm here. Marlowe.'

The name fell like a dead weight and the whole ship seemed to shake.

'Marlowe,' Poley repeated.

The other man looked at him. He had been right to choose him for Deptford; he was sure of that. But something had gone wrong. And he didn't know what.

'There's many a slip,' the projector murmured, topping up his own wine, but not his guest's. 'In my line of business, things happen. A careless word here, a glance there. I would say the ways of the Lord are strange if I believed in such things.'

'We had an agreement,' the younger man said. 'You and I.'

There was a scraping sound, of steel slicing through the air and Poley's dagger was in his hand before the tip of the blade bit into the planks of the table between them both. It quivered there, its brass-studded hilt dancing in the candle flame. Poley leaned back, further from it than his companion.

'Reach for it,' he said.

'What?'

'The dagger. Make a grab for it.'

'No, I ... why?'

Poley shrugged. 'To prove that you can,' he said. 'To prove you can beat me. No doubt you're disappointed that the Muse's darling still lives. No doubt you hold me responsible. Let's not waste our time with those oafs Skeres and Frizer – they were only there for ballast anyway. Well, go on, man. I'm ... what? ... Three feet further away from it than you are. I don't stand a chance.'

The younger man used his years to grab the hilt, but even as he did so, a second dagger hissed in the darkness, slashing his cuff and hand and he recoiled, dripping with blood and cursing under his breath.

'As I said,' Poley's smile was like a grinning skull, 'in my line of business, things happen. If you want Marlowe dead, do it yourself. And no, before you ask,' both daggers had already disappeared, 'I don't give refunds.'

'I *have* tried,' the other man said, nursing his wound.

'And I've either been *very* unlucky or Kit Marlowe really does have the Devil at his back.'

Poley chuckled. 'That he does,' he said. 'I'll tell you what I'll do, seeing as how you've had such bad luck; when I come back from the Low Countries, I'll finish the job. No extra charge.'

'You will?'

'I will.'

Marlowe and Dee went back a long way. Marlowe would say seven years. Dee would say millennia. He tended to take the long view of these things. Although the mob had made a good job of wrecking the house, Dee's sanctum had remained more or less unscathed, the few louts who managed to get that far having run out in terror for no reason they could bring themselves to share. Marlowe looked around and was pleased to see the cockatrice and the basilisk still held their posts guarding their master, with only minor damage to scale and feather. The scrying dish still held centre stage, the black pool within it currently a-tremble. Marlowe pointed to it.

'You were expecting me, I see, Doctor Dee.' He smiled. The old man looked ill and tired and it was sad to see.

'Always, Kit, always. I was perhaps the one man in London who didn't mourn your death, not because I don't love you but because I knew you weren't dead. I searched the ranks in Heaven and Hell and you weren't to be found.'

'You forgot to check Purgatory?' Marlowe laughed.

'That's a point,' Dee said with a smile. 'I didn't think of that. But anyway, the outcome is the same, you haven't left this mortal coil. Unless ...' he looked hopeful, 'you did and then came back. Wouldn't that be something!'

'I have been in purgatory many times in my life,' Marlowe said, 'but I have always had my feet on the ground. However, when my time comes, you will certainly be the first person I shall tell.'

'Thank you,' Dee said. He knew it was a serious promise, firmly given. He looked forward to it. 'But let's hope that won't be for a while,' he added, politely. 'What happened, anyway? Why did the rumour spread? Where did it come from? Is there some …' he looked carefully left, right and behind him, giving special attention to the cockatrice, which bridled theatrically. 'Is there some *projectioning* afoot?'

'Always,' Marlowe said. 'As you and your mirror probably know, I was planning to leave England for a while. I was even considering going to … Scotland.'

Dee was horrified and clutched at his beard.

'But before I could, I was … well, set upon, I suppose. I didn't see it coming, although I knew the men I was drinking with were rogues to a man. But, and not for the first time, Nicholas Faunt had a hand in the game and so … here I am.'

'And here you are with a problem,' Dee pointed out. 'Presumably, now you are clearly alive, the men who sought to kill you will try again.'

'As always, Doctor Dee, you have hit the nail on the head. There has already been a death, of a man who tried to make himself as much like me as he could. Vanity is not a cardinal sin, I know, but pride is, and he strutted around the place like a peacock and paid the price. Then, one of the conspirators at my death was found dead, killed in the same way as the other poor, deluded fool. So, yes, you might say that they are still on my trail. Not many know I am not dead, but of course, it only takes one, if their lip is loose.'

'Let me see,' Dee said, 'if I can guess who you have told. Come to the mirror.'

They leaned over it and the surface trembled so that their reflections broke up into shivering slivers. Dee passed his hand over it and the surface stilled, but their reflections had gone. Instead, a scene emerged from the inky black to show Tom Sledd, arms all over the place like a windmill, directing his crew building a set.

Dee chuckled. 'I didn't need the mirror to know you had told Tom!'

'No, indeed,' Marlowe said. 'It was a risk, though. Tom has never heard a secret he isn't keen to share. And he doesn't hold his drink too well, either. Still, I think it should be all right.'

'Right,' Dee said, dubiously. 'Who's next?' The mirror

showed a dark room, where a man slumped over a desk, his ink stained fingers clawing at his scanty hair.

'Shaxsper,' Marlowe nodded. 'Yes, I told him and to be fair to the man, I don't think he would talk. He and I may have need of each other before this year is out and Will always did have an eye to the main chance.' He peered at the image. 'Can you ...' he twiddled his fingers ... 'make it clearer? Closer, somehow?'

Dee pinched his fingers together and then flung them wide. The image grew and the manuscript on the table sprang into sharp focus.

Marlowe looked closely, 'What's that ...? "Thou toad, thou toad, where is thy brother Clarence? And little Ned Plantagenet his son?" What kind of gibberish ...?' He sighed. 'He doesn't get any better, does he? And what's he done to his finger? Look, there's a bandage.'

'Perhaps he's moonlighting, helping Sledd. Are you ready for the next?'

'Yes. Go on.'

The mirror this time only needed a glance. It was Philip Henslowe, counting money. And then it drew back and the whole cast of the Rose were there, clamouring for their pay.

'Did you tell all of them?' Dee was surprised.

'No,' Marlowe said, shaking his head. 'But I suppose this was bound to happen. Next.'

This time the mirror showed a peaceful scene, of Michael Johns sitting in his sunlit garden. A sparrow pecked at crumbs he had scattered at his feet and the two could almost feel the warmth and serenity.

'Of course,' Dee said. 'Dominus Johns. Is that where you are staying now?'

'I am. It just feels ... safe. I don't see my family these days and the Rose is so ... unpeaceful. At Michael's house I can sit or sleep or read and he lets me do it. The food is simple and if I eat it or not it doesn't matter. He doesn't bother me.'

'It sounds ideal,' Dee said, somewhat wistfully. He loved his wife and his late blessings of children, but sometimes he wished for quiet. 'Are you going back there tonight?'

'Tomorrow, if you can find a bed for me here.'

Dee chuckled. 'We only have one bed chamber these days, but if you don't mind, I can make you a couch down here. It will be comfortable for your body but … most people are a little put off by the cockatrice. He can be a little … judgemental.'

Marlowe glanced up at the stuffed creature on his perch. The creature glanced back.

'We are old friends,' Marlowe said. 'A couch here will be perfect. Are there more people to show?'

They turned to the mirror which showed in quick succession Faunt, Cecil, Frizer and Poley, Poley looking a little tempest tossed. Then, a dark room with a silhouette against a dim window. Marlowe caught his breath.

'Who *is* that?' he asked.

Dee stared into the mirror. 'I don't know,' he whispered. 'The dark has nothing to do with lack of light. This image is dark with hatred. Sin will coalesce sometimes to make my mirror dark, it swirls and swirls and masks the picture. I have had images sullied by them all in my time, gluttony, sloth, pride, wrath, envy, lust and greed. I don't know which ones are at work here, but they are dark, very dark …' He looked up, his face full of concern. 'Find this man, Kit. Find him, and kill him. Before he kills you.'

The mirror gave a final shiver and became blank, before their reflections formed again.

'So … was this man someone else, someone we hadn't yet seen? Because if so, I can cross so many off my list.'

Dee turned away from the mirror and walked towards the door. 'It would be a marvel if it were true,' he said, 'that men only come once to my mirror. But it isn't an exact science, I'm afraid. It reads men's minds and sometimes, dark and light is in the same skull and the mirror will show someone twice, or even more. Why, I remember one time …' and so, reminiscing and walking together, the two made their way up the clammy stone stairs, to light, food, Jane and her children. For a while, at least, Marlowe could almost forget he was a dead man walking.

Will Shaxsper stood in the centre of the wooden O of the theatre. All right, it wasn't the Rose. It wasn't the Curtain. It wasn't even the Theatre, but it was *a* theatre and it didn't look as though the Puritans had had the chance to close this one down yet.

'Well, Master Shaxsper, what do you think?' Henry Bark wasn't exactly Philip Henslowe either although he had read about the great ma in the *King's Lynn Remembrancer* and knew what miracles were performed nightly in the name of the Muse south of the Thames.

Shaxsper was feeling guilty already. He was seriously in hock to Henslowe to the tune of a number of advances. And now that Marlowe was back, he couldn't see his own theatrical efforts getting off the ground any time soon. Even so, a man had to make a living. He had a wife to support and, at the last count, two children. The pie-powder court of Stratford-on-Avon would be on his heels if he stayed away from them much longer. He glanced at the man next to him, beginning to doubt the wisdom of his bringing him along at all.

'Adam?'

The Lord Admiral's man pursed his lips and tapped the oak beams. 'It needs work, Master Bark,' he said.

'Yes, yes, of course,' Bark grovelled. 'But I have the best carpenters on either side of the Wash, Master Proud, the best painters in Lincolnshire, the finest fitters of the Fens. We'll make this the perfect setting for the Lord Chamberlain's Men ...'

'We'll have to think about it,' Proud said. 'We're staying in the town for a day or two. Master Shaxsper and I are collaborating on a play and it has a naval setting, so Lynn would be a good choice.'

'Naval setting?' Bark repeated. 'More suited to the Lord Admiral's Men, I would have thought.'

'Yes,' Proud snapped. 'But Shaxsper and I will do the thinking, thank you. We'll be in touch.'

The London men took their leave and went in search of the nearest tavern. 'The Lord Chamberlain's Men, Adam?'

'Hmm?'

'Bark. He mentioned the Lord Chamberlain's Men. Had he misheard you?'

'The man's a dolt, Will – and his theatre is shite, too. Tom Sledd would have kittens looking at that timber.' He caught the look on the Warwickshire man's face and laughed.

'Let me buy you a flagon or two,' he said. 'I haven't been entirely honest with you.'

Will Shaxsper was a country bumpkin at heart, Warwickshire born and bred. This jolting, rutted journey to Lynn was as far north-east as he had ever been and the bravest thing he'd ever done was to take the low road to London. Several people had not been entirely honest with Will Shaxsper and he was blissfully unaware of most of that.

When the ale arrived in the leather flagons, Proud confessed. 'Today,' he said, 'the Lord Admiral's Men. Tomorrow, the Lord Chamberlain's. The next day … who knows?'

'I see.' Shaxsper raised his cup to Proud's. He knew that men like Alleyn and Burbage couldn't be trusted – they were actors, after all; they lied for a living. Neither could Henslowe, worshipping Mammon as he did. But playwrights? Well, playwrights were honest men, salts of the earth, God's creatures. Look at Will Shaxsper. All right, he'd all but abandoned his family and wasn't too fussed about whose lines he pinched. Nor ideas. Not plots. Then there was Marlowe, the Muse's darling, all fire and air. Yes, he was quick with a dagger. All right, he probably spied for Walsingham and Burghley. And he didn't believe in God. And there were even more rumours about ,,, but that wasn't true; just malicious gossip. No, playwrights were honest men through and through, on the side of the angels in the theatrical world. And now, here was one of them, Adam Proud, another university wit like Marlowe, a man of letters and quite possibly a genius, planning to jump ship, as it were, to abandon not only the Lord Admiral, but Philip Henslowe too.

'Will, Will,' Proud leaned forward, as if reading the man's mind. 'We none of us have long in this vale of tears. A man has to make his mark where he can. And where. Of course, London is the theatrical capital of the world and of course, Kit Marlowe is the world's greatest playwright. But all that could change. That's why, when I heard of Master Bark and his theatre, it piqued my interest. I thought you'd want to be in on what could be a whole new world in the drama.'

There was an infection in Proud's face, a fervour in his voice. Shaxsper was with him all the way.

'Kit Marlowe is a genius,' Proud said. 'Philip Henslowe is too. Howard of Effingham's a great man. But we're young men in a hurry, Will, you and I, playwrights both. We can't sit back and wait for dead men's shoes. And if it's not Master Bark's theatre and it's not the Lord Chamberlain's Men, so be it. There'll be other opportunities. What do you say?' and he patted the man's hand.

Shaxsper hissed and withdrew it.

'Something wrong?' Proud asked.

'I must have caught a splinter or something on Bark's woodwork,' Shaxsper said. 'Hurts like Hell.'

Marlowe and Michael Johns left Lincoln's Inn a little before noon. The dominus had finished for the day and both men intended to spend the afternoon with John's books, always a pleasure in the summer sun streaming through the latticed windows.

They had just reached the door in the alleyway to the side of John's house when Marlowe caught his old mentor's arm.

'Did you leave that door open?' he asked.

Johns chuckled. 'This is London, Kit,' he said. 'Nobody leaves their doors open here.'

'Then, wait.'

Johns watched in horror as Marlowe pushed in front of him, a dagger blade gleaming in the alley's half light. The playwright pointed the tip at the lock. It had been worked, scratches along one side of the plate, the job of an expert. He held a finger to his lips and eased the door open. The passageway ahead was deserted and Marlowe's footfalls on the flagstones were muffled by the rows of books that flanked one wall. Beyond them, a door led to Johns' study. It was shut.

With Johns close behind him, Marlowe eased this second door open and a smile crossed his face. 'No tricks, now, Nicholas, please,' he said.

Michael Johns peered round the corner to see Nicholas Faunt sitting in his favourite chair, sliding a dagger into the sheath behind his back.

'Apologies for your lock, Dominus Johns,' he said. 'I'll get a locksmith to see to it at once.'

'No, Master Faunt, you won't. But you would oblige me by explaining why you're here.'

'Looking for Marlowe,' Faunt said. 'I'd like a word.'

'How did you know I'd be here?' Marlowe asked.

Faunt tapped the side of his nose. 'We have our little ways,' he smiled. 'And anyway, you weren't here, were you? Hence the need for a little lock-picking. Tell me, Master Johns, is your garden secure?'

'Secure?' Johns frowned. 'Master Faunt, I teach law at Lincoln's Inn. That's hardly a walk on the wild side. What need have I for security?'

'We live in a dangerous world, Doctor,' Faunt said. 'For instance, I happen to know that there are those at Thavies who are eaten up with jealousy at the larger pensions and amenities given to Lincoln's. Who knows when that kind of thing won't boil over into violence?'

'What do you want, Nicholas?' Marlowe asked.

'If we could go into the garden?' Faunt suggested.

'Anything you have to say to me …' Marlowe began but Johns held up his hand.

'That's probably not strictly true, Kit,' he said. 'I'm sure there are many things that Master Faunt could say which are far too sensitive for my ears. Go into the garden, gentlemen. There is no one to your left, a retired apothecary to your right who is as deaf as a badger and the Foundling Hospital beyond that. In this instance, I don't believe that walls have ears.'

'Very well,' Marlowe said, 'and I'm sorry about this, Michael.'

Johns waved his hand, brushing the matter aside. He knew that Kit Marlowe's world was not his and hadn't been since they both left Cambridge.

The garden was as quiet as the house. From somewhere over the wall came a low chanting hum of the Foundling boys at their Latin. 'Amo, amas, amat …' The sound of it took Marlowe back to Canterbury in the dear, dead days, when all was splashing through the puddles of the Dark Entry on his way to the King's School and the roar and rattle of the Star as he carried the foaming pots. Above all was the hiss of the dominus' knotted rope as it bit into his flesh. Kit Marlowe loved Latin but it left a bitter taste in his mouth each time he spoke it.

'Did you really have to kill Nicholas Skeres?' he heard Faunt's voice cut into the echoes of the past.

'What?'

'I thought we had an agreement,' Faunt said. 'At Deptford. There were to be no reprisals. Let sleeping dogs lie.'

'That was my understanding too,' Marlowe said.

'But Skeres …'

'Fell foul of somebody other than me.' The playwright sat down on John's bench, his back to the elm that shaded the garden. 'You might have known that from the manner of his passing.'

Faunt sat opposite him and shrugged. 'It didn't sound like you,' he said, 'and, frankly, I don't care whether Skeres lives or dies. But I gave my word to those reprobates and that makes it my business.'

'Nicholas,' Marlowe said, 'you know as well as I do that men like Skeres – and Frizer, come to that – have enemies that stretch from here to the Black Deeps. The pair of them have fleeced more passers-by than you and I have had hot dinners. Any one of the coneys could have got nasty, sought revenge. I don't envy you trying to get to the bottom of that lot.'

'I'm not trying to do anything of the sort,' Faunt said. 'I just wanted to hear you say you weren't involved.'

'I wasn't,' Marlowe assured him, 'but while I've got

you here – Robert Poley.'

'Ah.'

'I talked to Skeres. And I talked to Frizer. They both pointed their fingers at Poley.'

'Of course they did. You and Poley have a history, don't you?'

'Before Deptford, I promised to kill him if I met him again, it's true.'

'But you don't think he's behind Deptford?'

'No, no, I don't. But I do think he knows who was. And I hoped you might know where I can find him.'

'Am I my fellow projectioner's keeper?' Faunt smiled.

'You know Cecil's plans, or at least the ones he chooses to share.'

Faunt looked at the man whose life he had saved. Did he expect him to go out on a limb yet further? Ah, well, in for a groat, in for an angel. 'Vlissingen,' he said. 'The last I heard, Poley was going to Vlissingen.'

'Not the old coining ploy?'

'The ways of Sir Robert Cecil are strange,' Faunt said. 'It's not for us to query them, Marlowe.'

'No, no,' the playwright said. 'Perish the thought.'

'Will you go after him?'

'I could go to Cecil direct,' Marlowe said. 'If, as I suspect, he and his duplicitous dad are behind this.'

'Kit,' Faunt was serious. 'We don't know that. And I cannot sit back and let you kill the Queen's Privy Councillors. You won't succeed and if you did, it would cause chaos. You'd dare God out of his Heaven.'

Marlowe smiled. 'That I would,' he said.

'You know, this is rather good.' Ned Alleyn was leafing through the *Blasphemer's Tragedy*. 'It could turn out to be Marlowe's best yet. Particularly when I give the Blasphemer my own special polish.'

'You think Henslowe will cast you?' Adam Proud asked. 'I'm the new boy around here; I don't know how these things work.'

Alleyn's chill glance would have crushed a weaker man

but Proud brazened it out. 'Does Master Sackerson shit in his pit?' the actor asked. 'I was born to it, Proud, born to it.'

'I'm sure you were,' Proud said. 'But Henslowe could be a problem.'

'Henslowe? Why?'

'From what I know of him, he's his own man and keen on that. I just can't see him throwing in his lot with the Lord Admiral's Men. Aren't we cutting the ground from under his feet?'

'Not if he continues to buy the nonsense that we feed him, that he has full impresarial control and so on.'

'But you've already taken the decisions over casting away from him.'

'I've always done that. Marlowe writes the stuff and I improve it. Henslowe's just a bean counter.'

'But Marlowe's dead,' Proud pointed out.

Alleyn looked at him. He had to admit, he didn't altogether trust university wits, they were all too full of themselves. And this one was, after all, an outsider. 'What if I told you that wasn't altogether accurate,' he said.

'What?'

Alleyn closed to his man. They were sitting in the tiring room of the Rose. Tom Sledd's team were putting the finishing touches to the Tamburlaine set on the stage behind them and one or two of the hautboys were going through their paces in the pit. Unless the walls were listening, the two of them were alone.

'There *was* a bit of bother at Deptford,' Alleyn confided. 'God knows what about; some playwright thing, I expect. Touchy lot, playwrights – oh, present company excepted, of course.

Proud brushed the slur aside.

'It must have been pretty serious, though, because Henslowe swore us all to secrecy. Since you've come on board, so to speak, I don't see why you shouldn't be in the know. And Marlowe's changed his appearance.'

'Has he? To be honest, I don't think I would know him if I met him, changed appearance or not. I hear he was a bit of a natty dresser, that's about it.'

'Well, he looks like a damned Puritan these days,' Alleyn told him. 'Goes by the name of Brackenbury. How long he'll keep it up, God only knows.'

'Yes,' Proud nodded. 'No doubt he does,'

'Oh, I say, though, Proud. You won't talk about this, will you?'

'I wouldn't dream of it. Anyway, to be honest, Alleyn, what with one thing and another, I don't have much time to talk to anyone not from here. Is it like that for you?'

Alleyn looked down his nose at Proud. He tried not to spend too much time with anyone from the Rose, except for rehearsals, which he didn't bother with as often as he should, he knew. He had an altogether more high flown circle of, if not friends, exactly, then at least acquaintances. He became introspective. Was it his imagination, or were the women older these days, less pulchritudinous. Was he more desperate? Could it be, Heaven forbid, that he was getting *older*? He gave himself a shake and allowed himself a smirk.

'No, Proud, no. It isn't like that for me. Not at all.'

CHAPTER 10

The flag was hoisted a little before noon, shifting in the breeze that drifted from the river. It was true – the theatres really were open again and *Tamburlaine the Great*, both parts, was available to celebrate the fact. The groundlings of Southwark and beyond gabbled together on their way to the Rose, the whole stinking mass of humanity that was London, delighted that the world, once upside down, was righted again.

One or two, certainly, still wore the beak masks of the plague doctors, but even they were rubbing shoulders and other things against their fellow play-goers and Philip Henslowe could hear the sound of money rattling all the way to St Paul's. The dolly-mops were out in force, the wayward sisterhood of the Winchester geese. They declined to wear the yellow garb of their calling, making it easier for them to mingle with the crowd and more difficult for the Watch to pick them out. A pat on an arm here, the subtle lifting of a shift there; coins were pressed into palms and the beasts with two backs slunk off into a dark corner. Mustn't frighten the horses.

Ingram Frizer wasn't sure he should have come. If Marlowe wasn't out to get him, *somebody* was. And that somebody could have been alongside him now as he trudged along Gaunt Street; to his left, to his right, perhaps even behind. Frizer half-turned. A cripple hobbled there, a soldier-pensioner by his tattered coat. But was he? Was that crutch a snaphaunce with powder in the pan, a wheel-lock to blast said Frizer to eternity? With his practised eye, he saw a fellow coney-catcher lift a purse with a dexterous flick; there was one groundling who would not be able to buy a ticket at Henslowe's turnstile.

The ale was flowing freely and the smell of the roasting chestnuts in their braziers added to the atmosphere. So, they were a little mouldy this time of year, having been stored in a sack since November, but who would notice? The green all burned off before anyone got to eat them. It was like a holiday, the start of a brave new world. If only, the more wistful among them thought occasionally, the great Kit Marlowe could have been there to see it.

The great Kit Marlowe doubted whether he should have been there too. He was, in his own way, as marked a man as Ingram Frizer. But *Tamburlaine* was his and he wanted to see what tricks Ned Alleyn had added to ruin his masterpiece. The greatest living actor was strutting his stuff on the stage already, in his copper breastplate and crimson Venetians. He let the ladies of the middling sort hold his hand briefly and hob-nobbed with the wealthy who took their places on stage, left and right, as the sun set and Tom Sledd's people lit the flares. The groundlings had to make do with a wave, but that was good enough for most of them.

'Look,' one of them nudged her friend. 'Did you see that? He waved at me.'

'Bollocks!' was the friend's rejoinder. 'He was waving at me!' Then she yelled, 'Love you, Ned!'

Richard Burbage winced. He was trying on his crown as Mycetes, King of Persia, reminding the assembling crowd that he was an Important Member of the Cast. He was prepared to sit this one out, to accept second billing to Alleyn, because Henslowe had promised him the role of Barrabas in *The Jew of Malta* later in the run. Marlowe's mighty lines were already rumbling in his head as he looked down on the eager faces beaming up at him. 'Fie, what a trouble 'tis to count this trash!' And, talking of trash, what *did* Alleyn look like in that codpiece? As for Alleyn himself, he had already ignored

Marlowe's reminder that Tamburlaine was lame – every account said so; but Ned Alleyn would have none of it. The world's greatest actor limped for no man.

'Good crowd, Kit.' Will Shaxsper stood alongside the man in the seats among the gods, not far from where Philip Henslowe was laying out his counting house.

'Gratifying,' Marlowe said, 'considering they've all seen this before.' He turned to the Warwickshire man. 'And talking of new stuff, which we weren't, how's your *Richard III* coming along?'

Shaxsper's face said it all. 'It's the princes bit, Kit,' he said. 'That other tosh by whatshisarse had them killed on stage, if you remember, but the audience didn't like it. No doubt many a groundling would cheerfully murder their own brats, but you don't like to see it done for entertainment, do you?'

'Reportage, then,' Marlowe suggested.

'You what?'

'The murderer – what's his name? Tyrrell? Have him telling the audience about the bloody deed. Two little boys. Prayer books on pillows, that sort of thing. Wring their withers, Will. There won't be a dry eye in the house.'

'You … er … you couldn't have a look at it, could you? You know, just a few pointers?'

Marlowe laughed. 'Of course,' he said. 'Oh, Mother of God!'

Shaxsper followed Marlowe's pointing finger. 'Jesus!' was the Warwickshire man's response. They were both looking at Zenocrate, daughter of the Sultan, who was actually Bennie Blomfield with shoulders like a dray horse. 'Where did Sledd find him?'

Tom Sledd was watching the same scene. To be fair, he hadn't wanted Blomfield for the part at all, but Henslowe had insisted. The Blomfields owned a fair slice of the South Bank and their little boy had ambitions in the world of theatre. Too young for the big parts and too wealthy for the spear-bearers, a female lead would be ideal until his balls dropped.

''Ello, darlin',' various groundlings greeted Ben. 'Get

yer tits out.'

Ben took it all on the chin, which was more or less where his false breasts were and he paraded in as stately a manner as he thought befitting for the daughter of a Sultan. In fact, he hadn't really been sure what a Sultan was until he had read Master Marlowe's script. And even now, he had his doubts. Slightly behind him, as was fitting, Zenocrate's maid, Anippe, alias Tommy Slattery, skipped as daintily as he assumed maids of the Persian persuasion did, back in the olden times. Clustering in the wings behind Sledd's flats, the Virgins of Damascus were climbing into their corsets. They were actually the boys of the choir of St Mary Overie, glad to have a change of role from endless Byrd and Tallis; Master Marlowe didn't write musicals.

The orchestra were warming up as nicely as the chestnuts, but with less mouldy bits, except for the crumhorn who hadn't done enough practice. Even Master Sackerson, dozing the evening away in his pit, caught the odd shawm and hautboy and smiled to himself. All was right again in his world too.

Then, a trumpet shattered the moment and the great bear roused himself. He raised his nose to the wind. He could smell horses long before he heard their hoofs, clattering over the cobbles and thudding in the mud. The cavalcade trotted through the groundlings, who scattered, grumbling and muttering on their way to the turnstile.

'Make way!' somebody shouted. 'Make way for the Lord Admiral!'

Philip Henslowe heard that too and it broke his concentration. Not much could make the impresario lose count of his money, but the *second* arrival of Howard of Effingham in as many weeks surely did.

'What's going on?' he barked to an underling.

'It's the Lord Admiral,' the clerk said, clearly in awe.

'I know it's the bloody Lord Admiral!' Henslowe told him. He was already on the stairs that led to the gods. 'Marlowe. Shaxsper. Did either of you know about this?'

Marlowe shrugged. Shaxsper was about to deliver something of a prologue, but Henslowe cut him dead. 'I know he's muscling in on the Rose,' he snarled, 'but he doesn't have to live here.' And he thundered down the stairs, batting his audience aside. Furious as he was, he suddenly remembered Marlowe's very existence was not known to those who he now rather unceremoniously knocked out of his way and he hoped nobody had heard him use the name. He glanced back. Nobody was looking at Marlowe, nor the gleaming forehead of the Midlands idiot next to him, so he assumed all was well. On the other hand, it occurred to Henslowe, what was a Puritan doing at the theatre at all? Well, it was all too late now and he had other fish to fry.

The fanfare continued and those with seats in the theatre rose and stood to attention. The groundlings, already standing, craned their necks and jostled each other to see the hero of the Armada, in his scarlet velvet and gold robes, striding onto the wooden O. Spontaneous applause broke out, with whistles and cheers. Only one man spat volubly on the ground; his brother had died a broken wreck in one of Her Majesty's warships, abandoned by the very man who bestrode the narrow world like a colossus now.

By this time, Alleyn was in the wings, ready for his entrance. 'Has somebody come on?' he murmured to Burbage at his elbow.

Somebody had indeed. Tom Sledd's men were busy turfing the stage-sitters out of their places. The great and good of London they may have been, but nobody was as great and good as the Lord Admiral and he seemed to have brought his whole household with him.

Alleyn tutted. He basked in the adulation of the Privy Council, but protocol dictated that he had to bow to Effingham the first time he came on. That not only passed the limelight off the world's greatest actor, it destroyed the whole authenticity of the piece. He knew Marlowe would be fuming. He, Alleyn, was Tamburlaine the Great, for God's sake, conqueror of Persia and the scourge of God. He could have had the Lord Admiral for breakfast.

The noise subsided. Those who had been evicted from the stage were given a seat somewhere – *anything* so that Henslowe would not have to give anybody their money back.

The orchestra struck up and to rousing cheers, the Prologue bowed first to Effingham, then to the house in general.

'From jogging veins of rhyming mother-wits,' he began, 'And such conceits as clownynge keeps in pay, We'll lead you to the stately tent of war, Where you shall hear the Scythian Tamburlaine ...' There was the usual mixture of cheers and boos depending on whose side the groundlings were, 'threatening the world with high astounding terms And scourging kingdoms with his conquering sword. View but his picture in this tragic glass ...' And Kit Marlowe thought of John Dee and his dark mirror again. 'And then applaud his fortunes as you please.'

The audience did indeed applaud, whistling and stamping their feet. Tom Sledd, watching in the wings, pushed forward his youngest protégé, the one carrying the placard that said 'Actus I, Scaena I' and he duly circled the O for the crowd's benefit. Next time, Sledd vowed to give the job to somebody who could actually read – he had better things to be doing than stand here making sure the right card went out at the right time.

To those who were gripped by Marlowe's mighty line or Ned Alleyn's performance, the First Part of Tamburlaine shot by. And it seemed no time at all until Sledd's boy was scurrying on with his placard reading 'Finis Actus Quinti et Ultimi huius Primae Partis'. Alleyn had just promised to marry Ben Blomfield, the prospect of which didn't do much for either of them. And everybody in the audience got down to the serious business of wenching and fornication, drinking and squabbling, pillaging and looting – everything the Puritans hated and which, according to Henslowe, never happened, in theatres with the gravitas of the Rose.

'What do you think, Kit?' Shaxsper felt bound to ask.

'Not bad,' the author nodded. 'Ask me again after Part 2.'

From his place near the orchestra pit, Ingram Frizer was within purse-lifting distance of the Lord Admiral, but it was more than his life was worth to try anything there. Stationed behind his eminence was a coterie of some of the nastiest-looking bastards he'd ever seen, with helmets, breasts and backs and bristling with weapons. It was getting so an honest cut-purse couldn't make a living these days. He couldn't help noticing, however, that Lizzie Wallace, queen of the geese, was sitting at the Admiral's right hand, careful that that right hand wasn't up to *too* much wandering in full view of what seemed to be half of London. Frizer heard Effingham purr into her ear, 'Do you think there'll come a time, my dear, when women will play women on the stage?'

Lizzie looked horrified. 'What an idea, my Lord,' she trilled. 'Personally, I'd rather sell oranges.'

'Quite.'

And before anyone knew it, Sledd's lad was back on with his 'Actus I, Scaena I.' But this time, it was upside down.

By the end of Act 5, Scene 3, you could have heard a bodkin drop in the Rose. Tamburlaine was dying. And nobody died like Ned Alleyn.

He raised himself up on one arm from his couch, 'Farewell, my boys! my dearest friends, farewell! My body feels, my soul doth weep to see Your sweet desires deprived my company. For Tamburlaine, the scourge of God, must die.'

Before he had flopped backwards, there was an almighty crash in the gods and the whole theatre shook. There were screams and cries of shock and all eyes were turned to the rafters. Ingram Frizer couldn't help himself; he shifted the knife from the small of his back and helped himself to a weighty purse hanging from the belt of a member of the Cordwainer's Guild. There was a God, after all.

People were scurrying up steps to the highest seats in the galleries. The ring of steel around Howard of Effingham tightened as his guards went through their paces, halberds flashing outwards like some murderous hedgehog. Lizzie Wallace found herself on stage after all, booted out of her seat by an over-zealous bodyguard.

Philip Henslowe bustled onto the stage. 'It's all right, everyone!' he roared, although his voice was lost in the uproar. 'It's just a loose casement, that's all. A collapsed shutter. Nothing to worry about. On with the play!'

The play had only five lines left and the actor who should have spoken them, Harry Wallop, playing Amyras, had vanished into the crowd at the earliest opportunity, convinced that the whole roof was coming down. As the man responsible for that roof, Tom Sledd was bounding up into the galleries, fighting his way through the rattled, frightened crowd.

'It was a gun,' he heard someone say.

'The Armada,' somebody else added. 'The Admiral's here and the Dagos know that. We all knew they'd be back.'

'No, it's the Irish,' another worldly-wise commentator threw in.

'Don't talk bollocks,' somebody told him. 'The Irish haven't got a navy.'

'It's not from the river,' one of Henslowe's own clerks assured everybody. 'It's an attack from the south.'

'Quiet, all of you!' Sledd yelled and waited for a modicum of quiet. It was hot up here in the gods, but a section of the wall had collapsed and a large block swung in the air at the end of a chain. The last time Sledd had seen that, it was hanging over the stage to hoist timbers into position. Somebody had moved it. And somebody had made it swing.

'No, you can't have your money back.' The barked decision marked the arrival of Philip Henslowe. 'All you people, get out of here. There's nothing to see.'

But there was. Through the hole in the paster and timbers, the moon shone bright on the waters of the Thames and the silent black spire of St Mary Overie. But it wasn't sleeping London that everybody was looking at; it was the bodies lying in the rubble, their heads a mass of fresh blood, their faces unrecognizable. Tom Sledd was about to tend to them when an ashen-faced Adam Proud was at his elbow. 'My God,' his voice was barely audible, 'It's Kit. Kit Marlowe. And William Shaxsper. I saw him. I saw the man who did it.'

There was a ringing in Kit Marlowe's ears that wasn't coming from St Mary Overie. Everyone inside the Rose heard a sergeant bellowing at the retreating, bewildered crowd, 'The Lord Admiral has left the building,' but Kit Marlowe didn't hear that. Neither did Will Shaxsper, clinging to a broken beam alongside him. Both men had been thrown sideways by the impact of the iron block, still swinging on its creaking chain above their heads. They were covered in plaster, wattle and daub and Shaxsper's head was bleeding.

They poked their heads back inside the gallery and Sledd and Henslowe helped them in.

'Kit …' It was Adam Proud who found the words first.

Even after the shock of what had just happened, Marlowe recognized the face in the half-light. 'Adam Proud,' he shook the man's hand. 'I heard you were around.'

'What in God's name happened?' Henslowe wanted to know. The gawping sightseers had gone now and the five of them were alone at the scene. Far below on the stage, actors still in costume stood around, looking up at what was left of their roof. The orchestra, realizing that their precious instruments were secure, waited for the word from Henslowe as to what was to happen next.

'Master Proud knows,' Sledd said.

'There was a man,' the Corpus Christi alumnus said. 'I was supposed to be with the Lord Admiral's entourage, but I was late and decided to squeeze in up here. I'd missed half of the first part – sorry, Kit – and I went down in the interval for an ale.'

'Then what?'

'The man I saw was standing back there, under your window, Master Henslowe. Kit, Will – you must have seen him.'

The playwrights looked at each other. 'No,' Marlowe said. 'Nobody.'

Shaxsper was dabbing the blood off his forehead. 'Light's not good up here,' he said.

'At one point,' Proud went on, 'and I couldn't tell you exactly when, this man left his perch and pushed the gantry, the block towards the wall. It knocked you two over and took the timbers and plaster with it. I tried to grab him, but he slashed at me with his dagger and jumped out through the hole.'

Proud held up his arm, his doublet sleeve ripped with a clean cut.

'That means he was out on the ledge with us,' Shaxsper realized.

Marlowe craned his neck to look out. 'Above us,' he said, 'there's a beam. From there, with a bit of effort, he could have hopped across the thatch. But it's a long way down.'

'Not if he'd got the ropes ready,' Sledd said. They looked at him.

'Look, the gantry is out of position. I've been using it on stage for set building, but it shouldn't be up here. Somebody deliberately moved it.'

'Somebody who knows the theatre,' Marlowe said. 'This man, Proud, what did he look like?'

'Um … half a head taller than me. Dark hair. Beard. Carried two knives.'

'Poley,' Marlowe muttered.

'Who?' Henslowe asked.

'No one,' Marlowe said. 'No one at all.'

'I can only apologize,' Marlowe said.

'What for?' Philip Henslowe was still counting his ill-gotten gains from the opening night and was basking in the warm glow of money.

'A hole in the upper wall of the Rose and two of your audience dead.'

'Oh, that. I thought you were talking about the rather dead bit in Part I, Act 3, Scene 2.'

Marlowe smiled to himself, but not outwardly. Henslowe's gallows humour covered the fact that the impresario had a heart after all. He had already arranged to pay for the funerals of the men who got in the way of the block and tackle. 'Don't fret yourself, Kit,' he said. 'Bits have fallen off the Rose before. And in London, men die every day – it's the way of the world.'

'No,' Marlowe said. 'This is out of the ordinary. And it has to do with me.'

Henslowe looked at his favourite playwright, his cash cow. 'Poley?' he said.

Marlowe looked at his favourite impresario. 'What?'

'You said "Poley" last night, as if that explained everything.'

'Master Poley and I go back a long way,' Marlowe said. 'My Nemesis.'

'What are you going to do about it?'

'Find Poley.'

'You know where he lives?'

'The Marshalsea, the Clink, the Compter – you name it, Philip; there isn't a London prison that hasn't been honoured with Robyn Poley's presence.'

'Good Lord – but surely he's not always Inside?'

'No, not half enough of his time is spent there – he's too fly for that. He's out – for instance he was watching a play by Christopher Marlowe last night – I just need to pinpoint where he is now.'

Leadenhall Market was bustling as ever that Saturday, blissfully unaware chickens squawking on their way to the slaughter, fidgeting in their cages alongside the pale, dead sides of pigs, stiff in their cold lard, hanging head down with their blood dripping into the gutters. The cries of London were louder than ever – 'Fresh pork. West Country cheese brought in this very morning. Get it while it's cold. Watercress. Lovely watercress.' The flies of summer were swarming thick and fast, drawn to the butcher's axe and flashing knife.

Kit Marlowe had no interest in any of this. He turned down the offers of several flower girls that had nothing to do with flowers and passed on the haunch of venison that was available, complete with flies, at a knockdown price. He'd forgotten how difficult it was to find his quarry in the labyrinthine tangle of alleys off Gracechurch Street. Every step he took carried him further into darkness, which was oddly fitting considering the character of the man he had come to see.

A huge oaf answered the studded oak door, with the

build of a butcher in the nearby lanes. 'Yes?'

'Machiavel,' Marlowe said. 'To see Master Phelippes.'

The door was slammed in Marlowe's face and he waited. When it was opened again, the same oaf stood there. This time, he was more loquacious. 'They say that Machiavel is dead,' he said.

Marlowe smiled. 'No, no,' he said. 'My soul is but flown beyond the Alps.'

The door closed again. Then it re-opened. This time, a wizened little man filled the space, his pock-marked face the colour of old vellum, his long hair thin and yellow. Only his eyes danced, a piercing blue in the skull-like face.

'Kit Marlowe,' he said. 'I'd heard you were dead.'

'It's a commonly-held belief, Thomas,' he said. 'Sorry about the *Jew of Malta* quotation – or adaptation, to be accurate.'

'Ah, old habits,' Phelippes said. 'If you'd been Francis Bacon, I'd have used some tosh of his as a password – oh, no offence, of course.'

The men shook hands and Phelippes led Marlowe along a winding passageway and down stone steps. In the half darkness here, the playwright could make out columns that supported the roof, cold stone encased in even colder marble. Phelippes lit candles and offered Marlowe a seat.

'Impressive,' the playwright said. The walls were covered in scraps of vellum and parchment, all of them with cyphers and scribbles at every angle.

'You are sitting in the heart of Roman London,' Phelippes told him. 'This was the Mithraeum, the soldiers' shrine. Appropriate, I've always thought, that they still slaughter cattle on the streets above, where the great bull died.'

'Fascinating,' Marlowe said, 'but I didn't come to talk about ancient animal sacrifice.'

'I guessed not,' Phelippes said, pouring a cup of wine for them both. 'Bit early in the day for you?' he checked.

'Never,' Marlowe smiled. 'You'd heard I'd died. I'd heard you had given all this up.' He waved a hand to the hieroglyphs.

'Oh, I've had my share of the spying game,' Phelippes told him. 'Babington; Throckmorton; how many plots can one man foil in his lifetime? But,' he sighed, 'once a cryptographer, always a cryptographer.'

'You still work for Robert Cecil?'

Phelippes shrugged. 'The Little One sends me work every now and again. I like to keep my hand in.' The cryptographer leaned forward. 'Kit, you and I have hunted down more Papists than Father Robert Parsons preached about. What do you want?'

'Poley.'

'Ah.'

'Last I heard he was in Vlissingen. You wouldn't know anything about that, I suppose?'

Phelippes shook his head. 'I keep away from foreign affairs,' he said. 'Unless it has an impact on the safety of the realm.'

Marlowe laughed. 'That sounds like something out of Francis Walsingham's playbook,' he said.

Phelippes laughed too. 'I miss the old boy, you know, Kit.'

'As do I,' Marlowe said.

'No, espionage isn't what it was. Not like the old days.' Marlowe looked at Phelippes. The man couldn't yet be forty, but he looked a hundred. And the old days was only three years ago, when the Queen's Spymaster died. 'Why do you want Poley?'

Marlowe and Phelippes went back for ever. He saw no reason for subterfuge. 'I want to kill him,' he said, 'before he kills me.'

Phelippes tutted and shook his head. 'I do hate to see boys squabbling among themselves.'

'Come on, Thomas,' Marlowe said. 'It's how it is and always has been. People in our business don't have friends – at least, not for long.'

'Present company excepted, I hope,' Phelippes said.

'Always.'

'If you really want to find Poley, you could always talk to the Little One.'

Marlowe smiled. 'Let's say that Robert Cecil and I are a little … off hooks at the moment?'

Phelippes pursed his lips and placed his hands together. 'Do I take it you don't believe that Poley is in Vlissingen?'

'He may have been,' Marlowe said, 'but I think he's back now. Here in London.'

'Then try Spitalfields, in the shadow of St Mary Matfelon. The place is a rookery, full of rogue Irish and similar lowlife. I understand he has a safe house there.'

Marlowe nodded. 'I'm not sure it'll be safe much longer,' he said.

Marlowe knew this part of London well. For years before Deptford, he had lived in Hog Lane, Shoreditch and beyond the city wall stood the open tenterground in what had been the churchyard of St Mary's Hospital. St Mary Matfelon was no longer the white chapel shining in the sun, but a rather dilapidated building, with weeds sprouting from its ogee arches and gargoyle corners. On his way there on foot, like the penitent Puritan he was supposed to be, he had left Aldgate and walked past the fine houses of the aldermen of the City, shuttered windows to shield their occupants from the July heat. As he moved further east, over the burial grounds of the Romans, the property became less salubrious. By the time he reached the church, a shanty town lay strewn on both sides of the road, rough planks and piled stones covered with sacking and held together with rope.

Ragged children ran to him, filthy from head to foot, their hands outstretched for alms. They were all gabbling in a language he didn't understand and crowding around him as their mothers and fathers looked on suspiciously. It was an alien world beyond the wall, neither London nor Essex, but something more like Limbo.

'Irish,' an English voice grunted. 'They're talking Irish.'

Marlowe looked at the man. He was an Artilleryman of the Royal Train by the badge on his scarlet tunic and he was dragging a leather case of cannonballs to the Artillery

Ground.

'What do they want?' Marlowe asked, although he knew the answer already.

''Your money, Master,' the Artilleryman said. 'They all believe every Englishman is rich as Croesus which is why they're all over here in the first place.' He aimed a boot at the nearest urchin. 'Bugger off,' he snarled. He stood still, looking at the rookery slum across the field. 'What a shambles,' he said. 'They're supposed to be weavers, though I've never seen 'em with a shuttle in their hands. Are you going in there, Master?'

'I'd planned to, yes.'

'Well, good luck with that,' the Artilleryman grunted. 'If it's kirtle you're after, you'd be better off in Southwark any day of the week. They say the Irish only do it standing up.' He paused. 'And backwards.'

Marlowe had seen the large, half-timbered building in the centre of the rookery from half a mile away. A sign swinging from chains over its front door read The Wrestlers and it was an inn like any other. In Marlowe's experience, innkeepers the length and breadth of the country knew everything and everybody. If anybody had news of Robert Poley, it would be here.

'A flagon of your finest, landlord,' he said, holding up silver, 'and a little information.'

'Now, Master,' the man said, in the cocksure vowels of the Essex marshes. 'Ale we have. Information, well ...' At the same time he was eyeing Marlowe's coins and had the look of a man who had his price, rather like everyone else in Gloriana's England.

'Robert Poley,' Marlowe said quietly.

At the middle of the afternoon, The Wrestlers was not doing much trade. Scruffy men lounged around a couple of tables, their dogs on the flagstones at their feet, dozing in the sun streaming in through the grimy windows. Pot boys, which Marlowe had been once, waited for orders from the innkeeper.

That innkeeper shrugged now, polishing his leather

cups once he had given Marlowe his quart.

'Let me put it another way,' Marlowe said, taking a sip, 'you are serving the Irish here.'

The innkeeper bridled. 'Some of my best customers' he said, 'though I grant you, I wouldn't want my daughter to marry one.'

'You're missing the point, landlord,' Marlowe said. 'The Irish are Catholics to a man. And while a man's faith does not in theory lead to his death, in practice it often does. Not to mention the Recusancy Laws. How many of your customers, I wonder, have paid their fees recently? Let's see …' He turned to the men at the table. 'Gentlemen …'

'All right.' The innkeeper knew when to cut his losses and wave a white flag. 'No need for any trouble.' He jerked his head upwards and to the left. 'Third door on the landing,' he said. He leaned in to Marlowe, 'And you didn't hear it from me.'

'Hear what, Landlord?' and Marlowe took another swig and made for the stairs.

The third door was just like all the others and Marlowe pressed his ear to it. He heard a tittering female laugh. Poley was not alone. He stepped back against the rail and launched himself with his right boot crashing into the woodwork. The door swung back and there was a scream. Two people were scrabbling off the tester, one naked, one still in his Venetians, cod-piece apart.

'Who the Hell are you?' the man wanted to know, grabbing a sword and ripping it free of the scabbard.

'I was about to ask you the same question,' Marlowe said. He looked at the girl, still a child, with a mass of red hair, clutching the bed clothes to her modesty. 'See yourself out,' Marlowe said and waited until she'd gone, scuttling off along the landing to the applause of the drinkers on the ground floor.

Marlowe slammed the door behind him. 'Robert Poley,' he said.

'What of him?'

'Where is he?'

'Who wants to know?'

'I do.' Marlowe was a little surprised to be asked the question.

'And, as you may remember I asked you not a moment ago, who the Hell are you?'

'Kit Marlowe,' Marlowe told him, 'University wit, playwright. Some call me Machiavel, some the Muse's Darling.'

'And a dead man,' the man growled, standing up and pointing his blade at Marlowe's throat.

'That too,' Marlowe nodded and the man lunged at him. Marlowe dodged aside and trapped the man's arm under his own, wrenching it back painfully so that the sword fell from his grasp.

'Tut! Tut!' Marlowe said. 'That's a Spanish school thrust. They did lose in the Channel, you know.' He jabbed his elbow back into his opponent's nose and the man crumpled, his eyes streaming and his lips covered in blood. Before he had a chance to recover himself, there was the point of a dagger pricking the skin of his throat. 'Now,' Marlowe murmured, 'I believe we were talking about Robert Poley.'

'He's in Vlissingen,' the man mumbled through swollen lips. 'On business.'

'What are you to him?'

'His ... amanuensis.'

Marlowe raised an eyebrow. 'Do you mean dogsbody?'

'Er ... well ...'

'All right, Master ...?'

'Appleyard.'

'Master Appleyard. Don't embarrass yourself with semantics.'

From the look on his face, that was the last thing Master Appleyard would do.

'When do you expect him back?'

'You know Robyn ...' Appleyard tried to grin but the pain beat him back.

'Seriously, though,' Marlowe pressed a little harder and Appleyard's head came up with an agonized gurgle. More blood was trickling onto his chest.

'Week Thursday, on board the *Terra Nova*. Tides, wind and God permitting, he'll be in Deptford by cockshut.'

'Deptford, eh?' Marlowe smiled. 'What comes around, goes around.'

'How's the head, Will?' Adam Proud was staring at the purplish swollen cut below Shaxsper's hairline.

'Aches like the devil, Adam,' the Warwickshire man said. 'Thanks for asking.'

'I'm still shaking like a leaf. Good thing Kit wasn't hurt, eh?'

'Absolutely. Look, Adam, I don't want to be an old stick in the mud, but …' He spread his arm over the array of papers on his table.

'A new play?' Proud enthused.

'Hardly new,' Shaxsper moaned. 'I've been working on it now for a month. *Richard III*.'

'Ah,' Proud looked scholastic. 'He was a bad 'un and no mistake.'

'He certainly was. And he's a gift for a playwright. That is, if a playwright had any gift at all.'

'Now, Will,' Proud frowned. 'Don't let the bastards grind you down. I know what you're going through.'

'Really?' Shaxsper didn't look convinced.

'Yes, really. I started writing at Cambridge, you know. Oh, clandestinely, of course. You'd have to walk many a weary mile to find anywhere more Puritan than Cambridge. They don't approve of the theatre.'

'Yes,' Shaxsper sighed. 'I'd noticed.'

'Well, if I can ever help,' Proud said. Shaxsper was slightly older than Proud, but he didn't know one end of a university wit from another and Proud knew that. In his experience, country bumpkins needed all the help they could get.

They heard the bells of Andrew Underscroft tolling and Proud was on his feet. 'I've got a meeting with the Lord Admiral.' He tapped the side of his nose. 'Plans are afoot.'

'Keep me apprised,' Shaxsper said and busied himself with the task that all playwrights have when the Muse has deserted them; he sharpened his quill.

On the stairs outside Shaxsper's rooms, Adam Proud came face to face with the greatest playwright in the world. 'Kit!' he beamed. 'How are you? I've just been checking on Will. I fear his head wound has slowed his creative genius.'

Marlowe laughed out loud.

'Kit.' Proud held the man's arm. 'Can I talk to you, man to man, as it were?'

'Difficult to do it any other way, Adam,' he said, 'but is an open stairway the place? Is Nones the time?'

Proud hadn't realised that Marlowe was such a Papist, but he let it go. 'I can't say this in front of Will, but … well, something odd's going on, don't you think?'

'In what way?' Marlowe asked.

'These deaths, around the Rose, I mean. That man Willoughy. The walking gentleman – Skeres, was it?'

Marlowe nodded.

'And now, nearly, you and Will. I was just wondering what sort of madhouse I'd stumbled into.'

Marlowe laughed again and slapped the man on the shoulder. 'It's the theatre, Adam, the wooden O, the roar of the crowd. If that world was sane, you wouldn't be in it and neither would I. Where else could you dabble with the devil like Faustus, conquer half the world like Tamburlaine, die for love like Dido or take on the Christians like the Jew of Malta? What are you working on at the moment?'

It was Proud's turn to laugh. 'Sorry, Kit. The Lord Admiral is a stickler for protocol. I can't divulge.'

'The Lord Admiral,' Marlowe mused, 'is a man to be wary of, Adam. As one Corpus man to another, don't get into bed with him.'

'There *is* a rumour,' Proud was whispering now, 'that the target in these deaths is … well, not to put too fine a point on it, Kit … you.'

'Really?'

'Look, it's not for me to say, but you and I; well, as you say, we're Corpus men both. We have a bond, Kit, an affinity. The Muse has touched us both.'

'What *are* you saying?' Marlowe asked.

'Shaxsper.'

'What?'

Proud twisted on the stair so that his back was well and truly turned to Shaxsper's closed door. 'He's a budding playwright, isn't he? He's just been telling me, he's trying to write *Richard III* and he's stuck. I mean, how can you *not* write *Richard III* – the man's a gift. Almost writes himself. That gives him a motive.'

'A motive for what?' Marlowe was lost.

'Murder. I *have* heard that Willoughby bore more than a passing resemblance to you. It was night if I remember and dark. Overcome with jealousy at your success and his own failure, Shaxsper lashed out and wallop! Into the bear-pit you went – or rather, Willoughby did by mistake.'

'And Skeres?'

'Hmm.' Proud gnawed his lip. 'You've got me there for the moment. Obviously, Shaxsper knew him, but I don't know more – yet.'

'Leave it to the Under-Sheriff,' Marlowe advised.

'Man's an idiot,' Proud grunted.

'If Shaxsper wanted me dead,' Marlowe went on, 'how did he arrange the little accident at the Rose the other night? You saw the man who did it.'

'I did,' Proud nodded, glancing behind him to make sure the door was closed. 'But how difficult would it be to pay someone to do the deed? It would take the limelight off Shaxsper, wouldn't it, if it was assumed that Shaxsper himself had been injured in a murder attempt? You're on your way in there now. Have a close look at the gash on his forehead. More than a touch of cochineal, if you ask me.'

'Kit!' The door swung open and Will Shaxsper stood just inside it. 'Oh, Adam. Still here?'

'I shouldn't be,' Proud said. 'I'll be late.'

'Any luck with the murder of the princes?' Shaxsper asked Marlowe.

Proud raised an eyebrow as he brushed past his elder and better. 'Told you,' he murmured.

CHAPTER 11

Robert Cecil swept through the chapel in Hatfield House. He hadn't come to pray – he hadn't done that for years. He ran his finger along the nearest pew … just checking for dust. It irritated the Queen's imp when his father retreated to Hatfield, which he was prone to do more frequently these days. All this, the great house, the priceless library, the deer-park and the water meadows, would be his one day. But his heart lay in Whitehall, with its bustle and its intrigue. And if there, it wasn't quite clear who to trust, that was how he liked it. He was, after all, cleverer than any of them.

And there was his dear old dad, riding that smelly, braying donkey again and with his nose stuck in a book. The summer sun was warm at Hatfield and the geese by the lake's edge gabbled at him as he walked, splay-footed as always, towards him.

'Father,' he called and waited until he was close enough to the man before the conversation continued. 'We haven't really resolved the Marlowe business.'

'Haven't we?' Burghley looked up from his book. The donkey was cropping the Hatfield grass, unmoved, as ever, by the genius of Aristotle.

'Rumours are still spreading,' Cecil said, 'that the man is bent on vengeance. With what he knows …'

'Dear boy,' Burghley spread his arms, 'the man doesn't *know* anything.' He, too, checked that the coast was clear.

There was no one in the meadows except the Cecils and they talked to no one but each other. 'All right, he shot his mouth off about us being atheists, along with Hunsdon and the Lord Admiral, but no one but deranged idiots took him seriously.'

Cecil blinked. 'But we discussed his elimination,' he said.

'We discuss many things, Robert,' the old man said. 'Spain. Ireland. The position of the Papists. Some of it comes to fruition, some of it doesn't. I don't have to remind you, dear boy, that the Privy Council is composed of some of the most hated men in England. We'd be naïve not to acknowledge that.'

'I know, father, but …'

'From what I understand,' the old man eased himself out of the saddle and the donkey brayed in gratitude. 'There *was* an attempt on Marlowe's life at Deptford.'

'From what *I* understand,' Cecil said, 'There have been several. In Whitehall, they're calling him the Man They Couldn't Kill.'

'Well, if that's true, it's nothing to do with us.'

Paranoia was Robert Cecil's middle name. He looked at his father. 'But Marlowe doesn't know that. I found a dead rat in my slipper the other day.'

Burghley looked at his boy. 'And you think that Marlowe sent it?' he asked. 'That doesn't sound like him. I would have thought a cutting epigram …'

'No. Well, yes. Oh, I don't know. I only know it's the sort of sign that malevolent people use to warn their enemies. If Marlowe believes we wanted him dead …'

'But, according to Effingham, he's already spoken to him. And that old bastard is still walking about, larger than life.'

'Funny you should mention that,' Cecil momentarily toyed with petting the donkey, then caught the frosty look in the beast's eye and thought better of it. 'The last near miss on Marlowe was last night at the Rose, during a performance of *Tamburlaine.*'

'Never seen it,' Burghley said. Nobody dismissed genius like the Queen's Treasurer.

'The point is that Effingham was in the theatre at the time. What if – and I don't say this lightly – what if the *actual* target was not Marlowe at all, but Effingham? And what if Hundson's next? And then us?'

Bot for the first time, the most revered of Elizabeth's statesmen, his misshapen little boy, was the right man for this job. But he had placed all his political eggs in one basket and he had no choice now but to take them to the farmhouse. 'If Marlowe comes for us,' he clicked a deadly blade from his left cuff, 'We'll be ready for him. Now,' he slipped the blade away again, 'Ethel and I have business with a bunch of carrots.'

The donkey brayed with delight. And, as Burghley led her away, he called back, 'It's as if she understands every word I say.'

'There's no doubt about it, Kit,' Tom Sledd was saying. 'Somebody's trying to take us down.'

The stage manager's men were busy in the gods, hammering and sawing, repairing the damage done by the heavy hook dangling from its chain. It had been moved now, down to the stage where it belonged and where, hopefully, it would do less damage.

'*Us*, Tom?' Marlowe raised an eyebrow. Suddenly, everybody was a victim.

'Well,' Sledd folded his arms, watching the work with a practised eye, 'stands to reason. That Willoughby bloke, hanging round the theatre, hob-nobbing with us all. Dear old Nick Skeres, theatre in his blood (although I hesitate to mention the "b" word) and now you and Will – nearly. I tell you, I'm watching my back in the smock alleys, I can tell you.'

'You think someone has it in for the Rose?' Marlowe asked. His own thoughts were much closer to home.

Sledd pulled the playwright gently away from the noise. He padded up to Philip Henslowe's eyrie and looked from left to right. Then he flicked out a bradawl and picked his master's lock in the blink of an eye.

'Er …' Marlowe frowned.

'Nah,' Sledd ushered the man in. 'What his

impresarioship don't know won't hurt him. It's just that it's quieter in here. Rhenish?'

'Tom,' Marlowe growled and the stage manager put the bottle down.

'Oh, all right. Let's talk facts. The Rose, along with all the other theatres, is closed by that arsehole Tilney.'

Marlowe nodded.

'Then, just as it's re-opened, along comes the Lord Admiral's Men looking for venues.'

Marlowe nodded again.

'Now, without going through Henslowe's books, I can't be sure, but I'd be pretty certain that the retrospective of the great Kit Marlowe is bringing in a pretty penny for them both.'

'So we can rule Henslowe and Effingham out, then.'

'We can. But what about the others?'

'Who had you in mind?'

'The other troupes. The Lord Chamberlain's lot. Lord Strange's. And don't get me started on the Blue Coat Boys.'

'They're children, Tom,' Marlowe reminded him.

Sledd tapped the side of his nose. 'I've got a mate, well, more an acquaintance, really. He's a schoolmaster. Works at Archbishop Whitgift's.'

'And?'

'He told me things that'd make your hair curl, Kit – well, recurl, I suppose. There's nothing more vicious, he told me, than a spotty kid whose voice is breaking. They're rebellious, their balls are dropping and they think they're immortal.'

Marlowe nodded. He had been in that position once, back in Canterbury. It all seemed rather a long time ago now. 'So?' he said.

'So, the Blue Coat School have a theatre. And an acting troupe to go with it. What if the ambitious little bastards are trying to muscle in on the Rose? Eliminate the opposition, so to speak.'

Marlowe couldn't see it. 'Why not hit Alleyn, then, Burbage?'

'Give 'em time,' Sledd said. 'Softly, softly. That's the

approach they're taking.'

'They're still children, Tom,' Marlowe reasoned. 'Whoever killed Willoughby and Skeres and swung that thing at Will and me must be built like an ox, not a schoolboy creeping unwillingly to school.'

Sledd blinked. He hadn't thought of that. 'It could still be the others, though – the Lord Chamberlain, Strange. And of course,' he leaned forward, looking Marlowe squarely in the face, 'we haven't considered the most likely yet, have we?'

'We haven't?'

'Tilney.' Sledd leaned back against Henslowe's table, his arms folded, like the cat with the cream.

'Tilney?' Marlowe echoed. He was certainly having more than his share of mad theories thrown his way today.

'Think of it, Kit,' Sledd warmed to his theme. 'Have you ever seen a man more Puritan in your life?'

'Well …'

'He'd squash a Papist like a bug. And he *hates* theatres. Oh, you and I know it's all good fun; not to mention a centre of creativity and the glory of the age, but all men like Tilney can see is filth and fornication. It was all right while the Pestilence was raging, the curmudgeonly old bastard could close 'em down and blame the Devil and all his works. But now, well, we're back and he can't abide that. Today the Rose, tomorrow the Curtain …'

'It'll take him a long time,' Marlowe chuckled.

'Don't take this lightly, Kit,' Sledd warned. 'The man's a monster.'

'No, he isn't, Tom,' the playwright said. 'He's just an over-promoted idiot. And you're missing the point. All those murders and attempts are not attacks on the theatres, they're attacks on me.' Marlowe shrugged. 'Just me.'

When Kit Marlowe was new to the projectioning game – and it *was* a game, he had never taken his eyes off that – he loved the cloak, he adored the dagger. He would slide along alleyways in the dark, a hood pulled well down so there was no reflected light gleaming off his eyes. He would wear soft shoes, velvet so his clothes gave off not so much as a rustle and all in all, he was the very parfit spy. Nowadays, he had had enough of that. He had the dagger still and knew that it would serve him well against all comers. The afternoon was too warm for a cloak so that was that. He rapped sharply on Phelippes' door. The door opened as always and the enormous oaf – a different one from last time and, if anything, just a threat bigger than the other – raised an eyebrow. Marlowe sighed.

'Marlowe. Christopher Marlowe. Master Phelippes, if you please.'

A voice rumbled up from the oaf's subterranean depths. 'I will …'

'Oh, for the love of God,' Marlowe muttered and pushed past. 'I was here just the other day, do you people keep no records …?'

A little man came through from the room at the back, alerted by the noise. He was used to a certain order of things once the door had been opened by the oaf of the day and things didn't seem to be going to plan. 'Oh, Kit … I didn't hear the password …'

'Password be buggered,' Marlowe said. 'I know you love all that nonsense, Thomas, and perhaps at another time, I will be happy enough to play the game. But last night, someone tried to kill me and Will Shaxsper by swinging a lead weight the size of a horse and cart at us when we were minding our own business watching *Tamburlaine*. Two other men have died that I know of – and that doesn't count the two poor unfortunates who fell from the gods at the Rose last night as Will and I clung to the wreckage. So you'll have to excuse me if I don't want to bandy words with …' he looked the oaf up and down as he stood there, staring blankly '… with …'

Phelippes smiled. 'Gervaise.'

Marlowe's eyebrows rose. 'Gervaise? Really? Well, bandying words with Gervaise here. I need you to do something for me, something I suspect only you can do.'

'I did wonder why I was seeing you twice in one week,' the Queen's cryptographer said, peering at his friend over his spectacles. ' You're spoiling me, Kit.'

Marlowe laughed. 'I promise I'll come back soon without a favour to ask, but for now, I assume you have some paper, a quill and ink?'

Phelippes nodded. 'Always.'

'Good. If we can get to work then …' He looked at Gervaise, who went off to sit in a corner. The enormous man picked up a book from his stool and then made himself comfortable, turning it to the light and adjusting a pair of tiny wire spectacles onto his nose. In his enormous hand, the book looked like a child's reckoner.

Phelippes followed his gaze and chuckled. 'Gervaise is full of surprises,' he said. 'Now, how can I help you?'

The road to Ware, like the road to Hell, was paved with good intentions. Lord Burghley had received the letter that morning, in the unmistakeable hand of his second son, the Queen's Imp, the Little One, the man who would effectively rule England one day. Burghley was used to plotting with the boy, giving his words of advice the gravitas that only an old man could acquire. But this was odd. The pair could have met in the silent, creepy cloisters of the palace of Whitehall or on the sunlit terraces of Hatfield, with or without the donkey. But the letter insisted on Tibbalds, the great house that Burghley had built on the Ware Road, with its fountains and its heraldry and its ceiling sprinkled with the signs of the zodiac. And what was even odder, was that Tibbalds was closed now for the summer, while the latest plaster dried on the new wing. There were groundskeepers, to keep back the jungle, but no one in the house itself.

The place stood square and in darkness now that sunset's gold had turned to night's purple. 'Come alone,' the younger Cecil's letter had said in the cryptograph squiggles that both men knew well. But this was Gloriana's England and God knew what footpads and cut-throats lurked in the Hertfordshire countryside. Burghley was not a young man and he hadn't used the sword at his hip in anger for years. True, he had replaced the plodding donkey with a fine, high-spirited stallion, an animal that Burghley hoped could outrun anything.

But, just in case, several hundred yards back, four men armed to the teeth and wearing the Cecil livery trotted in the shadows, trying to be as inconspicuous as possible. Burghley reined in on the slope of the lawn. Ahead, he could see the knot garden, trimmed and angled under the fitful moon. He could see a light, too, in the Orangery; and as he watched, the candle fluttered and swept to the left, up the stairs that led to the Great Hall. Burghley couldn't make out who was carrying it, but surely, it had to be Robert.

He let his horsemen catch him up and fan out around him 'Position yourselves,' he said. 'One in the Orangery, the rest in the Great Hall annexe – and take care you're not seen.'

He eased his aching body out of the saddle. A two hour ride, even on a balmy evening, was not Burghley's idea of a good time. The Orangery door was open and he crossed it to the stairs, waiting as his men scattered silently in the two passageways alongside it. The heraldry of the great and good flashed in gold and silver leaf from the candle on the table in front of him. Beyond that, little Cecil sat on a cushioned chair, one with a special box so his feet didn't dangle unseemly.

'What's going on?' the old man barked. His arse had chafed more than he'd realized.

'Father?' Robert Cecil looked as surprised as his old man.

'Why did you send me this?' Burghley pulled the crumpled letters from the purse at his hip and passed it to his boy.

Cecil peered at it, his large, dreamy eyes flashing in the candle light. 'I didn't,' he said. 'But while we're about it,' Cecil produced his own letter, 'why did you send me this?'

Burghley held the parchment close to his face. 'Never seen it before,' he barked.

'Then why …?' but Cecil's question got no further.

'I hate to see families squabbling,' a voice said in the darkness of a corner.

The Cecils looked at the Puritan standing there, arms folded, eyes bright.

'Marlowe!' they said in perfect unison.

'Choral speaking,' Marlowe smiled. 'That's rather good. Get in touch with Master Henslowe at the Rose. When all this politics is over, there may well be careers for you both in the theatre.'

Lord Burghley was not an impetuous man, but this fake letter business had rattled him. He might have expected Young Robert to fall for it, but not him. And, furious with himself, he drew his sword; he had put on the wrong doublet in his haste and the concealed blade was safely hung up in his press. Cecil was still sitting on his chair. Neither man was a match for Marlowe and they knew it.

'*You* forged them?' Burghley all but screamed.

'No,' Marlowe said, 'I have people for that. But the handwriting is rather good, isn't it? Fooled you both, at any rate.'

'What's it all about?' Cecil wanted to know.

'I wanted to talk to you both,' Marlowe said, 'and I thought an empty house, without servants, would be the ideal spot for a serious conversation.'

Burghley chuckled. 'You didn't think I'd come alone, did you?' He pointed the sword tip to the oak floor and clicked his fingers. From out of the wall, his thugs crashed forward, all of them with drawn swords, advancing on Marlowe.

'Of course not,' Marlowe said, 'any more than I have.' He clicked his fingers too and another swarm of men appeared from nowhere. In the half light, the Cecils did not recognize Ned Alleyn or Richard Burbage (which cut them to the quick). Neither did they know Tom Sledd or Adam Proud. And they'd never heard, of course, of the three thick-set walking gentlemen.

'And you will notice, my lord,' Marlowe said, 'that I have twice the number of lads that you have. And all of them …' he pointed to their right hands, 'are carrying guns.'

Marlowe circled his people, watching the Cecils carefully. 'I particularly like this one,' he smiled. 'It's a pistol-mace. South German, I believe. If the mechanism fails, the projections on the barrel can do a great deal of damage.

They're all primed, my lord, and the balls will cross this room in a fraction of a second. Your men's swords are useless.'

'Robert!' Burghley shrieked. 'Where are your men?'

'Um … I didn't bring any,' the spymaster whined. 'Your letter said "Come alone".'

'Yes, but it wasn't my letter, was it, you blithering idiot?'

Ned Alleyn found himself humming a catchy tune and the others were sniggering.

'Gentlemen,' Marlowe said, 'now that we have the practicalities out of the way, perhaps my people and your people, Lord Burghley, can withdraw. I've been here for a while and was surprised to find the kitchen so well stocked for a house that's empty. I'm sure that Lord Burghley wouldn't mind dispensing a little largesse – cakes and ale aplenty.'

The looks on the Cecils' faces said it all. Marlowe had outmanoeuvred them and they knew it. Burghley grunted to his son and they sheathed their weapons, their men, with the company of the Rose, heading to the great kitchens.

Marlowe sat down, the candle still guttering between him and the Cecils. 'Now, gentlemen,' he said, 'to business.' Burghley sat down too, his white and beetling brows arched in a frown. This, he knew was not going to be pretty.

'Is there a God, Lord Burghley?' Marlowe asked.

A strange sound, half snort, half laugh, emerged from the younger Cecil's lips.

'The scriptures …' the Lord Treasurer began. He had cut his teeth on rhetoric like this at Oxford years ago. It was meat and drink to him.

'I know what the scriptures say,' Marlowe said. 'The Old Testament, the New Testament, the Catechism. I have even read the Mohametan Koran. But that's all about faith. I am interested in fact, hard evidence.'

'Can you doubt the word of God?' Cecil frowned. Men like Marlowe were turning the world upside down.

'Certainly I can' the playwright said. 'The Bible is just a book as riddled with errors and assumptions as any other. Take my play *Tamburlaine*, currently playing at the Rose. I wrote it based on the word of writers who never met the

Scythian shepherd; writers who wrote long after he was dead. I hope I have written a play which entertains the crowd. But is it the truth? Emphatically not.'

'You are a member of the School of Night,' Burghley said quietly.

'Damned atheists!' Cecil chimed in.

'Yes, thank you, Robert,' the old man said. 'I think we have established that.'

'They are not atheists,' Marlowe told them. 'They are thinkers, philosophers and their thinking and their philosophy has made them doubt the existence of the Almighty. One of their number is the son of Baron Hunsdon, your confrere in the Privy Council. So I ask you again, Lord Burghley, is there a God?'

'Well, really ...' Cecil tutted.

'No,' Burghley said. His son sat there open mouthed and Marlowe wished that the old man would shout that from the rooftops.

'Good of you to agree,' the playwright said.

'I cannot be certain,' Burghley backtracked, 'but there are more things in Heaven and earth ...'

Marlowe explained, 'It was because Hunsdon's son knew how you all felt – you two, Hunsdon himself, Effingham – that I came to know of it. I may have been ... shall we say, indiscreet ...'

'That Christ and John the Baptist were lovers,' Cecil blurted out.

'No,' Marlowe said. 'I never said that, nor do I believe it. But you were afraid, you leading Privy Councillors, you four horsemen of the Apocalypse, that I would expose you, tell the rest of the Council, the Queen, the Church. So you had me report to you every day back in May, threatening me with Master Topcliffe and his dark arts. You leaned on my friend Tom Kyd. Tortured him. He's a broken man.'

'Sorry about that,' Burghley mumbled.

'Then you came to a decision. You couldn't put me on trial, not even in the Star Chamber, because I would have talked about you and your beliefs. So you decided on Deptford.'

'Deptford?' Cecil and Burghley looked at each other, innocence itself. 'What do you mean?'

'Two walking gentlemen from the Rose, Frizer and Skeres, egged on by Robyn Poley.'

'Poley?' Cecil blinked.

'Come, come, Sir Robert. Poley is a stone cold killer. A former colleague of mine. You hired the three of them to kill me.'

The Cecils frowned, looking at each other again. 'No, Marlowe,' Burghley said slowly. 'I'd swear it on the Bible, except that wouldn't mean much to you and me, would it? If Poley and the others tried to kill you, the order did not come from me.' He looked at his son, an interrogative eyebrow raised. 'You?'

Cecil looked at him for a moment and then shook himself. 'Me?' He was outraged but Marlowe could tell acting, good or bad, when he saw it and this seemed real. 'Me? Of course not. For one thing, if *I* had ordered it, you really would be dead.' He nodded to his father who nodded back. His little son could be a cold bastard when he liked, but no one could accuse him of being inefficient. 'Sorry, Marlowe, you will have to carry on your hunt. Do let us know how you get on.'

Marlowe smiled. 'I will, Sir Robert. I most certainly will.' He raised his fingers to his lips and blew. At his call, his men came running, some still with crumbs around their mouths, more than one still carrying a goblet. In a whirl of capes and Venetians and boots of soft Cordovan leather, they were gone, Ned Alleyn alone pausing in the doorway to deliver a deep bow.

The Cecils sat there for a moment more, eyeing each other in the gathering dark. Finally, Cecil broke the silence.

'They seemed very well dressed, for guards. And a little … theatrical?'

Burghley looked at his son, in whom all his hopes resided, and sighed. He put his head in his hands. ' You think, Robert?' he said quietly to himself. 'You think?'

Marlowe's party of heavies had coalesced into groups as they rode the road back to London, the hard mud road a silver ribbon under the moon. They had a show to put on tomorrow afternoon and couldn't linger, although Ned Alleyn did have fond memories of a very compliant widow in Ware, who had a great bed. But that was a reminiscence to be followed up another day. The walking gentlemen brought up the rear, as was their habit, talking amongst themselves of this and that. Alleyn and Burbage, as always were riding together and yet apart – they liked to keep each other in sight, so they could be sure that, whatever they were doing, they were doing it the very best. Currently, it was riding with one shoulder thrown back and the other hand nonchalantly on the pommel with the reins looped through the fingers as if they and the horse were one. A centaur, a magnificent being whose beauty was only eclipsed by the sun, possibly. The fact that the road was full of holes and pitfalls made their progress somewhat more lurching than the centaur image would imply would not feature in the tales they would tell when they were making merry with a couple of geese after the performance tomorrow.

Adam Proud rode between them, trying to make small talk. This was never easy when around the greatest actors of their age, any inadvertent word out of place could cause either havoc or stony silence and before they reached Hoddesdon he had opted for silence.

At the head of the little band, Marlowe and Tom Sledd rode knee to knee in their usual companionable way. Their horses were as in step as their riders and Marlowe all but closed his eyes and listened to the harness and the saddle creaking, the soft clip clop of the hoofs on the packed road surface, turning to dust now summer was well and truly here. Tom sang quietly to himself, his days playing a girl in Ned Sledd's troupe never quite forgotten.

'Summer is a'coming in,' he sang, 'Loudly sing cuckoo. Grows the seed and blows the mead and springs the wood anew. Sing cuckoo.'

Marlowe came in on the round, his first 'sing cuckoo' chiming in as Sledd sang his second. And so the round spread back to the walking gentleman, one of which, a noted counter tenor, added his own harmonies. For half a mile the verges rang with their song, which only faltered when, as always happened, someone forgot where they were and began to helplessly cuck when they should be cooing.

Marlowe laughed and clapped his friend on the back. 'Tom, you always know how to cheer me up.'

'Can't beat a good round,' Sledd said.

'Talking of rounds,' Alleyn called over the jingle of bits, 'isn't there an inn in this county? I'm dry as a virgin's …'

'The Partridge,' Marlowe called back. 'A mile or two.'

'Thank God,' Burbage grunted. 'My arse has completely gone to sleep.'

'I couldn't help but notice,' Marlowe murmured to Sledd, 'not much singing from our noted actors there.'

'We kept going for almost as long as I've ever known it last before,' Sledd said. 'Martin at the back there has such a lovely voice we could scarcely go wrong. Oh, and you, of course,' he added, hurriedly, though Marlowe never made much of his glorious tenor. 'But if either Alleyn or Burbage had opened their mouths, we would have been all over bar the yelling and putting our hands over our ears within a couple of notes. They both sound like donkeys with their balls caught in the door.'

'Do they?' Marlowe chuckled. 'I don't think I had ever thought about it. Their speaking voices are … well, they are a bit declamatory,' and he flung out one arm and mimed Alleyn at his most florid, but silently; both men had famously short fuses when it came to mimicry, though they indulged in it themselves almost constantly. 'But I think I always just expected them to be able to sing.'

'People who can sing always do,' Sledd said wisely. He dropped his voice so that Marlowe had to lean in to hear. 'Henslowe decided once, do you remember, to do a musical evening one Christmas, for charity.'

Marlowe straightened up. 'Henslowe? Charity?'

'Yes, his favourite one. It's a children's charity.'

'The Henslowe children's charity.'

'Exactly so. Anyway, he had some music specially written and everything and then he had the bright idea of getting Alleyn to sing *The Coventry Carol* to a swaddled Christ Child as he rocked Him to sleep. Stop me if you've heard it.'

'Not sure where I was when this happened. I might have been …'

Sledd patted his arm. 'I know. I know. Anywhere. But anyway, he went to a singing teacher and everything. Refused to rehearse, said his teacher would tell him if it was going well or not. So, comes the night, the flute plays a bar or two intro and … well, you know how it goes …'

Marlowe beat three four in the air and sang low under his breath, 'Lully lullay …'

'Yes, you've got it. So, the moment comes, the Alleyn ladies in the pit are straining forward and he opens his mouth and …' Sledd leaned back and slapped his thigh. 'Donkey with its balls caught in the door!'

Marlowe gave a shout of laughter and the two collapsed over their saddle pommels, one laughing with remembrance, one picturing the scene.

Behind them, Alleyn was watching their dark shapes with narrowed eyes. He poked Proud in the ribs.

'They're laughing at me.'

Proud knew that Alleyn thought the world revolved around him, but he didn't know it was this bad. 'Whyever do you think that?'

'Well, look at them. Laughing like two boys in the school yard.'

'Just two friends together, I would say,' Proud told him. 'They must have so many memories to share. And just think, until a few weeks ago, Tom thought Kit was dead.'

'We all did,' snarled Burbage.

'What I mean is,' Proud turned to him, 'Tom must have been so sad and then so happy. Things like this make a man look back over good times.' Proud sighed to himself. Would he never hear the end of having to make peace between these two? Working for the Lord Admiral's Men was something he had always dreamed of, but babysitting two grown men who should know better was bordering on a nightmare.

'I heard him humming the *Coventry Carol*,' Burbage

said, leaning forward to speak across Proud. 'You weren't at the theatre then,' he told him as an aside.

'I didn't hear it,' Alleyn snapped.

'Well, you wouldn't, would you?' Burbage snapped back. 'You have ears like a flannel when it comes to music.'

'I'll have you know ...' Alleyn swallowed his annoyance. He couldn't claim with any honesty that anyone had ever praised his singing. He allowed himself to slump in the saddle. 'I hate Tom Sledd. I hate Kit Marlowe. I think I'm going to go and be a farmer. Apples, that's what I'll farm.'

'Did I just hear Alleyn say he wants to start an apple farm?' Sledd asked Marlowe.

'I believe so.'

Sledd sighed and looked at the waymarker by the side of the road. 'Oh, God. It's another hour and a half, if not more. I may have had to kill him before we get back to the Rose.'

'Look,' Alleyn whispered to Proud. 'Look at Sledd, all eyes a-swivel behind him. He hates me. I wouldn't be surprised if all these deaths have just been him trying to get rid of me.'

Proud sat low in the saddle and closed his eyes. An apple farm was sounding good around now.

The Partridge looked very unprepossessing in its darkness. The local drunks had long ago staggered home and mine host had locked and barred windows and doors. The clatter of horses in his yard and the shouts and whistles of their riders brought him to life, however, and his entire family were up and dressed in minutes as doors were opened, bedcovers beaten to remove dust and bugs and jugs of ale frothed in the midnight hour.

Both Alleyn and Burbage eyed the host's family, but the wife had a most unnerving turn in her eye and neither daughter was yet remotely of bedding age. Damn.

Bed itself, however, was welcome for them all and after as much bread and cheese as they could handle, they all flopped onto one, except for one of the walking gentlemen who had to make do with a downstairs table.

CHAPTER 12

The next day, after what seemed like days, but had actually been only a few hours, the motley crew clattered into the stable yard behind the Rose and dismounted gratefully. Before they went in, Marlowe took Sledd aside.

'Tom, I couldn't ask you this when the others were about.'

'Wise choice. Alleyn has ears like a bat.'

Marlowe opened his eyes wide. 'But … the story about the carol …'

'Oh, yes, I intended him to hear. He needs bringing down a peg or two when we can. But what did you want to talk to me about?'

'My situation. I established last night that the Cecils had nothing to do with Deptford.'

'All right,' Sledd nodded.

'And that got me thinking. Where was Shaxsper last night?'

'Will? He would have come, you know. Only he really hit his head …'

Sledd paused. 'Come on, Kit, you can't seriously thing … Will loves you.'

'Might he not be jealous, do you think?'

Sledd roared with laughter and eventually had to lean on a wall. 'Kit, of *course* he's jealous of you. We're *all* jealous of you. We all want to kill you sometimes as well, but none of us has tried. I promise. Shaxsper doesn't have a nasty bone in his body. If he had, he would have smacked that whining wife of his upside the head with a shovel long ago. No, really, Kit, it isn't Will. I promise.' He stood upright and wiped his eyes on his sleeve. 'Kit. It isn't Will. Look somewhere else. Look at … I don't know. Look at whatsiface, Frizer. He has done time for killing you, after all. Perhaps for once the coroner got it right, just a bit too soon. Or perhaps, how about this? And you're going to have to excuse me but I say this a lot, mainly to Alleyn and mainly under my breath. Maybe it isn't all about you this time. Perhaps …' he suddenly hugged him, patting him on the back, 'perhaps it's all been a misunderstanding. Mistaken identity. Perhaps someone has just gone, you know,' he tapped his temple, 'mad. It happens. Anyway, you must excuse me. I have a play set to straighten.'

Marlowe leaned against the wall for a while once Sledd had gone. The three Ms. Mistaken identity. Misunderstanding. Mad. He sighed and pushed himself away from the warm bricks. Well, that was enough of that for one day. He felt that a little Alleyn baiting might improve his mood. He pushed open the door at the back of the Rose.

'Lully, lullay, thou little tiny child' he carolled. 'By-by, lully, lullay …'

There was a roar from Alleyn, and the door swung to.

The Golden Boy was surprisingly empty after the afternoon's show. There had been no extra dramatics this time, with cranes swinging through walls and people ad there had been a proper curtain call when any number of dewy-eyed ladies were given proof that their darling Tamburlaine was not dead after all – look, there he was, larger than life and bouncing in front of everybody else. The usual crowd had gone on to the Boy, throwing their slops to Master Sackerson on the way, but most of them had left early and in the snug under the staircase, Will Shaxsper and Ingram Frizer sat drowning each other's sorrows.

'My wife doesn't understand me, Ing,' Shaxsper was saying, looking gloomily into the bottom of his tankard.

'Whose does?' Frizer nodded. 'I gave up on women

years ago. No, it's Nick I miss.' He sighed. 'I just don't seem to be able to get over it.'

'Got a mouth on her like a ratchet,' Shaxsper was saying, 'and unpleasant with it.'

'We went back, you know. Brought each other up you might say. Old Nick could spot a coney a mile off.'

'Shottery, her people come from. Only we called it Shittery.'

Frizer looked at him. 'Passes for humour, does it,' he asked, 'in Warwickshire?' He looked into his tankard, Shaxsper seemed to have something in the bottom of his, so it didn't hurt to check. 'Paul's is the best place to find 'em, wandering the aisles, gawping at all the sights. They virtually had signs around their necks saying "Help yourself to our valuables. The purse is on the right.'

'I never touched those deer, you know,' Shaxsper said, 'in Charlecote. Never poached in my life.'

'And when we both got gigs at the Rose, well, we thought we'd died and gone to Heaven. All them purses and plackets, watches and trinkets *and* pay *and* everyone clapping. They say crime don't pay, but of course it do.'

'No, the Hathaways were something else. People said to me on our wedding day, "Look at her mother, Will. And that'll be you one day, twice over." Course, I didn't listen. Now it's this bloody play.'

'What, *Tamburlaine?*'

'No, my *Richard III.* It's going nowhere.'

'Oh, that. Poor old Nick wrote a play once, you know. It was called *Hey Nonny Know*, about this smartarse who thinks he's cleverer than anybody else.'

'I just can't get the feeling of menace,' Shaxsper droned on.

Frizer paused and dipped his biscuit in his beer. 'He asked Burbage to have a look at it. Course, he laughed at it. I ask you. What a pizzle!

'Marlowe's given me some tips,' Shaxsper moaned. 'How does this sound for openers? "Now is the winter of our discontent made glorious summer by this sun of York." Get it, *sun* of York and he's talking about Edward IV, *son* of the duke of York. Good, eh? You've got to hand it to Kit. The man's a genius.'

The play's first line was "Was there ever a man so gifted as I?"' Frizer caught Shaxsper's face. 'All right, so it's not iambic pentameter or whatever, not Marlowe's mighty line, but it's streets ahead of *Ralph Royster Doyster,* I think you'll agree.'

'Definitely. So, all in all, I can't make a go of *Richard.* I've got to go back to her, Ing. Back to Shittery and all that goes with it.'

'Oh, I expect I'll find somebody else to catch coneys with,' Frizer said. 'It'll be all right.'

And both men bent their heads again and looked for something impossible at the bottom of their tankards.

In the gallery overhead, two other men sat drinking, watching the pair below.

'That's a marriage made in Hell,' Nicholas Faunt said.

'Why do you say that?' Marlowe asked.

'Since your demise, Kit,' Faunt closed to him, 'I've been keeping my ears open in the corridors of power. Times are a-changing and there are more Puritans in London than you and I have had hot dinners. Trust me, there'll come a time when the theatres will be closed for good. The Rose won't exist and neither will you.'

'Well, that's comforting, Nicholas,' Marlowe smiled. 'What's it got to do with those two?'

'Who pays the ferryman?' Faunt asked. 'Who paid Frizer and Skeres?'

'Poley,' Marlowe said.

Faunt nodded. 'And who paid Poley?'

Marlowe chuckled. '*That's* the question,' he said.

Faunt leaned back, still looking at the pair under the stairs. 'Could it be a disgruntled playwright, whose green eyes are watching your every move? Shall we have a word?'

'I'd rather not, Nicholas, if that's all right with you. If I question everyone, I'll suspect everyone and that doesn't help with clarity.'

'As long as you're sure …'

'Very sure. Let me know how you get on. And … Nicholas.'

'Yes?'

'Be gentle with him. He's got writer's block, you know.'

Faunt gave the playwright a look that said it all, but also promised that there would be no rough stuff, or at least, not as yet. 'I'll not bother him now. I never question a man in his cups. Tomorrow will be soon enough.'

'Agreed. But don't forget to …'

'Let you know. Don't worry, you'll be the first to know.'

'Suppose you and I have a little chat, Shaxsper.' Nicholas Faunt was not at his most generous today. Their lordships in the palace of Whitehall were edgy and if the Cecils were edgy, *everybody* was edgy. Faunt had come up the hard way; as the secretary of the Queen's spymaster, Francis Walsingham, he had been, literally, at the cutting edge of every cynical plot to overthrow Her Majesty. He was not a fanatic. He wasn't even a Puritan. What he was was a man with a reputation, and part of that was that he could turn on a groat, without warning.

'Master Faunt,' the playwright was, as ever, surrounded by crumpled up pieces of parchment, his fingers stained with ink, his mind elsewhere. 'I'd offer you some refreshment, but …' He waved a hand to indicate that there was nothing to offer; even the rats had left the building.

Faunt sat himself down. He didn't know how Shaxsper made a living. He'd written some average poetry, ending, predictably, with a rhyming couplet. He had co-written *The Tragedy of King Henry VI*, but, like the man himself, it was a play of many parts. But William Shaxsper was a Warwickshire man and that in itself rang alarum bells in Faunt's head.

Shaxsper didn't know how Faunt made a living either. However he did it, he was no playwright, grovelling at the hem of Philip Henslowe, fawning around Alleyn and Burbage. Rumour had it that Faunt was a projectioner, an agent of the Queen herself, the right hand man of the younger Cecil, who ruled the land along with his dad. One thing was certain; Nicholas Faunt had never set foot inside Shaxsper's rooms in Shoreditch before. Yet, today, here he was.

'To what do I owe the pleasure?' he asked.

'With clichés like that, Shaxsper,' Faunt said, 'I'm not surprised you aren't exactly making your mark with the Muse.'

Damn! Shaxsper thought – another good line that had gone to somebody else.

'Marlowe,' Faunt said.

'Kit? What of him?'

'Somebody's trying to kill him.'

'And me,' Shaxsper whined. 'That swinging counterweight at the Rose – it nearly got me too.' He pointed to the graze on his forehead.

'Hmm,' Faunt nodded. 'Nearly came unstuck there, didn't you?'

'What?'

'It was actually quite ingenious, putting yourself in harm's way like that. I expect you didn't intend the block to come so close, did you? Which is why, if you want to kill somebody, you'd be better off with one of these.' He tapped his right cuff and a stiletto blade slid into the palm of his hand.

Shaxsper winced. He'd felt the tip of one of those before and knew what damage could be done.

'Tell me, Master Shaxsper, why did you leave Stratford?'

'Oh, you know, the lure of London. I always wanted to be a playwright, Master Faunt, and … I don't know if you know Stratford, but it's hardly a metropolis, centre of culture, that sort of thing.'

'No other reason?'

'No, I …' Will Shaxsper wasn't about to tell this sinister visitor that his marriage had fallen apart and he couldn't stand his children.

'Your father,' Faunt badgered him. 'John, isn't it?'

'Yes,' Shaxsper said, not liking the way this

conversation was going.

'Glover by trade?'

'That's right. Look …'

'Would I be correct in assuming that Master Shaxsper the glover is of the Catholic persuasion?'

'Certainly not, Shaxsper said. 'Well, except in the sense that we all were once.'

'We?' Faunt raised an eyebrow. 'All the Shaxspers?'

'No, no. Everybody. Before the break with Rome. In my grandfather's time.'

Faunt chuckled. 'Yes, that, in my experience, is what most Papists claim, the clever ones that is, as they face the Gyves or the Rack. Tell me, Master Shaxsper, which of these instruments of persuasion would you prefer?'

Kit Marlowe had felt so sorry for Will Shaxsper the night before that he'd rattled off the seduction scene in *Richard III*, with the hunchback wooing the widow of the man he'd personally stabbed to death in his bloody mood at Tewkesbury. H was halfway up Shaxsper's stairs with it now, hoping to cheer up the man who had fallen through the wall with him just nights ago.

The last person he had expected to see was Nicholas Faunt; somehow, he didn't equate his questionings with broad daylight. Faunt, in his mind, was a dawn or dusk man.

'He's not your man, Marlowe,' he said, by way of greeting.

'I didn't really ever suspect he was,' Marlowe said. The thought had sleeted through his mind, yes, but he had never really believed in it. 'I didn't really think you would question him, in all seriousness.'

'He has the motive, though, don't you think? I would have expected him to hate your guts. He's living on scraps and handouts. His family, like most of the bloody country, are Papists. And here's you, the Muse's darling *and* with a long-running play series at the Rose coming up, if all that isn't a motive, I don't know what is.'

'But now you've changed your mind?'

'I have.'

'Why?'

Faunt chuckled. 'I have my ways,' he said.

Marlowe barged past him, expecting to find Shaxsper slumped at his table with blood oozing from a throat wound. In fact, the man was sitting upright, his face frozen, staring at the door through which Nicholas Faunt had just passed.

'Er … nice of Master Faunt to visit,' Marlowe said.

'Yes.' The Warwickshire man's voice was barely audible. 'And we shall never speak of it again.

The *Terra Nova* dipped past the Black Deeps, the salt trickling along the timbers and dripping from the gunwales. The Channel had been a bitch for the last week, the winds as contrary as any ever seen in June. It was as though God did not want her to reach landfall.

Landfall was Deptford. The tower of the church of St Nicholas loomed to larboard, the eyes of the skulls on the gateposts watching her Majesty's palace of Placentia and the cormorants plunging in the river's roll. The anchor chain rattled and jarred as the ship swung out of the weather into the lea of the Deptford Yards. There were shouts and the groaning of the capstan as men, hard as the timbers they hauled, dashed along the quayside and took the strain.

Jack Biddle watched them all. Most of them he knew. Half of them he had fleeced on a regular basis for years either directly with a flick of his knife or more convivially over a tankard of ale and a hand of lansquenet. Odd, some men noticed, how often the cards fell for Jack Biddle; just lucky, they would guess.

Jack Biddle didn't know the *Nova*'s passengers, but he'd been a Watcher now, man and boy, since Noah had sailed his Ark this way all those years ago, taking his animals above the Flood. And he knew the type and what to look for. There was the wool merchant, fat, expensively dressed in Flemish silk, specially imported from further East. Around him, his people clustered, clerks with swatches and samples, lawyers with quills, ink and attitude. There was the horse dealer; Biddle could smell the liniment from where he stood, his back to the Mermaid's snug. He had people too, men with bow legs and measuring sticks, bollock-loppers and teeth-taps, all the tools of their trade.

The Papal legate came as something of a surprise, bearing in mind how the Bishop of Rome was regarded in England these days. But there was no mistaking the broad hat with its ample flounced and the scarlet robes trailing down the gangplank. *His* people appeared to have filled the entire ship; gaunt clerics of the Catholic persuasion, looking apprehensively at the grim faces along the wharfs. Heretics like them were routinely burned in England and no one was surprised when a Queen's messenger arrived, accompanied by that vicious bastard Hiddlestone, the under-sheriff. Biddle toyed with telling his visiting eminence that the man had no jurisdiction here at all, but drawing attention to himself was something Jack Biddle just didn't do.

There. There he was. That had to be him. dark eyes darting left and right, an expensive sword at his hip. And instantly, Biddle knew that the dagger at his back would be the partner to a second up his sleeve. He walked slowly, back ramrod straight, head tilted for the merest sound that was out of place. The last man off the boat had two servants scurrying behind him, laden with leather and a spare Colleyweston. There was lace at the man's throat, clean and starched and no one would ever guess that he had been buffeted, along with everyone else, across the Channel over the past days.

Biddle watched as the man threw coins to an ostler by the Mermaid's stables and mounted a horse. Biddle flicked his fingers and a lackey slithered around the corner.

'Get a message to Master Marlowe,' he said. 'You'll find him at the Rose. Marlowe, mind – on one else. Tell him, the man he is looking for is making for London on a tall bay. Tell him Robert Poley is here.'

'Well, it's difficult without Kit.' Tom Sledd was standing, as he often did, in the wooden O. Around him the towers of *Tamburlaine* still stood, but Adam Proud was the Admiral's man and the Admiral had plans.

'What is?' he asked.

Trying to build a set for *The Blasphemer's Tragedy* was

like pissing in a bucket – water, water everywhere. 'Look, do we have to do this?' Sledd wondered aloud. '*Tamburlaine* is going well. Can't we extend the run?'

'The Lord Admiral will have it,' Proud said. 'I think he wants to make his mark in the world of theatre. After all,' he winked at Sledd, 'the old bugger won't be going to sea again any time soon. Anway, we can ask him.'

'Who?'

'Kit. We can ask him how he envisaged the set.'

'Umm …'

'Tom,' Proud patronized. 'It's me, Adam. You know and I know,' and he dropped his voice, 'that Kit walks among us – whatever the outside world thinks.'

'Sorry,' Sledd said. 'You know the theatre world, Adam; not to mention the other side of Kit's life. Can't be too careful.'

'The other side?' Proud looked blank.

Sledd tapped the side of his nose. 'Uh-huh,' he shook his head. 'That's a bottle I'd rather leave corked. The man's … what do you call that thing? An enigma?'

Proud chuckled. 'Oh, yes, he is that.'

'I've no idea, Tom.' Marlowe was lounging in the green room, on the ottoman where Tamburlaine spent his leisure moments on stage when he wasn't scourging God and slaughtering people. Ned Alleyn wouldn't have been pleased to see him there – when Ned Alleyn played a part, he became very proprietorial; that was *his* ottoman as surely as his gilded cod-piece was.

'But you wrote the *Blasphemer*, Kit.' Sledd was confused. 'I thought you could picture the scenes.'

'Oh, I could,' the playwright told him, 'if I had the first idea of what the play was about.'

'You what?'

'I didn't write it, Tom,' Marlowe said. 'The first I heard of it was from a stationer at Amen Corner. He was selling it in a Marlowe collection; except that it wasn't Marlowe.'

'Well, that's peculiar.'

'Isn't it, though?'

'Have you even read it?' The stage manager was trying to make sense of the whole thing.

'I have,' Marlowe nodded, 'and it's not bad. But,' he smiled and raised an index finger, 'it's not Marlowe.'

'Shaxsper!' The light of day dawned on Sledd's face. 'Shaxsper's pretending to be you.'

Marlowe laughed. 'That'll be the day,' he said. 'No, it's not Will either. It's not his style. But why the sudden interest?'

'The Lord Admiral wants to put it on. Old Marlowe is great, of course, but a *new* Marlowe … All the other theatres will be empty.'

'I see,' the playwright nodded. 'What does Henslowe think?'

'Well, I don't see a problem with that,' the impresario said, perched in his eyrie as he was. 'I knew the Lord Admiral's intentions, of course, but I think we can carry off a month or so more of *Tamburlaine*. What does Kit say?'

Tom Sledd was going round in circles. 'He told me to see you,' he said.

'Well, bearing in mind he's supposed to be dead, I think we'll have to leave him out. On the other hand, I don't want to raise it with the Admiral until I have to. An untried Marlowe is a risk. What if it doesn't work?'

'Kit didn't write it.'

'What?'

'*The Blasphemer's Tragedy*. Kit says he didn't write it.'

'Where is he?'

So it was that the Rose echoed with the sounds of three men arguing under its rafters. After nearly an hour of pros and cons, it was Henslowe who had the last word. 'The bottom line,' he said – and he was a man who dealt habitually in bottom lines – 'is the Admiral's final decision.'

'Well, next week, obviously.' Howard of Effingham was being kitted out for a new masque to celebrate Her Majesty's thirty-fifth year on the throne. He didn't really have the body for

Neptune and positively refused to be given a fish's tail. The Lord High Admiral, hero of the Armada, flapping about like a fish out of water? Don't be ridiculous. He was happy enough to have silver scales on his arms and legs and of course, the nautical crown graced his heroic brow perfectly.

'Next week, my Lord?' Henslowe could scarcely believe his ears.

'Well, possibly the week after. A new Marlowe, eh? We'll make a killing.'

'But there is a *slight* problem, my Lord.'

'Oh, what's that?'

'Marlowe didn't write it.'

Effingham frowned and waved away the scale-fitting flunky. 'That's all for now, Hartnell,' he said and he closed in on Henslowe. 'How do you mean, he didn't write it?'

'It's not a Marlowe, my Lord. And he wants nothing to do with it.'

'Does he now?' Effingham frowned a little and gnawed his lip. His icy glance hit Adam Proud, standing at Henslowe's shoulder. 'You're very quiet, Master Wordsmith.'

'I don't understand any of this, my Lord,' Proud admitted.

'Who does?' Effingham spread his arms in exasperation. For a moment, he tapped the table he stood by, then he took off his crown. 'All right,' he said, 'this is what will happen. If Marlowe wants nothing to do with the *Blasphemer*, that's fine. He's supposed to be dead anyway. Proud, you will take over.'

'My Lord?' The playwright stood there, mouth open.

'Take over. Do any tweaks and rewrites as necessary. Work with Henslowe on the directing. No, on second thoughts – plays don't work when run by committee. *You* direct. Henslowe, sit this one out.'

It was the impresario's turn to fume. 'We had an agreement, my Lord,' he said firmly.

'Agreement?' Effingham snapped.

'I was to have full commercial and directorial control …'

'That was *then*, Henslowe,' the Lord Admiral told him.

'*So* last month. You can still cast the thing, but Proud does the rest. Are we clear?'

'We should clear this with Kit,' Henslowe persisted.

Effingham rounded on him. 'Kit Marlowe is dead in the water, Henslowe. I prophecy that by Lammastide, no one will remember so much as his name.'

'But you had Tamburlaine!' Burbage snapped. When it came to petulance, he was in a drama class of his own.

'Of course I did.' Alleyn was going through his fencing moves, parrying the air in sixte and riposting as only he could. 'That was a given.'

'Well, now,' Burbage sneered, 'the flares will be on me. *I've* got the Blasphemer. Henslowe's just told me.'

Alleyn paused in mid-lunge. It didn't do his quadriceps much good but he wasn't going to let Burbage see that and he pranced through the pain. 'Tell me, Dickie, me old thespian – you have read the play?'

'Of course.'

Alleyn stood up, facing him. 'And you're going to play Brabantio?'

'Naturally.'

Alleyn laughed. 'I doubt that very much,' he said, 'but I think you're missing the point, Burbage.'

'Oh?'

'Brabantio may be the Blasphemer, but he's a cypher, a bit player, one up from the prologue. The *real* hero, the drawer of the crowds and no doubt the ladies, is Herminius.'

'Herminius?' Burbage frowned.

'Of course,' Alleyn took up the pose again. 'And Herminius will be played by moi, naturally.'

Dr Gabriel Harvey had never lost touch with Cambridge University, his alma mater, but he much preferred London. If he was brutally honest with himself, which he hardy ever was, that was because London was not saturated with huge intellects like his. Academically, it was a smaller pond and he swam around in it like some giant carp, untroubled by the minnows he met every day. There were *some* intelligent people in Lincoln's Inn, of course, but they were all lawyers and, by definition, motivated by greed. Harvey was altogether on a higher plane and he was just congratulating himself on that score when there was a knock on his door.

'Come in.'

Strangers didn't usually approach Gabriel Harvey. He had people for all the little things that irritated everybody ese, including a perceptive gatekeeper who kept the riff-raff out. So this man must be someone of importance, even though he had not been announced.

'Can I help you?' the dominus looked the man up and down. He had no idea who he was.

'I hope so, Dr Harvey,' he said. 'I'm looking for Kit Marlowe and I know that you and he were … acquainted, back in the day.'

Harvey sat upright. This was unexpected. 'Christopher Marlowe is dead, Master …?'

'Poley,' the stranger said. 'Robert Poley. Secretary to Sir Robert Cecil.'

A thousand images flashed through Harvey's brain. Cecil was the dwarf who ran England with his venerable father. 'Secretary' meant a hundred different things, depending on the context. And why should a lackey of one of the most powerful men in the state want to talk to Kit Marlowe? And why had he come to Lincoln's Inn?

'I'm flattered,' Harvey said. The man could smarm for England.

'Don't be,' Poley said. 'You and I know perfectly well, Doctor, that Kit Marlowe is as alive as you and me.'

'Alive?' Harvey felt the ground sliding beneath him.

'Alive,' Poley nodded. 'The last time I saw him he was standing in the upstairs room of an Ordinary in Deptford. A sort of colleague of mine, Nicholas Faunt, came to his rescue because I was about to cut his throat.'

Harvey's own throat bulged as he swallowed hard. People like Poley, he knew, walked among honest folk in Gloriana's England, but he never expected to meet one. And in his own chambers. 'I haven't seen Marlowe for years,' he said. 'Everybody I've spoken to thinks he's dead.'

Poley chuckled. 'Ah, the Puritan rumour machine,' he said. 'Well oiled as ever. Tell me, Dr Harvey, as a little background – back in Cambridge, what was Marlowe to you?'

Harvey saw a way to deal with this man. He couldn't see any weapons on him, but that told him nothing. If Poley was prepared to cut Marlowe's throat, he'd cut anybody's. 'Do I take it,' he asked, 'that you and Marlowe are not on particularly good terms?'

Poley smiled. 'Very perceptive of you, Doctor,' he said.

'He was a prize shit,' Harvey sneered. 'An upstart crow if ever I met one. Never met a rule he obeyed. He was a mere scholar at Corpus Christi whereas I was Lecturer in Law. Oh, and Logic. Not to mention Hebrew. He spent all his time avoiding lectures, rolling around the town drunk and translating that most filthy of Roman poets, Ovid.'

'Tut, tut.' Poley shook his head.

'If you say he is alive,' Harvey was more relaxed now, leaning back in his chair, 'then I must believe you. But I have not seen him. Nor do I wish to.'

Poley looked at the man for a moment, then he stood up. 'Very well,' he said. 'It was worth a try. Should Marlowe be in touch,' he pulled a card from his doublet, 'be so good as to give him this. I can be reached there any time, day or night. Oh, and give him this too, would you?' Poley drew back his right hand and slapped Harvey across the face. The impact threw the man backwards and his chair slid from under him so that he lay a dazed and groaning heap on the floor, his last breath knocked out of him.

'I'll see myself out,' Poley said.

'Needs work, Harry.'

Harry Temperley knew that perfectly well. He may have been only seven, but in his head he was forty-eight and knew exactly what was expected of him. His father was Sir Hugh Temperley, the foremost landowner in Berkshire and a knight of the shire. When little Harry was four he had been presented at court and the great and mighty queen, he discovered to his horror, was a ghastly old woman not that much taller than he was, with black teeth and a powder-white skin. Even more bizarrely, her hair was bright red.

'Right back to the chin,' Harry's mentor was telling him. 'You'll never be the next Robin Hood if you draw a bow like that.'

'Try it this way,' a voice made them both turn. The new arrival stood alongside the boy and helped him slide the next arrow into the nock. 'Back straight. Legs locked. Now, line up the arrow tip with the bull. Slide, further, further. You should feel your fingers against your ear. Now!'

Harry let fly and the grey goose shaft hissed through the air, the tip thudding into the gold at the centre of the target. There were whoops and cheers all round and Harry's mother and sisters dashed over to cuddle and make a fuss of him.

Henry's mentor fumed inwardly, while smiling at the boy's prowess. Through his teeth, he hissed, 'Thank you, Kit. And, by the way, what the Hell are you doing here?'

'I might ask you the same.' Marlowe was muttering too, beaming at the feathered and gowned ladies who beamed back at him, 'because you certainly aren't teaching the boy anything to do with archery.' He looked at the man. 'How've you been, Jack?'

Jack led the newly-arrived Puritan across to a stand of bows, away from the fluttering Temperleys and their servants. Behind them, the great house fluttered too, with flags in honour of the thirty-fifth year of Gloriana's reign and the dogs of the household basked and rolled in the sun.

'Well,' Jack said. 'Until a few moments ago, I was fine, earning my crust as Master-at-Arms to the young Temperleys.'

'Yes, yes,' Marlowe laughed. 'But come on, Jack. It's me, Kit. What are you *really* doing?'

Jack looked left and right, just in case. 'The usual,' he said, 'eavesdropping on a suspect family.'

'Any joy?'

'Not much,' Jack shrugged. 'Oh, there are still the usual Papist icons here and there around the house, but they're in the open, nothing clandestine. All the services I've attended have been in the church just over the hill. The vicar seems straight as a die. Whitgift man if ever I saw one.'

'Waste of time, then?'

'Probably,' Jack said, pretending to inspect a bow. 'But you know Burghley – no stone unturned. His little boy's even worse. He'll have us all nosing our way into every household soon, just to make sure there are no Papists under the bed.'

'There are rumours of a second Armada,' Marlowe said. 'With perhaps a little help from the Irish.'

'I know,' Jack said, 'but the Temperleys came over with the Conqueror, for God's sake. Geoffrey Temperley carried the king's banner at Agincourt. They're loyal as ivy to oak.' He looked at Marlowe. 'And none of this explains what you are doing here. Is Cecil checking up on me?'

'Not that I know of,' Marlowe said, 'although with your archery tuition, perhaps he should be.'

Jack ignored the slur. 'Incidentally,' he said, 'I heard a rumour that you were dead.'

'Oh, that little thing,' Marlowe chuckled. 'No, it's just a ploy dreamed up by Philip Henslowe to boost sales, get arses on seats.'

'Well, I'm glad,' Jack said. 'So, if you're not nosing around on behalf of the Cecils, and you're not a ghost, what brought you all the way from London?'

'Robert Poley.'

'Ah.'

'You and he were thick as thieves in days of yore, Jack. Where is he?'

'Days of yore, indeed,' Jack said. 'And I don't care for the "thick as thieves" bit. Poley *is* a thief, I'll grant you, but he's no friend of mine.' He looked into Marlowe's eyes, 'or yours, I'll wager.'

'Let's just say Robyn Poley and I have unfinished business,' Marlowe nodded.

'No, it's been months.' Jack was testing bowstrings and looking quite convincing to the untutored eye, though he could no more recognise a loose one than fly to the moon. 'The last I heard, he was hanging around with the Bacons.'

'Was he now?'

'Jack.' A female voice made both men turn.

'My lady.' Jack half-bowed. 'Er … may I introduce …'

'Robert Brackenbury, my lady,' Marlowe completed the gesture, 'of the Worshipful Company of Archers. Forgive me for not introducing myself earlier, but the display was underway. Your boy – Harry, is it? – has great potential. The Company is always looking for new talent, however young.'

And Lady Temperley gushed as only doting mothers can.

'Out there!' Tom Sledd shouted over the thud and rattle of the hammering.

'What?'

He had barely glanced at the man over his shoulder, but now he paused and took in the velvet and lace, he realised that, all in all, he was an unlikely shit-shoveller. The jakes at the Rose had been giving trouble for days and it was high time someone took that in hand, so to speak. Summer was well and truly here and the smell and the flies were not the best of welcomes for the theatre crowd on their way to see *Tamburlaine*.

'I'm sorry,' Sledd took the nails out of his mouth. 'I thought you were the sh … the night soil man.'

'And I thought you weren't Blind Jack of Southwark,' the stranger said. 'I'm looking for Kit Marlowe.'

Sledd looked at the man with fresh eyes. He was broad and tall with a Spanish swept-hilt rapier at his hip and no doubt a dagger under the expensive Colleyweston. 'Kit Marlowe's dead,' Sledd said.

'And I'm the Archbishop of Canterbury,' the stranger said.

'Your Grace,' Sledd half bowed.

The man closed to him. 'I didn't realise you were the Rose's Will Kemp,' he said. 'You're actually Tom Sledd, aren't you? Stage manager, or whatever?'

'What of it?'

'Rumour has it that you and Marlowe are like peas in a pod. If anyone knows where I can find him, it's you.'

'St Nicholas churchyard,' Sledd said, 'Deptford.'

'Really?' The man's tone had changed. 'What happened? I thought you were joking.'

Sledd thought for a while and in the end decided to brazen it out. 'A tavern brawl,' he lied. 'A fight over a reckoning. Some arsehole stabbed him.'

'That arsehole being …?'

'Who are you?' Sledd asked.

'Kit was a friend of mine, back in the day.' The man's lips quivered. 'Many was the quart of ale we sank, the tables we played.'

'You haven't told me your name,' Sledd persisted.

The stranger beckoned him closer and led him around the corner of a tower, Persian princes for the use of. And he whispered in his ear, 'My name is Robert Poley, pizzle,' he murmured, 'and we both know that whoever's lying in that churchyard is not Kit Marlowe. Tell me, Master Sledd … Tom. Is there a Mistress Sledd? And a couple of little Sleds?'

The stage manager nodded and swallowed hard. The tip of a main-gauche blade was pressed into his shirt just above his belt buckle.

'One thrust of this and you're dead,' Poley said. 'One thrust and twist and it'll take you a day to die. The agony will be appalling, but …' he smiled, 'look on the bright side; at least you'll have time to say goodbye to the family.' The smile vanished. 'Marlowe.'

'He comes in here from time to time,' Sledd gabbled, seeing his life flash before him, 'but as God is my judge, I don't know where he lives.'

For a moment, both men heard the hiss of cloth as Poley's blade pricked wool and skin. Sledd felt it too. Then Poley eased back, sheathed the weapon and patted the stage manager on the cheek. 'Give Kit my regards,' he called, walking away. 'Tell him I'll see him some time. Soon.'

Tom Sledd was still standing there, where Poley had left him. In his mind's eye, he saw himself in a winding sheet, soaked with blood, with his nearest and dearest sobbing around his corpse. For a while, he didn't hear Adam Proud shouting in his ear not feel him tugging at his shirt. 'Tom! Tom! I've just seen him.'

'Who?'

'Where's Henslowe?'

'What?'

'Henslowe. Where is he?' The playwright looked agitated.

'Not here.' Sledd tried to focus. 'Who have you just seen?'

'That maniac who tried to kill Kit and Will; you know, the one who swung the gantry. I've just seen him riding away from here.'

'You have?'

'Yes. I was just getting out of my coach – oh, here are the set plans for the *Blasphemer*, by the way.' He thrust some scrolls in Sledd's general direction. '– and he was riding away.'

'Robert Poley.' Sledd nodded.

'Who?'

Sledd looked at the man. Had the playwright no idea how close to death the stage manager had just been? Did he have no heart at all? 'An old friend of Kit's,' Sledd said, numbly. 'Or so he claimed.'

'Old friend enough to want him dead,' Proud said. 'We've got to get this to the Under-Sheriff, get a warrant out for Poley's arrest.'

But Tom Sledd was shaking his head. 'The Robert Poleys of this world are like will o' the wisps, Adam,' he said, 'hovering over marshes like miasmic ghosts.'

It was Proud's turn to look at Sledd. God, that was good. Was *everybody* a playwright in this bloody theatre?

It had been a while since Kit Marlowe had been to the scrivenery. Once, it had been Thomas Phelippes' second home, where the old magician hobnobbed with fellow cryptographers, translators and dabblers in the black arts of mirror-writing and invisible ink. The Babington Plot had been exposed here, as well as a dozen other attempts to assassinate the Jezebel of England. And it was the creator of this miscellany of misfits that Marlowe had come to see today.

He flashed the queen's cypher to the grim-looking heavy at the gate and made his way up a winding staircase in the turret tower of Gray's Inn. Bustling High Holborn lay below him, street sellers carrying their wares, blissfully ignorant of the devilish skills contained in this section of the building. On the face of it, Gray's was just like the other three Inns of Court, crawling with lawyers obsessed with the lure of the groat, arguing minutiae in already dead Latin. But *this* part of Gray's was different, an inner sanctum where subversive minds fought fire with fire.

'Kit Marlowe!' The bearded man in his corner stood up and crossed the room. Marlowe was not ready for the tight hug, still less the kiss on the cheek, but it *had* been a while.

'Anthony Bacon,' the playwright held the man out to a little more like arm's length. 'How long has it been?'

'Too long,' Bacon said, ushering his guest to a chair and reaching for the Rhenish. 'I've been abroad, you know.'

'Oh, I know,' Marlowe said. 'Playing the old game for Walsingham.'

'Walsingham,' Bacon grunted. 'All that seems eternity ago now. I suspect the Spymaster's sorely missed. I know he was in France.'

'We shan't look upon his like again.' Marlowe took the proffered cup. 'To Francis Walsingham.' He held it aloft. 'No doubt he's snooping on God now.'

'Not if Satan paid him more,' Bacon laughed and raised his glass too. 'Francis Walsingham.'

'When did you get back?' Marlowe asked.

'Er … let me see. February of last year. I don't mind telling you, Kit, as somebody who's been out of circulation for a while, I haven't been very impressed with what I have seen.'

'The great game goes on, Anthony,' Marlowe shrugged.

'Oh, indeed,' Bacon said, 'and always will. But it's the game masters who trouble me. Burghley is older than God and that misshapen runt of his is no Francis Walsingham. When the wolves are circling, you don't need a shepherd who can't see over the tabletop.'

Marlowe let the mixed metaphor pass.

There was a tap on the door and a short, thick-set man swept in. He looked horrified to see Marlowe sitting there.

'Oh, William,' Bacon said. 'Master Marlowe here is an old friend and I'm nearly out of Rhenish. Fetch another bottle, would you?'

William looked a little confused.

'William is a mute,' Bacon said. 'Hasn't been in my service long. Not a bad thing to have silent servants, eh?'

Marlowe suddenly swept to his feet and crossed the room, colliding with the manservant. 'Vaya, lo siento, amigo. Descuidado conmigo.'

'Culpa mia,' the man replied, 'No se ha hecho daño!' And his eyes widened at what had just happened. Then he was gone, the door slamming behind him.

'A selective mute, then, Anthony?' Marlowe raised an eyebrow. 'No comment in English but he can gabble in Espagnol with the best of them.'

A man like Bacon knew when the game was up. 'Damn you, Marlowe,' he growled. 'I knew the mute thing wouldn't work out. How did you know?'

'That he's a Spaniard?' Marlowe shrugged. 'Something in his bearing. Something in what he's wearing. Would you like to explain,' he sat down again. 'One projectioner to another, what an avowed enemy of this country is doing serving wine in one of Her Majesty's Inns of Court?'

'Well, for a start,' Bacon said, refreshing their cups, 'he's not serving wine. And his English is appalling. I hope you're not thirsty, because we won't be seeing a top up any time soon.'

'Who is he?'

'Antonio Perez,' Bacon told him under his breath, 'and you didn't hear that from me.'

'Perez?' Marlowe frowned. 'There was a royal secretary of that name at the Escorial, the court of Philip of Spain.'

'That's him,' Bacon nodded. 'Used to nip in and out of the black curtains in Philip's closet along with his midget jesters.' Bacon sighed. 'You wouldn't believe how tangled Spanish politics is, Kit. Makes Her Majesty's court look like a game of pitch and toss. Dear Antonio fell foul of all that and Philip threw him in gaol, with a bit of help from the French, of course.'

'Of course.'

'I don't mind telling you it cost me a pretty penny to get him out. And now, I'm stuck with him. Umm … I need hardly tell you none of this can get out. We'd all of us have an appointment with Master Topcliff.'

'He's just passing through, I presume?'

'Oh, yes, yes. But … well, there is a complication.'

'Oh?'

'Well … er … I don't quite know how to put this, Kit, but …'

'But you and he are lovers.'

Bacon sat open-mouthed. 'How did you know?' he managed at last, the second time he'd said that in as many minutes.

Marlowe laughed. 'It's been nine years since Walsingham recruited me,' he said. 'You pick up a few trifles as you go.'

'You heard about that business in Montauban?' Bacon asked.

'Charges of sodomy with a page, wasn't it?' Marlowe checked.

'Dear Isaac,' Bacon smiled. 'It all sounds so sordid, doesn't it, in legal jargon? The law doesn't recognize love at its deepest.'

'There's not much the law does recognize,' Marlowe agreed. 'It is, at best, an ass, as doubtless somebody will say in print one of these days.'

'Yes, I became very fond of Antonio. I couldn't let him fester in some ghastly foreign oubliette. He's such a sweetie.'

'Adorable, I'm sure,' Marlowe said, 'and your secret's safe with me, Anthony; on one condition.'

'Name it.'

'The whereabouts of one Robert Poley.'

'Robyn?' Bacon frowned. 'Now, there's a name I

haven't heard in a while.'

'You haven't seen him?'

'No. You're the first of the old brigade I've seen since I got back. And Poley was never exactly a friend.'

'People like Poley don't have friends,' Marlowe said. 'They have targets.'

'And talking of that,' Bacon said, 'I had heard you were dead.'

'Everybody has,' Marlowe chuckled, 'though most of them don't recognize me in the first second as you did.'

Bacon shrugged modestly. 'A small skill, but it has saved my life more times than you could shake a stick at it,' he said. He waved a hand across the general area of his eyes and forehead. 'You are very memorable, Kit.'

Marlowe stood up. 'If Poley should be in touch with you, let me know, won't you? I can be reached at the Rose.'

'And at Lincoln's Inn, round the corner, courtesy of Michael Johns.' Bacon winked.

It was Marlowe's turn to be open-mouthed.

'Come on, Kit,' Bacon laughed. 'I may have been abroad for a while, but I haven't lost the old touch, you know.'

CHAPTER 13

'**A** Masque, my Lord?' Proud wasn't sure he had heard right.

'Yes,' said Effingham. 'You know – intelligent people making idiots of themselves in fancy dress. If I'm playing Neptune to mark Her Majesty's Thirty-Fifth, I've got to play it … er … him properly.'

'Were you thinking of the Rose, sir?' Proud asked.

The Admiral narrowed his eyes in thought. 'Not the theatre. Should Her Majesty accept my invitation, we can't have her traipsing the same streets as the riff-raff who live there. No, I thought perhaps Gray's Inn. They have a reputation for that sort of thing. We can use Henslowe and his people, though. Professional actors, musicians, that sort of thing. You'll write it, of course.'

'I am flattered, my lord,' Proud gushed. 'And strictly between us, we don't really need Henslowe, do we? Too many cooks, and all that?'

Effingham raised an Admiralish eyebrow. 'Don't let's run before we can walk, eh, Proud? Henslowe has been putting on this kind of thing since before you were a twinkle in your father's eye.'

Proud looked mulish and Effingham sighed. He had eight children that he was aware of and probably many more that he was not. He had even visited the nursery once or twice and patted the occasional sticky little hand in a paternal sort of way. But dealing with actors and their accompanying ilk was worse than any gaggle of children he had ever met. He had always chuckled when he heard people compare a difficult task with herding cats. With this lot is was like herding weasels, just as slippery as cats but with a hidden agenda. He waved a hand towards the door.

'Just go and make some preliminary plans, Proud, there's a good fellow. You will have the final say in any dispute, you have my word on that. My man will talk to Henslowe and let him have an idea of the budget he will have to work to. But, listen, Proud. For reasons I won't go into here, we are not having elephants this time, is that understood? Because the masque we held for the … let me see, twenty-fifth, was it? Yes, the twenty-fifth anniversary, had elephants and there were repercussions, shall we say? Shovels. Spray. So, no elephants and for preference, no animals at all '

Proud avoided the sulky face this time. He was a fast learner. 'Understood, my Lord. Do you want to see the plans? The sketches?'

'Lord above, no. I have people for that. You, in fact. I'll turn up as Neptune and that will be enough. Just one thing, Proud. Make sure that my costume is the most sumptuous and at the same time not the most ridiculous in the room. That's my only stipulation.'

'And no elephants.' Proud thought he had better check. His Lordship had been quite adamant.

'Goes without saying. Now bugger off, Proud. You're a busy man.'

Proud bowed and left the room. Sailors really got on his wick, but a man had to do what a man had to do. A Masque, indeed. He was above all this really, but … he began to plan. He wished Effingham hadn't mentioned elephants, though. He didn't seem able to get them out of his head.

Henslowe hated being interrupted when he was counting. He quickly wrote down a running total and put an inky forefinger on the relevant column.

'What?' he snapped. These days there were just too many damned people cluttering up his theatre. It had seemed a sound financial plan to team up with the Lord Admiral and his Men but if this was the result he would be tearing up the contract as soon as he could find it in the welter of paper on his desk.

'I have a message from Lord How …' the man began.

'Of course you bloody do,' Henslowe said, looking back at his columns. 'Just sling it there on that pile and I'll get round to it.'

Ambrose cleared his throat. 'His Lordship specifically asked, Master Henslowe, that I made sure you read it while I was present.'

'Oh, really.' Henslowe was not a particularly unpleasant man. He had his moments, but generally, he was well-enough liked by his employees and also tolerated quite well by his wife and Matilda when the mood was on them. But this idiot was trying his patience. 'And does your master not trust me, then, to do his bidding?'

Ambrose had not lasted in Effingham's volatile household without being a quick thinker. 'This is a particularly sensitive matter, Master Henslowe. It involves a great deal of money …'

Henslowe's head snapped round like a mongoose spotting a snake.

'… and, of course,' Ambrose dropped his voice and leaned forward, 'almost certain …' he looked right and left and leaned in even nearer, 'preferment.'

'Preferment?'

Ambrose put a finger to his lips. 'Almost certain.'

'Well, in that case, hand it over.' Henslowe held out a hand.

Ambrose took out the note from his purse and waited as Henslowe read it. He tutted to himself. These men with more money than he would see in a lifetime still had to mouth the words as they read them. It was a disgrace. He noticed Henslowe's eyes widen as he came to the number at the bottom. He could almost hear the calculations going on in his brain as to how much he could cream off the top. Ambrose had been doing the same for years and he silently doffed his cap to a master of the art. Henslowe looked up and smiled. His eyes shone like sovereigns in the sun.

'Tell his Lordship I would be delighted to help,' he said. 'I understand from this that I will be liaising with Master Proud. There is no mention of who has the final say, though, in any artistic disagreements.'

'I believe that would be you, Master Henslowe,' Ambrose said with a smile, wishing he could be a fly on the wall when this behemoth gathered speed.

'Well, I should think so too,' Henslowe said. 'These whippersnappers have to be kept in line, don't they? You run a household. I run a theatre. We know what's right and proper.'

'Indeed we do,' Ambrose said. 'You mustn't keep me, though, Master Henslowe. I have yet to visit the custodian at Gray's Inn, to thrash out the final arrangements for the day. Oh, and I have been asked to specifically say … no elephants, if you please.'

'A Masque?' Tom Sledd was aghast. It was bad enough, running one play while planning another, always looking to see what current piece of scenery could be wrangled into doing duty as something else, what costume could be ripped to bits and reassembled in such a way that the regular groundlings wouldn't notice. But a Masque! He had done the dratted things before and they never ended well. There were always tears before bedtime and now … 'Master Henslowe, really. Are you mad?'

'Mad? No, I'm not bloody mad. Everyone else is mad. Effingham is mad. Proud is mad. For all I know the theatre cat is also mad. All I am trying to do is juggle with more balls than a man has business to have. And when I can't juggle any more, I know who to call. And that, I'm afraid, is you. It's only for one night. How hard can it be?'

Sledd tore his hair. He had heard the phrase before but never actually done it until now. He wasn't going to do it again – it hurt! 'But that's the point, isn't it? Just for one night. Costumes. Rehearsals. Casting. Burbage and Alleyn strutting about like two cocks in the ring. All the geese done up to the nines out for the payday of their lives. People muscling in when they aren't invited. And you're going to tell me now that the Queen is invited, I expect.'

'Well, yes, she is,' Henslowe said. He couldn't quite see what that had to do with anything.

'My Molly has a friend who is an under under maidservant at Placentia,' Sledd hissed. 'She says the Queen never goes anywhere she is invited. She prefers to go where she isn't invited. Apparently, she laughs and laughs when she sees the state it throws the households into. She's a bit of an old besom, Molly's friend says.'

'But my Lord Effingham is a favourite, isn't he?' Henslowe said plaintively, seeing his preferment take a header out of his eyrie's window.

'She just likes to stay home these days,' Sledd said, with all the certainty of a man whose wife was a friend of an under under maidservant at Placentia. 'She's old, I suppose.' He looked at his employer with a wary eye. No one was sure how old Henslowe was. On a good day he could look as little as mid-fifties.

'Don't you look at me like that, Sledd,' Henslowe growled. 'Before this age thing goes any further, I am 43 next birthday.'

Sledd put on his blandest face.

'But we digress, don't we? What I need from you is a list of things you need to kit out the cast according to Master Proud's plans. They are a little high-flown, so make sure you rein him in a bit. He wanted a lake at the last talk we had. I don't somehow think the gentlemen of Gray's Inn would appreciate a flood. Do we still have those fake waves from *I Joined the Navy*?'

'That only ran one night,' Sledd pointed out. 'The censors …'

'Very narrow minded, yes, I remember. But do we have them somewhere?'

'Probably. I'll have a look.'

'Effingham is tricked out as Neptune, Proud says, so keep a nautical theme. But mind the mermaids don't offend anyone. You know how people are.'

'Do they have to be boys? Only I don't know whether we have enough.'

'Boys?' Henslowe was puzzled, then his brow cleared. 'No, no, you can use women for the women parts in this. Just don't tell the Master of the Revels. It isn't like a play. It's just … a bit of nonsense. Talk to Proud. Just get the thing done, under budget, in time. I know I can rely on you. So, why are you still here?'

And with a sigh, Tom Sledd went off to do what he did best, make a silk purse out of a sow's ear. With mermaids.

'A Masque? Intriguing. Who's invited, do you know?' Marlowe was sitting in the window seat of Michael Johns' study, watching the world go by.

'The usual suspects, I suppose,' Nicholas Faunt said. 'And yes, I do mean that literally. I hear the Queen is expected, but I doubt she'll come. She likes to be asked, but if she came everyone would be stunned. Effingham is going as Neptune, or so I understand.'

'Neptune. How very understated,' Johns commented, from his writing table in the corner. 'I would like to see that.'

'And so you shall,' Faunt said. 'I've had a word with Tom and he is in need of as many mummers as he can lay hands on. Adam Proud has gone slightly overboard … no pun intended … in his pieces and nothing short of an army will really fill the roles. So everyone is welcome, within limits. Tom has said that if you can provide your own costume, he would be grateful.'

Marlowe looked wistful. He was getting a little tired of his Puritan attire and had noticed that Michael Johns had been sharpening his clippers – the curl was starting to reassert itself as his hair grew. An evening dressed up and pretending – yet again – to be someone he wasn't would be a respite from his current searches for Poley. He was always there, lurking in the back of his mind, but he needed something else, if only for a while. This being alive again thing was sometimes very hard. He looked fondly at the two other men in the room and knew himself to be very fortunate in his friends. All he needed now was Sledd and Shaxsper and his little coven would be complete.

There was a tap on the door and it creaked open. A

head, all forehead and little hair, peered round the edge of it.

'Think of the devil,' Marlowe murmured.

'Come in, Master Shaxsper,' Johns said. 'Pull up a chair. We're talking about the Masque.'

'Oh,' Shaxsper said, 'you know about that.' He looked deflated. He had thought he was coming with news.

'All of London knows about it,' Faunt said. 'Tom Sledd has managed to get a tidal wave of gossip going among the geese and the acting fraternity and the world and his wife will be taking part. What about you, have you been asked to write anything?'

'No!' Shaxsper plonked himself down on a bench near the empty fireplace. 'No, I haven't. That's partly why I'm here. Adam Proud is doing it all. He's scribbling in the wings and handing out pages as he goes. He's got some hack musicians writing songs with nautical themes and they sound … well, they sound like something made up by a drunken sailor.'

Faunt smiled. There was nothing more nautical than a drunken sailor.

'But you have a speaking role, I expect, Will, don't you?' Marlowe asked.

'*No!*' Shaxsper's voice had risen to an exasperated shriek. 'I have been told that if I want, I can be a walking gentleman in one of the shipwreck scenes. *A. Walking. Gentleman!*' A vein stood out on the massive forehead, throbbing worryingly.

Faunt put out a hand. 'Do calm down, I beg of you. You will have a seizure at this rate. There are those in London who would give their eye teeth for a walking gentleman role in this. What would you have to do, specifically?'

'Drown.'

'Oh. Still, you can bring a bit of drama …' Marlowe was trying to help.

'I have been told,' Shaxsper said, in a sepulchral voice, 'that I just have to sink beneath the waves, no dramatics.'

'I see,' Marlowe said. There didn't seem much else *to* say. 'Are you going to do it?'

Shaxsper shrugged. 'There'll be food and drink, I assume.'

Faunt nodded. 'The best cooks in London have been called in,' he said, 'and the wine is from his Lordship's own cellar.'

'I'll be there, then, I suppose,' Shaxsper said, getting up to leave. 'But I'm not happy.'

When the would-be playwright had gone, the three men looked at each other. Many thoughts were sleeting through their heads but it was Johns, always kind about his fellow man, who spoke first.

'Poor Will,' he said. 'He came to London to seek fame and fortune and here he is, a silent drowning sailor in someone else's masque. It isn't exactly fame, is it, not as anyone would define it.'

'He came to London to escape his wife, if you ask me,' Faunt said. 'He never has a good word to say for the woman. Has anyone met her?'

Marlowe shook his head. 'I think there's money ...'

They fell silent. Even Michael Johns had considered marrying for money before now, but there were no takers.

'He'll be famous one day,' Johns said, optimistically.

'Even if it's for being a wife killer,' Faunt said, looking into his cup in a disappointed way. It was unaccountably empty.

'Uxoricide,' Johns said.

'Are you well, Michael?' Marlowe asked.

'Yes, why?'

'I thought you were clearing your throat.'

'Uxoricide. Killing of a wife.'

Faunt gave up waiting and went to fetch another bottle from the shelf above Johns' head. 'That's what I love about coming here,' he said. 'There's always something to learn. Even if the wine tastes like ...' he sipped and smacked his lips, 'seagull piss. Acid with just a hint of old mackerel. Where do you get this stuff, Michael?'

'Well, not from my Lord Howard's cellar,' Johns assured him. 'So we will sup much better than this at the Masque.'

'A Masque!' Alleyn was looking at the rough pages he had screwed up in his hand. 'I never thought I would live to see the day!'

'And no fee!' Burbage was outraged. 'We are actors of substance, Ned. I wonder they had the nerve!'

'Indeed, Richard, my old, dear friend.'

Burbage bridled. 'Old? I'm younger than you!'

'No slur intended,' purred Alleyn. 'I simply meant as in long-standing. No one understands an actor like an actor, don't you find?'

Burbage was getting suspicious. Alleyn was not normally this friendly. In fact, the last time Burbage remembered exchanging pleasantries with the man had been a good dozen years ago, when their voices had broken simultaneously and they had been reduced to the ranks of walking gentlemen after years as very successful maid servants and at least one duchess. 'So … you are not doing the masque, then?'

'Are you?' Alleyn checked.

'I … don't … know.' Burbage waited until the cat jumped.

'Well, do you know, I might,' Alleyn said. 'There is food and wine, I understand. Wine from the Admiral's cellar.'

'What's Proud given you? Is it a decent role?'

Alleyn tried to hide a smirk. 'It's a song.'

'A song? I didn't know you sang, Ned.'

'Not as a rule, not as a rule, dear friend. But … well, we all know Gloriana has a weakness for a nice baritone.'

'I always thought it was more what a baritone had hidden under his codpiece that amused the queen. Perhaps you'll strike lucky, Ned.'

Both men were silent, contemplating the possibilities. There was a knighthood in it, for sure, if the Queen took a fancy to their well turned calves. On the other hand, there was the lead-white face, the black teeth and the hair that spent the night on the bedpost. Unable to vocalise their thoughts, they both cleared their throats and wandered off, one stage right, one stage left.

'How is my Masque coming along, Master Proud?' The note seemed a little peremptory. It didn't even have the Admiral's elaborate seal on it. It just had Ambrose's squiggle at the bottom. The messenger stood to attention, waiting for a reply. Adam Proud forced a smile and dipped his pen in his ink pot.

'Splendidly,' he wrote, in a slightly shaky hand. 'We'll all be there in plenty of time on Wednesday. It will be a night to remember.'

He shook sand over the words and tapped it off onto his desk. He folded the paper and handed it over to the messenger. 'Thank you,' he said, handing the man a penny.

The messenger looked at it and rolled his eyes. Say what you like about these theatre types, they were tight as a weasel's arse.

'Deliver it straight away, please,' Proud said, already back to his rewrites. Then he looked up. 'What day is it today, please?' he said.

Tight as weasels' arses and also stupid. 'Tuesday, Master Proud.'

'Tuesday? *Tuesday?* Surely not.'

'Tuesday, as I live and breathe. I know this because my wife helps at the Lord Admiral's kitchen when they have a feast and she has been kneading bread since sun-up. Allowing six hours to rise, one to knock back and prove, then …'

'When I want a lesson in breadmaking,' Proud snapped, 'I'll ask for it. Now …' he flapped a hand, 'Off you go and deliver that message. I have things to be. Places to do.' He paused, listening again in his head. 'Or something along those lines. Just … go.'

The messenger left, vindicated. Tight as weasels' arses, stupid and also mad as March hares. Theatre folk; pah! If he never met another, it would be too soon.

'What are you wearing to the Masque, Kit?'

Will Shaxsper was lounging on Marlowe's bed while the playwright washed behind a screen. He had avoided the haircut, although Johns and Faunt had been very vocal on the fact that a true Puritan would never let his curls show like his currently were. His costume for the masque was hanging on the back of the screen but he wasn't going to reveal it yet. He had smiled nicely at one of the seamstresses at the Rose and he had to admit she had done him proud, especially in the time at her disposal. His sketch had been abysmal, but she had almost read his mind.

'It's a surprise.'

Shaxsper sighed. 'I have a costume.'

'Of course you have.' Marlowe's reply was muffled by the cloth he was drying his face with. 'You're a drowning sailor, aren't you?'

'Not any more. Proud has rewritten that bit. Decided it was a bit … dour … for a celebratory masque.'

Marlowe came from behind the screen. 'He's not wrong. I've been to quite a few masques in my time and while some of the performances can be dire, they aren't meant to be. But when you have the lady of the house performing a catch when she can't hold a tune in a bucket, it is never going to end well. But mass drownings – whatever was he thinking?'

'He was trying to smarm round Effingham, that's what he was thinking,' Saxsper said morosely. 'It was a re-enactment of the sinking of the *Trinidad Valencera.*'

'Any particular reason?' Marlowe thought back and couldn't remember that ship having been a personal triumph for Effingham.

'She went down off Ireland, or something. Proud has been trying to get in the good books of some little slut of a goose and she's from there. She was going to have a speaking role. Because of the accent.'

'Oh, I see.' Marlowe put on a clean shirt and then his doublet. He was hoping he wouldn't have to be a Puritan much longer. Poley was so close he could almost smell it. 'And now?'

Shaxsper smiled for the first time. 'And now, he has a cat in hell's chance of getting anywhere near her. Or at least, the bits of her he is interested in.'

'Proud is a bit of an ingenu, isn't he?' Marlowe sat down and gestured Shaxsper to join him in his simple breakfast. He sometimes thought it was his favourite meal of the day. Ever since school it had been the same, whenever he was in comfortable circumstances. Manchet bread, butter and honey. Milk so fresh it was almost lowing. It was hard to beat. Shaxsper usually broke his fast with whatever was left over from the night before and he had eaten some very strange things that way. He sat down and soon was nose deep in sticky butter.

'He's a pizzle,' Shaxsper said, indistinctly. 'Tom and I were saying the other day, for a man with no discernible talent, he has risen faster than a rocket.'

'And he will burn out just as fast,' Marlowe assured him. He pointed to his chin. 'You … you have something in your beard.'

'Oh,' Shaxsper wiped it with his sleeve, examined it and licked it. 'Honey. You do well here, Kit. Where is Master Johns?'

'Well,' the playwright chuckled. 'Unlike us, Will, Michael works for a living. This morning, I believe he is sharing his knowledge of Logic with some no doubt undeserving scholars. Lucky them. Unlucky him.'

'Is he coming to the masque?'

'I persuaded him to come. He isn't a man who looks for raucous company, but it will be the place to be tonight and I didn't want to think of him sitting in here and hearing all the shenanigans from down the road.'

'What's he coming as?'

'He is coming as my opposite.'

'Which is?'

'You won't catch me like that, Will. But on that subject, what are *you* now the story has changed?'

Shaxsper took another bite of bread and talked around it.

'Sorry? I didn't quite …'

'A … sardine.'

'Sorry, I still didn't … I thought you said sardine.'

Shaxsper exploded in a hail of crumbs. 'I did say sardine, Hell and Damnation take it. We are now doing a stately dance, according to Proud, in honour of Neptune. And I am a bloody sardine.'

Marlowe set his face at its most neutral. 'That sounds very …' But even he, the wordsmith of his age, was struck dumb.

'It sounds like what it is, a total disaster. You know me, Kit, two left feet when it comes to dancing. And dressed like a sardine, well …' he spread his arms and honey flew through the air.

'It will be wonderful, Will,' Marlowe said, spreading a second hunk of bread with glistening butter. 'Look, to cheer you up, you can have a glance at my costume before you go, as long as you don't tell a soul.'

Shaxsper's face lit up. 'Can I? I have to go now, as a matter of fact. We have a rehearsal this morning. Apparently, Proud is a little worried about the whale and whether it will fit through the doors. Tom has been having a measure up and he may have to make adjustments.'

'A *whale*?' Marlowe had to give Proud full marks for being a thorough-going over-reacher.

'Well, the story goes that Effingham has banned elephants and so Proud had to go one better. Now,' Shaxsper licked his fingers and wiped them down the front of his doublet, 'where's this costume of yours?'

Marlowe looked askance at the man. He loved him dearly, but he was a sloven of the worst water. 'Don't touch it.'

'Of course not.'

'Or even go near it.'

'No, I just want to have a look.'

'All right, then. It's hanging behind the screen.'

Shaxsper disappeared for a moment and came out, eyes shining. 'Kit, it's wonderful. However did you get it done so quickly?'

Marlowe tapped the side of his nose. 'I have my methods. Do you think it will work?'

Shaxsper laughed. 'It will outshine the stars in the firmament,' he said.

'That is the general idea,' Marlowe told him. 'Now, off you go, to see how a sardine measures up to a whale.'

CHAPTER 14

igh Holborn was thronged with more people than it usually saw on its cobbles in a week. They were converging on Gray's Inn for the evening of the year, some said of the decade. Those who remembered the Masque of 1583 were hoping for elephants, but realised they would probably be doomed to disappointment. The crowds who had just gathered to gawp were getting the evening of their lives. All the great and the good were there, carriages rolling up one after the other and disgorging totally unrecognizable people dressed in sumptuous clothes. To help the crowds know what wonders they were sharing, a flunkey dressed as a merman was perched on a dais, proclaiming the names of everyone who arrived but for all it mattered, he might as well have shouted names at random. But the crowds were happy and the great families were happy and generally, bonhomie filled the air.

The last carriage rolled away, to wait in handy mews and side alleys until the time came to fetch their illustrious passengers. Coachmen and footmen sat at their ease, lounging for once on the seats, some of them, with more understanding owners, actually inside. Some of the geese who didn't have roles in the masque, plied their trade amongst them and a good time was had by all. Especially Ingram Frizer, whose practised fingers were everywhere.

Then it was time for the foot traffic – the walking

gentlemen (and, for once, ladies) in the parlance of the Rose. They walked in a stately pavane down the middle of High Holborn, bowing to the crowd on either side, laughing and throwing tokens to the waiting people; roses, sweetmeats, scented scraps of cloth. It was as if flock of brightly coloured birds had landed in London and were flying at street level in a gracious murmuration. There were jewels made of glass, painted velvets, whispering silks but every one a credit to the dressmaker's art. Feathers bobbed, gewgaws sparkled but soon even that gorgeous vision had passed.

And still the crowds waited, shuffling their feet ready to mob the carriage they had been waiting for. They had been loyal subjects of Gloriana for thirty-five years now and most in the crowd had no memory of her father, the great, flawed Henry. She didn't come out much these days, but the rumours had been spreading that she would be at this masque in her honour and everyone knew how she loved her people. They knew that she would come. They had, after all, left their shops and houses and waited since midday to get a good spot from which to wave their flags and let her know how much they loved her. Just before they began to get restive, there was a distant clattering of hooves and the rumble of heavy wheels. The crowd perked up, a many headed monster with all its eyes trained on the road toward the river. That was the direction she would come from, for sure. She would have come from Placentia by water. That was how she would have come. The heads nodded to each other. Here she was. Gloriana.

The gilded carriage hove into view, pulled by four grey horses, their heads high and proud, snickering and blowing as the coachman pulled them up before the doors of Gray's Inn. The crowd surged forward as the carriage stopped and waited almost breathless to see their Queen descend. The footman jumped down and elbowed his way through the press to open the door. An elegant foot descended, shod in the finest white kid leather. It was followed by a well-turned calf and then the lissom body of a gorgeously dressed young man of aristocratic bearing. The crowd grunted to itself. Of course, the Queen would have someone to check the safety of the steps for her, it was too much to expect for her to take that risk at her age. They waited for the man to turn to guide her down but no, he walked away and the footman slammed the door and the carriage rolled away.

The silence was palpable and after a step or two towards the door, the man turned and raised his hand for attention.

'The Queen sends her regrets,' he said, 'but this evening finds her indisposed. The extreme love shown on this momentous occasion by her beloved subjects has simply been overwhelming and she has sent me to let you all know how much she loves and treasures every last one of you.' He looked around and saw a woman holding a baby. He swooped on her, Colleyweston cloak swinging, and scooped the child into his arms, kissing it extravagantly on its curly head. The crowd responded as all crowds will, with a soppy 'Awwww' and the mother dimpled prettily and took the child back.

Summoning up her courage, she asked, 'Who shall I say has kissed my little Stukely, sir?'

'Certainly, Mistress …'

'Westcott, sir.'

'Certainly, Mistress Westcott. Robert Devereux, the second Earl of Essex, at your service.' And, with a flourish, he disappeared through the doors of Gray's Inn.

After he had disappeared, the crowd were quiet. Then one voice broke the silence.

'Who?'

With a universal shrug, the massed subjects of Gloriana wandered away.

Mistress Westcott was the only one not disappointed. Her little Stukely had been touched by greatness. He would go on to great things, she was sure. Her happiness was not even dented when the man standing at her elbow said, 'Don't get too excited, Mistress. I always say, never trust a man whose beard is a different colour from his hair.'

And soon, High Holborn, still called Old Bourn by its older residents, was silent apart from the sounds of gaiety seeping through the walls of Gray's Inn.

Robert Devereux was not used to being upstaged, but then he didn't spend that much time in the company of players. Gorgeously attired though he was, he could barely hold a candle to the others in the room. His jewels were real, it was true, but the glass ones shone as brightly and in most cases were at least half as big again as his. His well-turned calf was nothing next to those of Ned Alleyn and Richard Burbage, who spent at least half an hour every morning flexing their most bankable features before a cheval glass. He pushed his way through the throng until he was at the throne of Neptune, who was looking very uncomfortable and was trying to scratch a wayward scale.

'My Lord Admiral,' Essex said, leaning in.

Effingham looked him up and down. 'Yes?'

'Robert Devereux, my Lord, second Earl of Essex.'

'I know who you are. I just don't remember you being on the guest list.' Effingham looked down his nose as best he could, bearing in mind that his beard was overlaid with fake seaweed. He knew that his gravitas was seriously impaired but he was sitting on a throne at least, which gave him an edge.

'I am here at the request of the Queen, my Lord. She sends her regrets, but … she is indisposed.'

Effingham leaned an elbow on the arm of his throne and leaned down to Essex's level. 'My dear Essex,' he said. 'I had no hopes that the Queen would actually grace our little offering tonight. As you see, no place is set for her on the dais to watch the show. No bowers, no thrones save this one … the only thing which would have staggered me would have been her walking in through that door. I am mildly flummoxed by the fact that she has sent you. Some lad who is only where he is today because his father died young.'

Devereux bridled. 'Oh, I say, my Lord, that's rather harsh.'

'But true. However, because we were not expecting the Queen, there is no seat for you to occupy. So I suggest you either bugger off back to Placentia to do whatever you do there or just mingle. The choice is yours.'

Devereux considered his options. An evening being

pawed by an old woman who seemed never to tire of fumbling about behind his codpiece or mixing with the hoi polloi. He sniffed the air. Not too bad. Some of them may even have had baths for the occasion, something which the Queen seldom bothered to do. There were some comely faces in the crowd as well, both male and female – he made his choice and decided to stay. Effingham, watching out of hooded eyes, gave himself a tick in the credit box; he hadn't got to where he was today without being a shrewd judge of men. And Essex was a man to watch – anyone who would make the beast with two backs with the Queen these days had more than usual self control.

From his raised position on his throne, Effingham had a good view of the crowd. They were a handsome lot, he had to give them that. Their costumes were superb, in the main. He had asked for a nautical theme or failing that something from the natural world and the throng before him had done him proud. He could recognise some, but there was a sea serpent undulating through the crowd which had him foxed. He could tell there were many bodies under the frills but the leader of the worm was encased from head to foot and he just couldn't work it out. Others were more obvious. Thomas Hariot was dressed in his usual sober fashion but wore a hat on which the planets circled, spinning whenever he turned his head. Henry Carey was there with his wife, Anne, though it had to be said he didn't look well. They were dressed in green, with exotic orchid hats. Effingham doffed a metaphorical cap to them, for choosing costumes which where flamboyant and beautiful and yet just like wearing normal clothes. He broke off his musings to attack his wayward scale again. He was sure the blessed thing was drawing blood and in such a very awkward place.

Over in the corner, the people of the Rose were beginning to gather and he was looking forward to the entertainment beginning. He had regretted appointing Proud as the main planner almost instantly. The man had barely left him alone from the moment he gave him the job. Rewrites. Rewrites of rewrites. Requests for more money, instantly turned down. Even sheaves of sheet music, for the love of heaven. Howard had an ear so tin that he hardly recognised the sound of a bosun's whistle but Ambrose had an unusually fine ear and he assured him that the tunes, though banal, would cause no offence. He could see Henslowe, got up like a dog's dinner in what was possibly meant to be a representation of a ship of the line. The one thing was that he looked as uncomfortable as the Lord Admiral was feeling, so he took some comfort in that. On the edge of the crowd was a striking figure, all silver and white. It was hard to see the detail, but the cloak seemed to be of some faint tissue, embroidered with circles and faint lines. The doublet was white, shadowed in grey but as the man moved, the patterns seemed to change and grow and fade as if lit from within. By his side was a man dressed in black so dense that he looked like a hole in the air. His face was hidden behind a veil and the two looked as opposite as two things could be. It was disquieting to be unable to focus on what were, after all, just two perfectly normal human beings in fancy dress. Howard looked away and when he looked again, they had gone. Or had they?

Suddenly, Proud was at his elbow. To Effingham's amusement, Proud has decided to dress himself as a merman, appearing to ride a seahorse. It wasn't an easy costume to carry off and Proud had failed almost entirely. The seahorse was tied around his waist and the merman's tail was curled around it. From under the seahorse's stomach, Proud's rather stocky legs stuck out, with green leggings intended to portray seaweed. He gave him full marks for trying, no marks for the finished effect. But the man was saying something, hard to hear in the hubbub and Neptune kindly bent down to hear.

'The performance is about to commence, my Lord,' Proud yelled in his ear. 'Shall you announce it, or would you like me to do it?'

'I believe Master Henslowe has made arrangements,' the Admiral said. 'Tell him we're due to start and meanwhile I will get Ambrose to assemble the seated guests.'

Proud stalked off, his seaweed legs stiff with annoyance. Henslowe, indeed! He went back to his assembled cast and clapped his hands. 'Positions, positions,' he said. 'All those who are not on at once, please go into the rooms stage left and right. Everyone else, positions, positions please.'

Ambrose was meanwhile herding the great and good into their seats and the lesser folk took up positions to the sides. Marlowe and Johns, moonlight and dark, were lucky enough to find a low windowsill and leaned on it, arms folded.

'Just look at Proud,' Marlowe muttered from the corner of his mouth. 'I think he might burst before the night is out.'

'What?' Johns inclined his head. 'I can't hear a thing with this netting round my head.'

Marlowe nudged him in the ribs and leaned closer. 'Nothing. I was just gossiping. Have you seen Cecil's costume, by the way? What an inspired choice. A mole, its little questing nose always busy, its paws always digging. And he also can just wear his ordinary clothes, with some pink gloves.'

Johns looked around vaguely. 'To be frank, Kit, I wouldn't recognise my mother if she were here. I really can't see much, either. When can we take these damned costumes off?'

'Midnight is the usual time, I believe,' Marlowe said.

'And what time is it now?'

'I haven't heard a clock strike lately but I think it's about seven.'

Johns let his head fall forward in defeat. Five more hours in his veil of darkness might just be four and a half hours too many.

'Once the entertainment is done, though, we could perhaps compromise and let you take the veiling off. I have business to do tonight and I don't want you falling over or cannoning into people while I can't guide you.'

'Business?' Johns leaned closer. 'Did you say business? What business?'

'Best you don't know, Michael.' Marlowe patted his velvet arm with his velvet gloved hand. 'Best you don't know.'

'Evening, Kit.' A sea serpent had insinuated itself to Marlowe's side, its head resting on his shoulder, its pricked tail curling round Michael Johns.

'Good evening. Do I have the pleasure of addressing Jörmungandr?'

The tail tipped back its hat and beamed at Marlowe. 'I knew you'd know! I said to Jane, Kit will know who we are.'

The sea serpent opened lazy eyelids and, looking beyond them, Marlowe could see the beautiful blue eyes of Jane Dee.

'Do I assume that the little Dees are making up the body of the world serpent?' he asked.

Little voices raised in greeting confirmed that he was right.

'Jörmungandr, can I ask a favour? I have some business to conduct this evening and Master Johns here is a little hampered by his costume …'

'Very nice, by the way,' Jane Dee's voice echoed from the serpent's head, its drooping whiskers wafting on the breeze from the window. 'Moonlight and night. Very effective.'

'Thank you,' Marlowe said. 'I think it works. But if you could just make sure he doesn't fall over or similar, until we can take the costumes off …'

Little voices from the belly of the beast were raised in protest.

'They don't want to take it off,' Dee explained. 'They rather enjoy being a serpent.'

'Who doesn't?' Marlowe said, leaning down to ruffle what he thought might be a head. 'But if you could, I would be very grateful.'

'Of course we will,' Dee said, replacing the serpent's tail on his head. 'It would be a pleasure. And afterwards, perhaps we can touch on transmutation for a while.'

The serpent's head fluttered its eyelashes at Marlowe. 'There, you see. A marriage made in heaven. Off you go, Kit, and do your business. And …' the head lowered and Marlowe planted a kiss on its papery brow, '… take care.'

'Don't worry,' he said. 'I will.' And, like moonlight behind a cloud, he was gone.

Henslowe stepped forward. He had seen more Prologues than most men had had hot dinners, but this was the first one he had ever delivered. It was at the specific request of the Lord Admiral and although nothing overt had been said, he understood the hidden message that this would rile Proud beyond measure and so simply had to be done. He had written it himself and had performed it once or twice for his wife, who had very kindly said that it would do very well indeed, and so, here he was, knees knocking with nerves, but standing centre stage and ready to proclaim. The lack of the Queen had been a disappointment at first, but now he was glad. She had been known to throw things.

'O, for a muse of fire that would ascend the brightest heaven of invention! A kingdom for a stage, princes to act, and monarchs to behold the swelling scene!' Damn! Henslowe realised too late that he should have cut that bit, with Gloriana not here and all. He had forgotten what comes next and glanced at the sheet of paper in his trembling hand. 'Umm … But pardon, gentles all the flat unraisèd spirits that hath dared on this unworthy scaffold to bring forth so great an object.' No. The words had gone again. He thought back to all the times he had cursed Alleyn and Burbage for having to use a prompter. He would never be angry with them again if the words would just come back into his head. 'Oh, yes, umm, the perilous narrow ocean parts asunder, piece out our imperfections with your thoughts. Admit me chorus to this history, who, prologue-like, your humble patience pray gently to hear, kindly to judge our play.' That was it! He had done it. Mistress Henslowe led the applause, realising as she did so that she had not taken a breath since he had walked onto the stage. She almost forgave him for the costumes, his and hers robins, his a magnificent brown velvet suit of clothes with a scarlet front, hers, just brown.

No sooner had Henslowe cleared the stage but Alleyn and Burbage came prancing on, mermen, like Proud but with more sparkle and glitter and with bravely bared chests. They led a whole host of cavorting sea life, from mermaids with carefully arranged blonde tresses glued down over pert breasts, to one rather sullen sardine. The whale, when it came on to its cue in the song, was underwhelming in the end, the scene-builders having done their best but somehow failed to capture the majesty of the animal. It looked somewhat like an upturned rowing boat painted blue, which was unsurprising as that was what it was.

But the audience was mellow, thanks to the circulating trays of goblets of the best the Admiral's cellar could provide and small gobbets of food, salmon from the Thames, smoked venison from Howard's country estates and a whole flock of larks' tongues in aspic. As the entertainment wended its way through increasingly dull scenes all written to praise the Queen but written in language so arcane and high flown that even Dee and Johns, undoubtedly the most intelligent men in the room, missed almost all of it. Indeed, the sea serpent's tail was dozing against night's inky shoulder long before the cast assembled on stage for the rousing final number.

Marlowe had not given up his search for Poley and he knew in his heart that Poley had not given up his search either. In some ways, it scarcely mattered who killed whom, as one man was already dead and the other had disappeared from his native country so comprehensively that he was, to everyone who mattered, also no longer among the living. But one of them would be no longer breathing by this night's end, Marlowe was determined on that. He had been scouring the figures at the masque since he had arrived. It was hard, amongst all the costumes, to find the man he sought, but he had quickly ruled out many as being too old, too short, too frail or otherwise not what he was looking for. He also felt that Poley would disguise himself in a way that did not displease his ego – he was many things, was Robyn Poley, but no one could ever call him shy and retiring. Not for him the simple costume of a hat on ordinary clothes. Poley would go for the grand gesture and so as soon as he saw Leviathan rising from the deep, he knew he had his man. The costume was imaginatively made, with a wide hood pulled down to almost shield the face to create the idea of a huge head emerging from the water, which streamed down all around the body, created of ribbons of blue and green. Small fish were sewn to the ribbons and all down the sleeves and the man's Venetians were studded with starfish and barnacles dusted with gold. Oh, yes, this was such a costume that Poley would revel in and Marlowe was soon on his trail. He realised that perhaps his moonlight costume would not be the easiest thing to follow someone in, but he didn't care – he would be confronting the man in any event, so whether it was soon or late, he didn't much care. Sidling round the room, behind the seated audience, he slipped through the door a heartbeat or two behind the spy and out into the dark corridor beyond. The music became a murmur and then a mere vibration on the air as he padded silently up a staircase which wound its way up into the darkness.

'I think that went well,' Alleyn said with unusual generosity to Proud, as they gathered in one of the disrobing rooms off the makeshift stage.

Proud looked at him and almost bared his teeth. 'Well? *Well?* It was a catalogue of disasters.'

'I wouldn't say that,' Burbage said, coming up on his other side. 'I think my portrayal of the forsaken merman had not a dry eye in the house.'

'Forsaken?' Proud's eyes were wide. 'Is that what you were doing? What brought forsaken into it, for the love of Poseidon?'

'Well,' Burbage waved an airy hand. 'It was a little … bleak, wasn't it?' He turned to Alleyn, who nodded. 'When a part is underwritten, I like to flesh it out myself. Give it some … depth.'

'Like the Blasphemer,' Alleyn chimed in. 'A one dimensional cypher if ever one trod the boards.'

'What?' Proud bristled. 'What do you two posing popinjays know about anything? Neither of you could act a … a … dish of frumenty off the stage. You,' he pointed at Alleyn, '*you* are just flashing your bits at everyone and hoping for a rich widow and *you*,' his finger quivered as it swung round to Burbage like a compass in a storm, 'you just stand there pulling faces like something demented. When I am running the Rose, you two are out. Do you hear me, *out.*'

'When you're what?' A quiet voice had joined the trio and they all spun round to see Henslowe standing there, as truculent as any robin after the last worm in the grass.

Proud looked him up and down. He was stepped in too far now – it would be far more tedious to go back than go over so he just went over. 'Yes. Yes, old man. When I am running the Rose, which will be tomorrow, at a guess. When I am running the Rose, these two are out and so are you.'

Henslowe had eaten better men than this for breakfast and the one thing he had learned early on was to not argue. Men like Proud were a groat a dozen and just leaving them to dig their own graves was a method which had never failed him. He was getting a little tired of being called old, but that too could be an argument for another day. As it was, he had noticed Matilda and Mistress Henslowe in earnest conversation as everyone mingled after the entertainment had ended and that really was something that could end his life as he knew it. This poltroon he would save for tomorrow.

'As you say,' he said to Proud. 'I'll see you in my office in the morning.'

Proud watched him go, a sneer across his face. 'He is finished,' he said to whoever would listen. Alleyn and Burbage had wandered off, but Shaxsper and Sledd were all ears.

'Did I hear you say you will be running the Rose?' Sledd checked.

'Yes. And you're out as well. Call yourself a stage manager? That whale was a joke.'

'Whales take a bit longer than twenty-four hours, as a rule,' Sledd said mildly. 'I think the spout worked well.'

'Very effective,' Shaxsper said. 'I got thoroughly soaked, as did the front row of the seating.'

'That was that idiot with the siphon,' Proud snapped. 'No one can do a simple job around here. And where was Marlowe, that's what I want to know. I thought he would be watching, eating his heart out that he wasn't asked. Because he gets asked to do everything, after all.'

'Well, he is dead, I suppose,' Shaxsper said reasonably.

'Oh, you utter … sardine!' Proud screamed. 'Everyone

knows Marlowe isn't dead. Can't we stop this nonsense?'

'Marlowe's alive?' The geese gaggled round Proud, patting at his costume, tugging on his sleeve. 'Is this true, Tom? Will?' Their eyes were shining.

Proud shrugged them off. 'Oh, for the love of …' and the swinging door into the corridor cut off the rest of what he was saying.

'Well,' Alleyn said, peering round a complaisant goose dressed as a sea anemone, 'he isn't very nice, is he, boys and girls?'

All Proud could hear on the other side of the door was their laughter. He had had enough of being laughed at. Quite enough.

Poley's costume had been well thought out. Although to a casual glance it was colourful enough, it nevertheless blended into the darkness almost perfectly. The gold paint on the barnacles on his legs was dull and didn't reflect the light. The ribbons were also matte and they didn't make a sound as the projectioner headed up and up through the building. Marlowe knew that he was glowing like the rising moon he was, picking up every scrap of light coming through the windows. The sun had set, but the sky was still light and every landing he passed seemed to feed the glow until he could almost light his own path. He didn't know quite what Poley was looking for, but he knew it would be something to which he had no right. Sensitive documents were stored in Gray's Inn and it could be anything. He was closing in on his quarry. At first, he had just seen a door swinging to, or a pair of heels around a corner, but now he could see the man's back as he went through a door at the end of the passage. Breaking into a stealthy trot, Marlowe was through it before it had had a chance to close.

He gasped. He was no longer hunting through twilight landings and stairs. He was out on a narrow balcony that edged the roof. A tower rose behind him, not very high, and the roof of a lower level chevroned down to his left. To his right, stood Leviathan, a dagger in his upraised hand.

The world serpent was sitting on the low windowsill, its head bent to cradle the sections of its midriff which were now fast asleep. Its tail was in earnest conversation with the dead of night. Jane Dee had never expected life with her husband to be very normal, but somehow this summed it all up in its extreme eccentricity. The conversation above her head seemed to hinge upon the nature of reality when applied to the transmutation of base metals, something she had heard many times before. She was a practical woman so had never pointed out to her husband that, should he ever succeed in transmuting base metals into gold, gold would become as worthless as … well, base metals. She would leave him to discover that, should he ever manage it.

Night suddenly looked out into the room, as best he could.

'Where's Kit?' he asked, anxiously.

'He had business, he said,' Dee told him. 'With Kit that could mean he would be gone five minutes or a year. There's no telling.'

'I know, but … oh, to Hell with waiting for midnight. This veil is driving me to distraction. Can you help me unwind it?'

Dee raised deft hands to undo the knots that held the veil in place and Johns emerged blinking into the light.

'Is it really bright in here?' he asked.

'Not particularly,' Dee said. 'It's the veil. It's made your eyes sensitive. Give it a moment.'

Johns looked around. 'There are some quite extraordinary costumes here tonight,' he said. 'All manner of beasts. I see mermaids are quite the fashion.'

'Jane wanted to be a mermaid,' Dee said. 'But it would have meant … well, it would have meant exposing more than a married woman with children should expose. So we went for the world serpent instead.'

'Leviathan has gone,' Johns said.

'How can you tell?' Dee asked. 'I didn't think you could see too well.'

'I looked particularly,' Johns said, 'because I assumed it was Nicholas Faunt.'

'No, it isn't Faunt,' Jane Dee said. 'He's over there, look, dressed as a tree. Well, a bush, more, I suppose.'

'How do you know Nicholas Faunt?' Dee asked sharply.

'Oh, you know, round and about,' his wife said, batting her serpent eyelashes in an attempt to change the subject.

'If Nicholas is the bush, then who was Leviathan?' Johns asked.

'I don't know,' Dee said. 'But Leviathan isn't the only person to have slipped out, surely. I would have thought anyone with an ear for music would have wanted to be elsewhere during that awful duet between Ned Alleyn and that girl dressed as a squid.'

'I don't trust Leviathan,' Johns muttered.

'I don't think even God trusted him much, did he?' Dee asked, trying to lighten the mood. 'Let's call Faunt over.' He whistled and gestured Faunt to join them. With difficulty, the bush removed itself from the clutches of an aged duchess dressed as a Dryad.

'Master Dee,' he said. 'Johns.' There was a pause. 'Mistress Dee.' The serpent averted its gaze. 'How can I help you?'

'Where is Leviathan?' Johns asked.

'Er … in the deeps, if I remember my Bible,' Faunt said.

'The one in here. The one in the hood.'

Faunt shrugged. 'No idea,' he said. He shrugged off some of his foliage. 'The thing about masques is they don't come round that often. I suppose the best thing we can say is that we won't be having any more of these. The old girl can't last much longer, surely.' He knew he was committing treason as he said it. But he was among friends.

'Ill met by moonlight, Robyn,' Marlowe said, taking a step back, feeling for safe footing.

'I have been chasing you round London for days,' Poley said. 'This was the only way I could be sure to get you to myself.'

'You only had to ask,' Marlowe said reasonably. 'We could have had a sit down, talked over old times. Had a drink perhaps. Ale, or have you developed a taste for the exotic while you have been away?'

'Let's not bandy words, Marlowe,' Poley sneered, throwing back his hood. 'We both know that all we want to do is put a knife between the other's ribs. And I shall be doing that, any moment now. But before I do, let me say that when I was asked to kill you, I didn't really need to be given money, although that was a pleasant extra. I would have killed you anyway. Killed you for being what you are. Arrogant. Untouchable. Protected wherever you go. Before you came along, *I* was the projectioner who everyone wanted to work with. *I* was the one who had the ear of those who mattered. I was on my way to fame – infamy perhaps, but fame in my eyes – fame and fortune. And then, you.'

'I never wanted to be a projectioner, Robyn,' Marlowe pointed out, steadying himself against the eaves. 'I was happy with my poetry, my plays. Enjoying a pipe or two, the banter of friends. Since that first day that I was summoned to Francis Walsingham's room, I have had to watch every word I speak, every move I make. I can never get drunk, make love, lose myself in someone's eyes. So, when people say "Marlowe's dead" they are not as wrong as you might think.'

Poley laughed. 'Don't try to make me pity you, Marlowe,' he said. 'I was talked out of killing you once before, so don't think you will do it again. You promised once to kill me and I know you meant it. So I will never be safe, while you live. It doesn't take a genius – or the damned Muse's darling for that matter – to work out that I will have to kill you. And as I have a knife in my hand and you don't even have one on your body … quod erat demonstrandum, as we used to say at school.'

'How do you know I don't have a knife?'

'I don't think you realise how very revealing your costume is, Master Marlowe,' Leviathan told him. 'Your cloak is tissue, your doublet fits like a glove. I wonder there is room for a layer of skin in your breeches. I made sure that I took a close look all around you when you arrived. You should have worn Johns' costume. Plenty of places for concealment in all that dead black.'

'You are cleverer than people think, Robyn,' Marlowe said quietly. 'No one can pull the wool over your eyes, that's for certain.'

'Being underestimated has often stood me in good stead,' Poley told him. 'But here, there is no need to estimate or underestimate. I have a knife and you do not. Your years with Walsingham have clearly taught you nothing. Take your bow on the world, Marlowe. This is the final curtain.'

The door into the great hall of Gray's Inn flew open and everyone turned to see who it was who had arrived so very spectacularly late. A flunkey stood there, still dressed as a merman, ready to speed the departing guests.

'My Lords,' he said, 'Ladies and Gentlemen.' Old habits were dying hard. 'I hesitate to interrupt but …' then the excitement took hold and he pointed wildly above his head, 'but two monsters are fighting on the roof. A monster of the deep, it looks to be, and … well, the moon!'

For a moment, no one moved and then all was chaos. The room emptied in an almost impossibly short time, leaving Effingham struggling with his tail and trident. A few of the guests who had visited the contents of his cellar rather too often were convinced that something was stuck to the ceiling and peered upwards in growing confusion. Almost everyone followed the flunkey outside. Only Johns and Faunt ran for the stairs.

Outside in the street, everyone looked up at the small turret that overlooked Gray's Inn. It was little more than a folly atop the building and was fronted by a small ledge with a low balustrade. Two men could be seen, some twenty feet above the cobbles, one with a knife raised, the other pressing back against the slates of an abutting roof. One was dark and menacing, the other shone like molten silver in the light of the rising moon.

After the first flight of stairs, Michael Johns was flagging. It wasn't his usual way to go hurtling about, climbing stairs at lightning speed. Flashing lights were in his eyes and his chest was hurting. Faunt was almost a flight ahead before he noticed. He went back down to where the dominus was leaning on the banister, a hand to his chest.

'Michael. Stay here. I can do whatever is necessary, you know I can.'

Johns shook his head. He swallowed hard. 'No,' he grated out. 'I just need a moment. Just a moment …'

'Stay here. Come up when you're able. I must go.' Faunt looked anxiously up the stairs. He thought he could hear voices from above. While he had been climbing, he had been counting turns but this had made him lose count. He wasn't even sure whether Marlowe and Poley – because it had to be Poley – were on the topmost floor. What if there was an attic? Another whole floor, even? He cursed himself for having grown a soft heart. Not so long ago, he would have gone on ahead, leaving Johns to his fate. But now, that just wasn't possible.

Johns shook his head again and stood up, squaring his shoulders. 'I can do this,' he murmured. 'I eat well. I barely drink. I carry enormous piles of books all over Lincoln's Inn. I climb stairs all the time. I don't know why …' He collapsed back again in a fit of coughing, which he tried to suppress behind a fist.

'It's the tension, knowing Kit is up there. But … Michael. You have to stay here. Or go back down. I just can't wait.' Faunt's ears pricked up. A door had clicked shut above them and he raised his eyes and locked the position in his head. Without trying to reason with Johns any more, he crept up the stairs like a cat and slid through the door he had heard closing like a shadow.

Down on his landing. Johns leaned back, his head resting on the wall, his chest heaving. He willed his heart to be still.

On their balcony, giving a strictly last and never to be repeated performance for the audience below, Marlowe and Poley locked eyes. The moonlight glinted on the blade and on

Marlowe's costume. Down below on the ground, Henslowe looked anxiously up but mixed with his worry for his most profitable playwright was a faint jealousy that, no matter how costly the flares or subtle the wardrobe, nothing he would ever put on could hold a candle to this. He hoped that somewhere in this crowd was an artist who would be able to commit it to canvas one day, doing it the justice it deserved. Marlowe put a foot out to balance on the balustrade and for a heart stopping moment lost his balance. Below him, the crowd gasped as one.

'Careful, Machiavel,' Poley sneered, taking a step nearer. 'I don't mind if you die falling from a height, but I really would prefer you to die on my blade. Also, of course, now that the crowds have gathered, I would imagine that your friends are on their way, pounding up the stairs. So, I fear we can't continue our little chat.'

'One thing, before we part,' Marlowe said. 'Something I must know. Who paid you to kill me, before Faunt outbid him?'

'I've kept his secret until now,' Poley said, 'and I see no reason to change that. So, you'll just have to die in ignorance. Perhaps Lucifer will take pity on you and tell you. Who knows? As for now, though, die bravely for the nice ladies and gentlemen, Christopher. Farewell.'

Poley tucked his hand in against his own belt and drew Marlowe in, as if to embrace him. There was a dull noise, not loud, but enough to chill the blood of anyone with acute hearing. The men stood together, swaying, Marlowe's head dropped on Poley's shoulder.

Poley pulled back and looked Marlowe in the face. 'How?' he said, on an outward breath. 'I looked everywhere.'

'But not up my sleeve,' Marlowe said, pulling the knife out from under Poley's ribcage. 'I always keep something up my sleeve, Robyn. Just unlucky for you that this time it wasn't a mighty line but a neat stiletto.' He pushed the man away and he fell onto the balustrade, looking up at him with misting eyes. 'Will you still not tell me?'

Poley smiled as a ribbon of red oozed out of the corner of his mouth. 'In Hell, Marlowe,' he said. 'I'll tell you in Hell.'

CHAPTER 15

Christopher Marlowe had killed men before. He had decided some years before to not keep count because it somehow didn't seem right, to count souls he had sent to perdition. But he did intend to remember this one, the time, the date, the phase of the moon when he had taken the life of Robert Poley, a man who had sworn to kill him and who he too had sworn to kill. He stepped back onto the landing, out of the eyes of the crowd, and spent a moment in reflection. He heard footsteps and opened his eyes, to see Nicholas Faunt approaching. Nicholas Faunt was always approaching, so that was not that much of a surprise. It occurred to him that Faunt was probably the one man in Holborn that night who didn't know what had just happened.

'Poley is dead, Nicholas,' he said.

'As you are still standing, I thought he must be.' Faunt said. 'Where is he?'

'Outside.' Marlowe gestured with his thumb. 'On a little balcony out there.'

'I'll see to it,' Faunt said.

Marlowe looked at him. 'Of course you will,' he said. 'Should I … wait for the Under-Sheriff?'

'The last I saw of him was dressed as a crab and in the crowd heading outside. I think he considers himself very much off-duty tonight. Wine has been taken, shall we say? He won't be much of a witness in the morning. But, Kit, can you go down to the next landing? Michael is there and in a bad way.'

'Michael? Why? Is he hurt?'

'He found the stairs a bit much. He … he just needs to have a sit down, I think. But if he sees you are all right, it will help.'

Marlowe went down to the flight below and found Johns clambering to his feet. The dominus saw his favourite student and held out a hand in speechless greeting.

'Michael,' Marlowe said, bluntly. 'You look awful. Those black clothes do not flatter a grey face at all.'

Johns laughed, but weakly. 'It was all a bit too much. I'm not as healthy as I thought I was. Perhaps I should … what should I do? Take up tennis, perhaps? Rowing?'

'I think perhaps just not coming to masques with me when someone wants to kill me would be a good idea. After that we could think of tennis, even though it's a French game. Can I help you down the stairs?'

'I can go down myself. Did Nicholas find the man he was after?'

'Man? What man?'

'He went along that landing, there. I assumed it was to find you.'

'No, I was higher up and to the front. Wait here. I'll go and see what he was doing.'

Faunt was out on the balcony, calling down to some of the men who were constantly in attendance on the Admiral. Although they dressed as cooks and servants, they were to a man highly trained and would deal with the mess on the balcony in a very discreet and timely manner. The crowd had gone back inside. Although it was summer and warm, some of the costumes were only made of paper and let in the draughts of night.

'Nicholas? Did you find the man on the landing?'

'What? Oh, did Michael tell you?'

Marlowe nodded.

'We were following you and I lost my bearings on how many turns the stairs had taken when Michael felt ill. I followed footsteps along there and then I lost them. A wayward pair of lovers, probably, looking for some privacy.

Don't worry about it. It was nothing.'

Marlowe went back onto the landing and down the stairs. Johns was ahead, taking the stairs one step at a time. About to join him, Marlowe thought again and went along the landing, into the dark. He strained his ears, listening hard. The silence was so dense that it sang in his ears. He stopped, dropped his chin on his chest and listened hard. He tuned out the beating of his own heart, the thud of conversation from below, the halting step of Michael Johns on the stairs. Yes, there it was, the rustle of cloth, then a hiss, a hiss he recognized. He ducked and so almost missed the thud as a man's shoulder crashed into him, knocking him off balance. The knife he had thrown had missed by a whisker. In the dark, his silver costume had made him a sitting duck.

Whoever it was had put too much into the lunge which followed the knife, and he had winded himself as well as Marlowe. He lay there, gasping for breath and scrabbling for the knife. Marlowe had left his embedded in Robert Poley's ribs, so he knew it was essential that either he got to the knife first, or he kicked it away where neither of them could reach it. He rolled over and grabbed his assailant's wrist, pulling his hand back from the knife. Using the inertia of the man's body, he swung round and kicked the knife away, sending it skittering down the landing and out of reach.

'Who are you?' he grated, as he pulled on the man's arm. There was no light on the landing but there was a window at the end, letting in the moonlight. He dragged him closer to the window and sat across his chest, pinning him down. 'Proud?' he said, peering down at him. 'Proud? Is that you?'

The would-be impresario and playwright looked up at him, one eye already puffy from its unintended impact with Marlowe's shoulder.

'Kit? I didn't know it was you. I thought … I thought it was someone else.'

'Anyone in particular?' Marlowe asked, still astride the man.

'I saw someone come down this way,' Proud said. 'He was acting suspiciously and so I followed him. Then you came from nowhere and I suppose I panicked.' He coughed. 'I don't suppose you could get off my chest, could you? I can't really breathe very well with you sitting on me.'

Marlowe didn't move, but took some of his weight on his own knees, to release the pressure. He still looked into Proud's eyes, trying to decide how much of a threat he posed.

Proud took a deep breath and wriggled slightly. 'That's better but could you get off me? I really don't feel comfortable. I feel as if you suspect me of something.'

'I do suspect you of something,' Marlowe said. 'It's just that right at this moment, I am not totally sure what that might be.'

'I told you,' Proud said. 'I heard something. And yes, I will admit, I was in a temper. The masque was a disaster, everything that could go wrong did go wrong. I just needed to get away from everyone. So I came up here.'

'And you heard something. Me. But I could just as easily have been one of the denizens of Gray's Inn returning to his rooms. I could have been a goose and her latest conquest looking for somewhere quiet. You could have killed a perfectly innocent person. As you would have, indeed, had you killed me.'

Proud looked contrite. 'I told you. I was in a temper. Please get off.'

'Well, Master Proud, I don't think I will. It seems to me I have a tiger by the tail. In a moment, the men summoned by Nicholas Faunt to recover the body of Robert Poley will be passing the end of this corridor and all I need to do is call …'

'Robert Poley is dead?'

Marlowe was surprised. 'You knew Poley? I wouldn't have thought your paths would have crossed.'

'Oh, *Poley*. I thought you said something else. No, I don't know Robert *Poley*. Not at all. Some roughneck, was he? Killed in a brawl.'

Marlowe cocked his head and looked down at Proud by the light of the moon. 'Killed in a tavern brawl in an argument about the reckoning, perhaps,' he said.

'I beg your pardon? This isn't a tavern.'

'No, indeed not. This isn't Mistress Bull's Ordinary in Deptford, is it? Where I was supposed to meet my end. But any old port in a storm, if I can stick to the nautical theme of the evening for a moment.'

'I'm afraid I …'

'I am afraid you are scuppered, Master Proud. Your anchor is fouled. You are becalmed. You are, in short, found out and will soon be in the care of the Sheriff of London.'

'What for?' Proud's previously rather ingratiating face had taken on a malevolent leer in the grey light streaming in through the window. 'I think you will find that I have done nothing wrong. Assuming for a moment that I did pay Poley to kill you at Deptford, he's dead now and Frizer was always just his lackey. He won't know. And I think you'll find that trying to see off Henslowe and take over the Rose isn't a crime. It's just fair business. I deserve it. I am the better man. I have always been the better man. At Corpus I was the better man.'

Marlowe looked down and felt sorry for him. He saw a man who had plenty but wanted more. He had talent, but wanted it to exceed that of others. He had an education beyond what many could dream of, but wanted it to carry him beyond its limits. He saw a little man in a bigger man's body. He saw someone who would always climb over dead bodies rather than work to succeed.

'I pity you, Proud,' he said. 'Have you ever been happy?'

'When I thought you were dead, I was happy,' Proud said. 'But not as a rule, I confess, no.' He let his body slump, his back go loose and his head lolled to one side. It took Marlowe by surprise and he knelt up a little more, to give his captive some air. With an almighty heave, Proud threw his hips in the air and catapulted Marlowe away. Too late, Marlowe remembered that Proud had always helped out around the theatre, carrying things which some men would have trouble simply lifting off the floor. He fell awkwardly and before he knew it, Proud was behind him, his hand over his mouth. Faunt's men were passing the end of the landing, carrying Poley's body on a makeshift stretcher, and they didn't even glance in their direction. Two floors beneath them, the band, released from the strictures of Proud's commissioned sea shanty dirges, were kicking up a storm and the sound of heels on the boards and the whoops of the dancers drowned out almost anything else.

'When I killed you again, that pointless popinjay Willoughby, I was happy then. When I got rid of Skeres, that blackmailer, I wasn't happy but I reached a kind of mild content. This masque got in the way of my plans. When the weight on the gantry didn't get you, I had planned something more … well, something more elegant. I was going to lure you to the theatre, late one night after the performance. I was going to send a message signed by Shaxsper. His handwriting is so chaotic a child of four could forge it. It would be to say he was going home to Stratford, back to his Nancy, and he wanted to say goodbye. You would have swallowed it, hook, line and sinker … nautical theme again, you see. And I would have killed you. Slowly. I had plans to … well, why spoil the surprise? I can do all that now.'

Proud moved his hand from across Marlowe's mouth. 'The trouble with you, Proud,' Marlowe said, 'is that you don't do your research, do you? Life, like plays, need research. There's poor old Will, trying to write his *Richard* and he reads and reads his Holinshed and gets so bogged down. But he does at least know his stuff. He wouldn't make a stupid mistake. Like you. You killed Willoughby because he had a passing resemblance to me. Did it not occur to you that if I was being declared dead left and right that, if I were still alive, I would change my appearance. Which of course, I did. So why kill the only man in London who looked like me?'

Proud didn't answer, but put a threatening arm around Marlowe's throat and applied some pressure. 'Go on,' he growled. 'While you still can.'

'Nicholas Skeres had not got the brains God gave sheep,' Marlowe said. 'If he tried blackmail, all you need have done was to say no. He would have had no answer to that. He would have taken an angel and wandered away, to carry on being a more or less harmless walking gentleman.'

'I think you underestimate him. He seemed intent on

doing me down, right from the start. Always wanting lines in the play, asking for more.'

'He was just stage struck. There was really no need to have killed him. Unless, of course, you rather enjoy it by now. When you swung that weight at me in the theatre, you didn't care how many others died.'

'We paid their widows handsomely. I don't expect they will mourn for long.'

'This may surprise you, Adam,' Marlowe twisted in his grip but it was implacable. 'It may surprise you to learn that some people love people more than money and power.'

'Romantic nonsense,' Proud said. 'Money and power are what all people want. And fame as well, for some.'

'I would rather have people,' Marlowe said, and meant it.

'That's easy for you to say, though, isn't it?' Proud said. 'The Muse's darling. The groundlings' darling. Everybody's damned darling. And for what? You never met a law you didn't break. Laws of God and man. And yet, you come up smelling of roses. You come to a masque, quite openly, dressed like the moon himself. While I have to wear this load of tat, got up like something washed up on the tide. The geese all love you, there isn't a man jack of the Rose company who doesn't follow your every word …'

'To be fair, they are actors. That's what they're supposed to do.'

'And that's it. They learn the words. They sound like angels when they say them. But mine … they can't even bring a whale in on cue.'

'There's the *Blasphemer's Tragedy*.'

'What's that got to do with it?'

'You wrote it.'

'Say that I did. But who would know? It has your name on it and if it didn't, there wouldn't be anyone in the audience.'

'I think you over-estimate the discernment of the audience of the Rose. Don't forget, *Ralph Royster Doyster* played to packed houses for weeks.'

The forearm tightened its grip. 'Enough of this,' Proud

hissed. 'I had planned to fillet you, bit by bit, until you had no blood left in your body, but I think in fact I will just strangle you, slowly, while you contemplate your end.'

Marlowe shrugged as best he could. 'I can face my end,' he said. 'I have had more time than you had planned for me to have and somehow, I can see that as my swansong. I have sent Poley to where he deserves and when I meet him there shortly I can tell him that I know who paid him to kill me. That will make eternity really annoying for him, I think, so that will amuse me for a millennium or two. But, you know, I would really like to die with London in my view, not the end of this dark landing. Could we go to the window, so I can see the old girl once more. I wasn't born here, or educated here, but I have lived my fullest here. It seems only right that she should see me into my goodnight.'

'It's a trick,' Proud said. 'You always have a trick up your sleeve.'

'I do, as a rule,' Marlowe said. 'But tonight, my trick ended up between Poley's ribs. I don't have another. I know you hate me, Master Proud, and that's a shame, because I have done nothing to you. But I would deem it the greatest favour if you would just let me watch out of the window while I die.'

Proud was silent for a while, thinking it through. Eventually, he said, 'You'll have to work with me, to get up. Any tricks, and I'll snap your neck like a twig.'

'I understand. I think if we both sit, then kneel. Yes, that's it. And now stand.' He coughed as Proud's arm tightened as they changed position. 'It's as well we're young and limber, eh? You couldn't do this with someone older. When you kill Henslowe, you'll have to be better prepared. Like I told you. Planning.'

'I don't plan to kill Henslowe,' Proud protested.

'Of course you do. Men like you, they don't stop killing. You have a taste for it now. Anyone who gets in your way will meet a sticky end. Take it from me.'

Proud dragged him across to the window, decked out by someone as a little reading nook. The low sill had cushions on it and a book, lying face down. Proud peered at it in the moonlight. 'Oh, what a shame. I thought it might be one of yours. The final irony. There,' he tugged Marlowe upright, his back arching to relieve the worst of the pressure, 'your city. Say goodbye.'

They stood, looking out over the silvered rooftops. From close by, a church bell started to toll.

'How apposite,' Proud said. 'The passing bell. How did they know, do you think?'

Without warning, a patch of darkness detached itself from the wall halfway down the landing and lunged at Proud, hitting him in the middle of the back. His arms flew up and Marlowe fell sideways, clutching his throat. Proud's shins hit the low sill and his hands crashed through the leaded panes. His balance in ruins, he fell through, clutching hopelessly at the edges of the window as he fell. The crash of glass was still on the air when there was a dull thud from below, followed by a scream.

Marlowe looked up at the man standing over him, a hand extended to help him to his feet. 'Michael,' he said, throatily. 'Feeling better, I see.'

'Right as a trivet,' the man in black said.

'What does that mean, exactly?' Marlowe said. 'I've always wondered.' And fell into step with his old dominus as they made for the stairs.

CHAPTER 16

Without much thinking about it, Will Shaxsper found himself singing along under his breath with the bell sounding outside hi dingy lodgings. 'When I grow rich, say the bells of Shoreditch.' When I grow rich! What a joke. He had never believed the old adage that the streets of London were paved with gold, but they were, at least, more inviting than the streets of Stratford.

It had been quite a while since he'd been back. His old birthplace was still there, but it was falling apart. Hell, it was falling apart when he was born. Because his father was such an arsehole, the entire Shaxsper family were despised, not just in the town, but in the county generally. Then there was Anne, the unlovely shrew, a woman whose face could turn milk.

So, London it had been, with its colour and its music, its poetry and its sheer *life*. But the Muse was not with William Shaxsper, the hated glover's son, with his flat Warwickshire vowels and his annoying habit of pinching other people's ideas. No the Muse was with …

'Kit.' The man looked up as Marlowe stood in the doorway. 'I didn't hear you come in.'

'It's those damned bells,' Marlowe laughed. 'How can you stand this, morning, noon and night?'

'Needs must,' Shaxsper shrugged. He didn't let Marlowe know that these were his third lodgings in as many months, on account of sundry misunderstandings with the previous two landlords.

Marlowe sat himself down, removing a scruffy pile of papers so that he could. 'How's *Richard* coming along?'

Shaxsper looked at him. Part of the Warwickshire man wished he had never mentioned the damned play. Part of him wished he hadn't let Marlowe write half ... oh, all right, three quarters, of his *Henry IV Both Parts*. But all that was water under London Bridge now and it was just too late.

'It's no good, Kit,' Shaxsper said. 'I've given it my best shot. God, I even toyed with going into business with Adam Proud, God rot him. Let's face it ...' he threw his quill down, 'I'm never going to make it as a playwright. I miss Anne. I miss the children. Hamnet is getting to the age when he needs his father. I even, in a strange way, miss Stratford.'

'But I,' Marlowe said in somebody else's voice, 'that am not shaped for sportive tricks, nor made to court an amorous looking glass. I, that am rudely stamped ...'

'Who are you quoting?' Shaxsper asked.

'You,' Marlowe said. 'Me. Both of us.'

Shaxsper was confused. 'What are you talking about?'

'I see your Richard character doing his own prologue. He sits on the edge of the O, whispering to the groundlings – you know how they love that. He tells them the war is over and it's all a weak, piping time of peace. Well, all that's for the milk sops, the weaklings, the meek who will never actually inherit the earth. He, Richard, has other ideas. He'll murder his way to the top, what did we say in *Henry VI*? 'Set the murderous Machiavel to school. Can I do this and cannot get a crown? Tut – were it further off, I'd pluck it down.' Marlowe smiled at his friend's confusion. 'It's all in here, Will,' he said. 'All of it. Richard will be the most Machiavellian villain since, well, Machiavelli.'

'Machiavel,' Shaxsper nodded.

'Aha,' Marlowe said. 'And there's the rub. Machiavel – Kit Marlowe – is dead, as everybody knows. He can't write *Richard III* or anything else ... But William Shakespeare can.'

'What?'

'Come on, Will. Remember when I first knew you.

You had such plans. You were going to use the name Shakespeare and take the theatrical world by storm.'

Shaxsper laughed, but there was no mirth in it. 'That was then,' he said.

'Yes. And now is now. All that is different is that Kit Marlowe is dead. Time for the Muse to take on another darling.'

'Do you think it'll work?' Shaxsper was dubious.

'It might not,' Marlowe said. 'So,' he stood up, 'you're probably right, Will. Fame and fortune – well, they're not all they're cracked up to be, are they? Far better to have a nagging wife with a ghastly family, snot-stained kids and the life of a parish clerk. Or, better still, a country schoolmaster. No, forget I mentioned it. Let me know when you're leaving, though. I'd like to say goodbye.'

Marlowe was halfway out of the door. 'Wait a minute. So, let's see if I've got this right …'

'I'll write the plays. You take the credit. You can flog whatever I write to Henslowe or Effingham or the man in the moon for all I care. But I have to live, Will. Shall we say, fifty-fifty?'

He held out a hand, but still Shaxsper hesitated.

'William Shakespeare,' Marlowe let the words roll around his tongue. '*Sir* William Shakespeare, the Bard of Avon.' He let his raised hands fall. 'Oh, well,' and turned his back.

He was halfway down the stairs when Shaxsper was at the top of them. 'How does sixty-forty sound, Kit, eh?'

AUTHOR'S NOTE

According to the historical record, Christopher Marlowe, playwright, poet and 'university wit' was stabbed to death in an Ordinary, an eating house belonging to Eleanor Bull, on Deptford Green on the evening of 30 May 1593.

The next day, a sixteen man jury heard evidence before the royal coroner, Sir William Danby, to explain how Marlowe died. The inquest, long forgotten and written almost entirely in Latin, was rediscovered by researchers centuries later and it raises more questions than it answers. This record claims that Marlowe arrived at Eleanor Bull's at about ten in the morning and spent the day drinking and walking in the garden in the company of three men – Robert Poley, Ingram Frizer and Nicholas Skeres. They played tables (backgammon) and after supper, a quarrel broke out between Frizer and Marlowe, ostensibly over who was going to pay the bill – 'the reckoning' – for the day's hospitality. Frizer was carrying a dagger in a sheath in the small of his back and Marlowe was lying behind him on the bed. Given to bursts of temper as Marlowe was reputed to be, he grabbed Frizer's dagger and hit him around the head with the hilt. The two men fought and it ended with Frizer's dagger being plunged into Marlowe's right eye socket. Death was almost certainly instantaneous.

Frizer was charged and imprisoned but released under the Queen's pardon in record time (twenty-nine days) and no further punishment followed. Today, most books on the period, even the well-written ones, contend that Marlowe was killed in a tavern brawl over a bill and that Frizer acted in self-defence.

All this would be acceptable if the three men with Marlowe in Deptford were anonymous travellers, but recent research has revealed that all of them, especially Robert Poley, worked for or on the fringes of Elizabethan espionage, as did Marlowe himself. There is nothing in Marlowe's character to suggest that he would lose his temper over what amounted to small change. He was almost certainly an atheist at a time when such beliefs, or lack thereof, incurred the death penalty by burning. He was undoubtedly a rebel – most of his plays were contentious and shocked polite society in his day and later. He may have been homosexual – and that 'crime' carried the death penalty too.

That Marlowe was a dangerous man cannot be doubted, but we have no idea why he was in Deptford at all. We know that he was arrested by Henry Maunder, the Queen's Messenger, on unspecified charges and that he had to report daily to the Court of the Star Chamber (in effect the Privy Council) in the weeks before his death. Coroner Danby worked for the Queen's government. He was a personal friend of Lord Burghley, the Queen's chancellor. Eleanor Bull, who kept the Ordinary, was Burghley's cousin. There is a sense of a net tightening on Kit Marlowe in May 1593 that makes the 'tavern brawl' seem an unlikely and superficial explanation.

Will we ever know what really happened at Deptford? Probably not, but today, Kit Marlowe is once again 'all fire and air', 'that pure elemental wit'. He is Shakespeare's 'dead shepherd' and the 'Muse's darling', he of the 'mighty line'. His ghost can be found in cobbled Canterbury, scholastic Cambridge, roaring London or anywhere where men's hearts and souls are free.

For more information, M.J. Trow and Taliesin Trow's gripping non-fiction account *Who Killed Kit Marlowe?* is available from Blkdog.

Other titles by BLKDOG Publishing for your consideration:

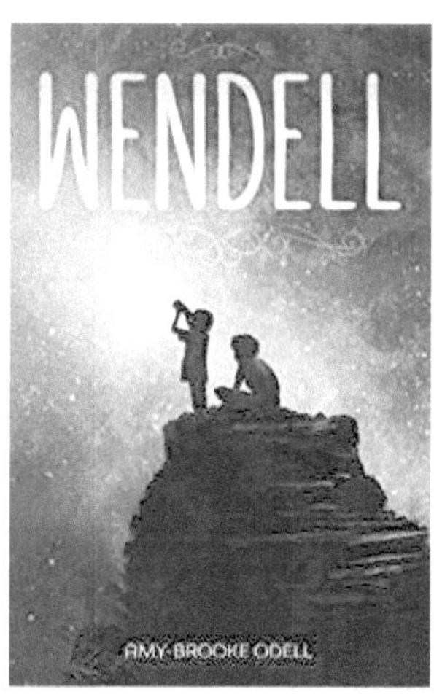

Wendell
By Amy-Brooke Odell

Wendell and his friends, both human and animal, embark on a journey to discover the truth about the Wind Folk and where his mother really is. His world of baseball, camp-outs, and fishing is rocked when he discovers that the adults in town know a lot more than they say, and sometimes those tales told around a campfire are true.

And, when it comes to the Wind Folk; it is said if you see one, you become one.

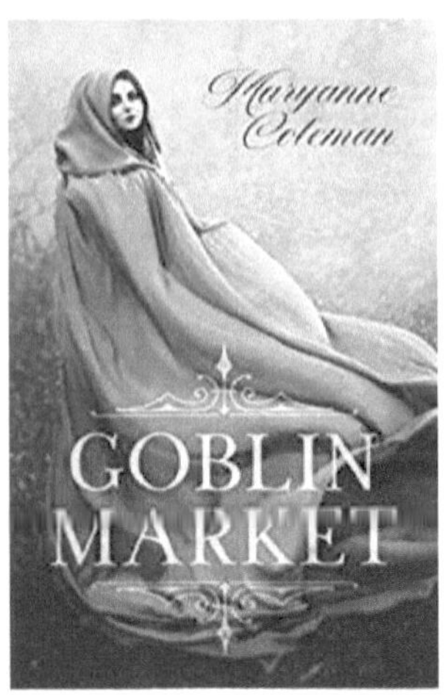

Goblin Market
By Maryanne Coleman

Have you ever wondered what happened to the faeries you used to believe in? They lived at the bottom of the garden and left rings in the grass and sparkling glamour in the air to remind you where they were. But that was then – now you might find them in places you might not think to look. They might be stacking shelves, delivering milk or weighing babies at the clinic. Open your eyes and keep your wits about you and you might see them.

But no one is looking any more and that is hard for a Faerie Queen to bear and Titania has had enough. When Titania stamps her foot, everyone in Faerieland jumps; publicity is what they need. Television, magazines. But that sort of thing is much more the remit of the bad boys of the Unseelie Court, the ones who weave a new kind of magic; the World Wide Web. Here is Puck re-learning how to fly; Leanne the agent who really is a vampire; Oberon's Boys playing cards behind the wainscoting; Black Annis, the bag-lady from Hainault, all gathered in a Restoration comedy that is strictly twenty-first century.

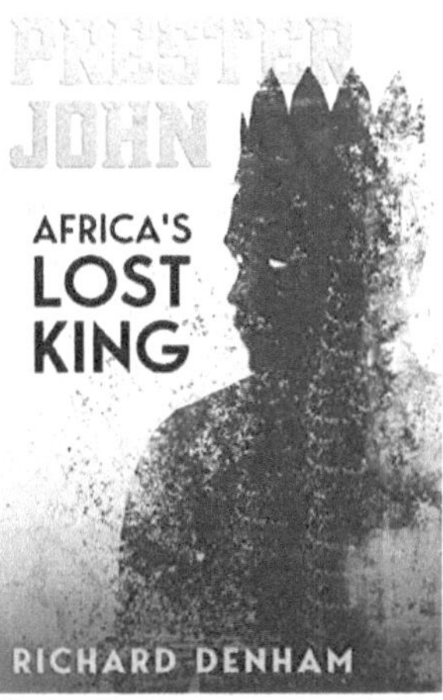

Prester John: Africa's Lost King
By Richard Denham

He sits on his jewelled throne on the Horn of Africa in the maps of the sixteenth century. He can see his whole empire reflected in a mirror outside his palace. He carries three crosses into battle and each cross is guarded by one hundred thousand men. He was with St Thomas in the third century when he set up a Christian church in India. He came like a thunderbolt out of the far East eight centuries later, to rescue the crusaders clinging on to Jerusalem. And he was still there when Portuguese explorers went looking for him in the fifteenth century.

Was he real? Did he ever exist? This book will take you on a journey of a lifetime, to worlds that might have been, but never were. It will take you, if you are brave enough, into the world of Prester John.

Fade
By Bethan White

There is nothing extraordinary about Chris Rowan. Each day he wakes to the same faces, has the same breakfast, the same commute, the same sort of homes he tries to rent out to unsuspecting tenants.

There is nothing extraordinary about Chris Rowan. That is apart from the black dog that haunts his nightmares and an unexpected encounter with a long forgotten demon from his past. A nudge that will send Chris on his own downward spiral, from which there may be no escape.

There is nothing extraordinary about Chris Rowan...

The Witch of Tessingham Hall
By Sinéad Spearing.

England 1657.

Alison, a folk- healer, stands falsely accused of murder by witchcraft, an allegation that sets in motion a powerful curse — "May your women forever wane!" — the spell haunting generations of her accuser's family, sending their women early to their graves.

London 2022.

Eden Flynn – an anxiety-ridden academic of Old English magic is invited for a job interview in the crypt of Southwark Cathedral, where her interviewer, the dashingly handsome geneticist Lord James Fabian, pulls her into the midst of his family secret: his sister is sick, and his daughter is showing signs of the same mental affliction.

Can Eden fulfil her part in the web which has been woven stronger and stronger over hundreds of years? Can she find the strength to break the bonds that bind her and Lord Fabian to the past? And can she live with the changes she will unleash?

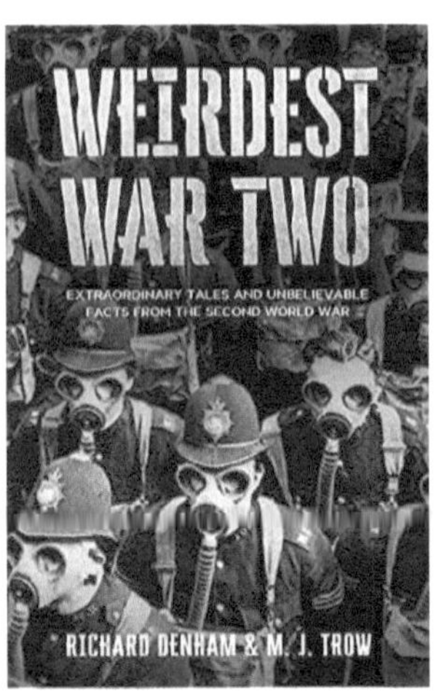

Weirdest War Two
By Richard Denham & M. J. Trow

Was Britain's Thermopylae really fought over a tennis court?

What happened in Canada during the invasion of Winnipeg?

How did the Night Witches terrify and torment the Axis?

Was Hitler actually sent to spy on the Nazis by the army?

Who was the schoolgirl who helped win the Battle of Britain?

Whether it's official Nazi propaganda dreamed up by Josef Goebbel's Ministry of Enlightenment or the 'scuttlebutt' of the US navy; tall stories from the officers' mess or attempts to escape from the grim reality of total war, the Second World War provides a fascinating glimpse into the mindset and ingenuity of a generation.

Have we now exhausted our supply of weirdness? With new information coming to light all the time from the classified archives in the corridors of power, we wouldn't bet on it!

www.blkdogpublishing.com

9 798224 938209